The Root:
Discovering Power

By Saqqarah

ME House
Metaphysicalerotica.com

Table of Contents

Books may be purchased by contacting the publisher and author at saqqarah@metaphysicalerotica.com or visiting http://metaphysicalerotica.com

Cover Design: ME House Graphics
Interior Design: ME House
Interior Layout: Maxxtwelve
Exterior Image: Dirk Czarnota and 123rf and ME House
Exterior Layout: Ultrakhan22
Printed by Amazon Createspace
Editor: Magpie Editing Services – Michelle Browne
ISBN-13: 978-1492714347
ISBN-10: 1492714348
1. Erotica 2. Metaphysics 3. Sacred Sex and Spirituality
4. Sacred Geometry
5 4 3 2 1
Printed in the United States

About the Author

Saqqarah, is a writer, musician, mother, nurse and artist. Drawing on her experience as an energy practitioner, she created "The Root" by receiving information from The Akashic Records and energetic downloads. This book is the first of seven in a series that highlights each chakra dysfunction and transforms it through sacred erotica. She invites readers to examine central themes prevalent in erotica fiction such as control, power, and domination and uses erotica to bring personal awareness, conscious relationships and personal transformation.

Her books and music can be found at Metaphysical Erotica, an online community that focuses on sharing creative artistic work centered on sacred sexuality. She is also the founder of the ME House which focuses on publishing metaphysical erotica novels, music and eBooks. She can be found at http://metaphysicalerotica.com

Other books by Saqqarah

"Sacred Fire: *Cultivating Power*" – due for release March 2014

The Mythrotica eBook Series

Greek Mythrotica – Vol 1:1 – "The Adventures of Aphrodite" – due for release October 2014
Greek Mythrotica – Vol 1:2 – "Legend of Royalty" – due for release November 2014
Norse Mythrotica – Vol 1:3 – "Circle of Power" – due for release November 2014
Norse Mythrotica – Vol 1:4 – "Mysteries of Magic" – due for release December 2014

Dedications

Thank you to my amazing friends and family for being so supportive during the birth of The Root and The Metaphysical Erotica community. Thank you for believing in me and encouraging me to continue even when I didn't know what the outcome would be.

And most of all, I give thanks to The Most High – Our Divine Father and Divine Mother – for inspiring me with words, story lines and insights. It is in aligning to our destined path that we come to know why we are here to serve.

Chapter One

Seventy people, clad in white, stood blindfolded and unaware, behind Tristan Alexander, as he kneeled with his head bent down in respect in front of a Tribal Council of twelve elders. Their silent gaze penetrated through the silver dust floating in the bright sunshine, assessing him as he murmured the ancient words, "Pater, Mater, Deus. Lumen quod intra te honoro."

These words rang clearly, meaning *Father, Mother, God. I honor the Light in You.* It was the greeting extended to all elder Lightworkers in the Tribe of Light Council.

The head of the council, a tall, regal looking man named Bjorn Cassidy stood up and beckoned him to come forward. Bjorn was also head of the Fire Starters. "Rise, my son. Please – introduce us to your initiates."

Tristan nodded dutifully, following the orders of Bjorn, who was examining each person with shrewd eyes. One by one, Tristan unmasked the seventy men and women. They rubbed their eyes, squinting against the brightness that blinded them, curiously looking around as if trying to place their location. It looked like any room - any place in the world – except for the large golden sphere that was suspended in the middle. The sphere held a symbol of the four directions in the center. This symbol appeared on all the robes of the elders, uniting and binding them together.

The dry air made their throats parched, but the smell of rose and amber wafted around them, lifting their senses. It felt otherworldly and strange, and the strangers hugged one another for security.

"Welcome, young Lightworkers, to Terra Quattro. This will be your temporary home for the next six months as you undergo your initiations...."

Bjorn's words felt mechanical and rote in Tristan's head. He had heard the same speech for fifteen years now. He could recite it perfectly with his eyes closed. Sighing wearily, his mind wandered to the challenges of this most recent assignment. As he jetted around the globe, discovering the Lightworkers that were already activated and waiting for initiation, he found that his travels were beginning to take their toll. He felt fatigued and burned out.

Many Lightworkers he met along the way were already awakening. Most of them had no idea what had happened to them, let alone what initiation meant. More than twenty people refused to follow him to Terra Quattro and undergo the trials. He didn't blame them. They were not easy, and did a damn good job of breaking your spirit down.

His reminiscence was interrupted as Bjorn called him to step up front. He knew this routine. As soon as he delivered the young initiates, he would receive his next assignment and leave again.

"Tristan," Bjorn voice was brisk and direct. "You had one hundred people on your list and only seventy made it here? What happened?"

Tristan looked up and met his steely gaze. "The Corona beat me to it. They seemed like they were one step ahead this time."

A hushed whisper of discomfort and concern ran through the tribal council. They had every reason to worry.

Bjorn raised a commanding hand and uneasy silence settled over the council. "I see. It would seem that even our best tracker gets beaten at times."

Tristan flushed, his neck red with embarrassment. His blue eyes blazed defiantly as he looked back at Bjorn. He hated to lose.

"With all due respect, Chief," he began. "There are over a hundred trackers scouring the globe for these Lightworkers. Many of us are also working within the structure of The Corona, infiltrating their society for secrets and weaknesses. We're doing the best we can."

"'Best' is not good enough when you're under a deadline, Tristan," Bjorn responded stiffly. "Either way, we'll have to double our efforts, keep training and keep searching." He looked amongst his council members who nodded in agreement, murmuring to each other in support.

Bjorn picked up a large manila envelope and tossed it to Tristan. He caught it with thoughtless grace. His next assignment.

Although this package seemed lighter than usual. Opening it, he looked at the list and picture. There was only one – Harmony Mendelson. He looked at the council with confusion and suspicion in his eyes.

"What is this?" he demanded. "Some kind of a joke?"

They looked at one another uncomfortably, shuffling as their robes swished around them. "Tristan – this is your next assignment. This is not a joke. This one is as important, if not more important, than your previous ones."

"You want me to find this half-breed and bring her to the light?" he replied scathingly. "Why?"

"Because she holds a very special genetic key inside that is monumental for our revolution," Bjorn answered, his voice softer. He didn't want to insult or alienate Tristan. He was, after all, their best tracker and most gifted Earth keeper.

"But why only this one? You've given me a list of thousands before."

"This one is a very special case. There are two forces you'll have to overcome: The Corona and Emily Morgan. We need you to bring this woman and Emily back. The time has come."

Tristan remained silent, looking at the pictures of the lovely woman, seeing nothing and seething hotly inside. This assignment felt impossible, and he felt resistance surge through him.

"You couldn't have sent John Michael or Raphael Jean for this job?" he asked half-heartedly.

An elder woman with silver streaked long hair stood up. Myalene Mays – head of the Air Traders began to speak softly. "Tristan, we know this touches a raw nerve for you, having to deal with Emily Morgan, but we need her back to the council. Furthermore, we have word that The Corona already has their sights on Harmony Mendelson. Your window is tight on this one."

"Not only that," Bjorn interjected. "It is imperative that you prepare for the completion of your Elemental Trials. You've been holding out for fifteen years, and we have received word that you will need Harmony to help you prepare."

"Damn!" Tristan whispered.

A tense silence held the room as Tristan examined the contents of his manila envelope one more time. There was the possibility that he would refuse. They reserved the right for him to exercise his Divine Will, but they needed him. He knew it. Releasing a sigh of frustration, he stuffed the papers back into the envelope and gazed at each Tribal Council member. His eyes finally settled on Bjorn.

"When do I leave?"

Bjorn raised his right hand and closed his eyes, chanting quietly under his breath. A golden sphere of light with bright geometrical patterns of pyramids, star tetrahedrons and Mobius strips grew from his hands. A gasp rippled through the seventy new initiates as they watched in awe. The sphere began to float above Bjorn's hand, turning and glowing, and drifted lazily towards Tristan. He raised his hands to receive the glowing orb, allowing it to hang above him, before it descended down into his crown chakra and disappeared. His eyes were closed as he absorbed the energy. As he opened them, they were filled with light causing a silver glint to appear in his ocean blue eyes. He had received the download necessary for his mission to be successful. Nodding his head toward the council in affirmation, he turned around to face the new initiates.

"You will be fine here. The Tribe of Light Council will help you train and connect to your gifts. Next time I see you, you will be one of us."

"The plane is waiting outside," Bjorn said, his voice more gentle this time. "We wish you the best of luck. May Gaia protect you wherever you go."

With a final nod to the Council, Tristan whirled around and headed for the exit which led him outside to the sunny strip of land that held a small charter plane. Before entering, he took one final look around Terra Quattro.

An extensive aqueduct system fed the lush gardens surrounding the property. The buildings were eco-friendly with straw-bale insulated adobe construction and solar panels outfitted on the rooftops. It was sustainable and completely off the grid.

Nestled amongst a fortress of mountain tops which obscured its view, this place was virtually invisible as it blended in with its terrain. As a matter of fact, it didn't exist in any map and satellites were unable to find it. That was how they intended it.

Tristan entered the small private jet, settling into a large, plush leather seat by the window. He opened the contents of the envelope again, gazing at the lovely, green-eyed beauty who stared back. He took in the details of her wild, wavy hair, the curve of her full lips, and the hint of a smile that hid behind them. But it was her eyes that held him captive. They looked like emeralds – brilliant and piercing. He felt a strange stirring inside – one that he had not experienced in a very long time.

The sound of the plane's engine roared to life as the vibration of the blades turning began to fill the cabin. He closed his eyes. He could feel it. His window was narrow, and he needed to hurry.

~~~~~

Weaving along the busy traffic of the highway known as Loop 1, Harmony was heading towards her client's home up in North Austin. She moved to the driving rhythm of the dance music blaring through the speakers of her gold Toyota Forerunner. She sang along to the music, losing herself in the lyrics about lost love and redemption. The vibration of an incoming call interrupted her. The caller ID identified it as Clara, her best friend and also a fellow massage therapist.

She knew why Clara was calling, and was almost tempted not to answer it. But she knew better. Clara was persistent and would keep calling and texting until Harmony picked up. She turned the volume down and switched over to her phone. *Thank God for Bluetooth! I hate to talk and drive!*

"What's up, honey?" she answered smoothly.

"Oh my God! I've got the best news ever!" Clara squealed. "You're going to be so stoked!"

"What?" she asked wearily. She and Clara had different ideas of what *stoked* meant.

"I just got a job at NET Media as one of their massage therapists in the Wellness Department!"

"Yay! Congratulations!" Harmony was vaguely familiar of the advertising and marketing firm, having seen their featured articles in glossy magazines and promotional sponsorships throughout the city.

"And guess what? I told them you were available to be a fill-in, as needed therapist!"

She froze. "You did what?!?"

"I know right?" Clara sounded happy and excited. "I knew that you wouldn't have the guts to apply for the job so I brought your resume down to their HR department."

"Oh no…"

"And they want to see you tomorrow. 11 am. Sharp."

"Why, Clara?" she groaned. "I'm totally fine working on my own clients. I like this freedom. I don't know if I'm cut out to work for some corporation."

"Don't think about it that way! They're an amazing company! And you get paid super fat!"

"What's super fat?" she asked suspiciously. She had been working on her own for over ten years, and 'super fat' was a variable amount in the holistic trade. It could range from a twenty dollar meal at Magnolia Café to the electric bill getting paid off.

"You get $75.00 per client, and you're guaranteed three-four clients per day. And the best part – most of the massages are only an hour long. You get huge breaks through your day."

"Sounds too good to be true."

"And get this, they work with your schedule and even let you float to different satellite offices."

Harmony was quiet. She did like the idea of having a steady gig and a consistent paycheck. With these down times in the economy, people were cutting out luxury items like massage. But still – she enjoyed her independence and being able to call the shots.

"Just give it a chance, will you?" Clara pleaded with her. "I have a really good feeling about this."

She couldn't deny that Clara might have a chance of being right. Her friend's highly intuitive abilities were scarily accurate sometimes.

"Ok – fine. I'll give it a chance. I'll do the interview tomorrow."

"And then we can celebrate afterwards!"

"Celebrate? I haven't even gotten the job yet."

"Oh don't worry," said Clara smugly. "You will."

"Thanks, Clara, for that vote of confidence."

"Oh and don't forget – we're going out for dinner and drinks with Mike and Todd Wenzley." Mike was Clara's boyfriend of two years. He worked at NET Media as a graphic designer and got her the job interview with the Wellness Department. Harmony liked Mike well enough, but she wasn't so sure about the other guy.

"Ugh...really? As if I don't have enough to worry about with this job interview – you guys want to set me up on a blind date?"

"Harmony – Todd's totally cute!"

"I don't care! What if he's a creepazoid? You know my history with men."

"You mean your *short* history with men. Honestly, girl, I don't know anyone who is so shy about being around men. You're positively beautiful."

"Yeah, but I have this stellar pattern of meeting love-'em and leave-'em guys. It's really getting old."

"So change it!" Clara challenged. "You know you can."

"I don't know. It's just that the guys I meet carry so much ick on them. I wish I couldn't see it. Maybe I would be blissfully ignorant of how toxic they are inside."

"Well, just give him a chance, ok? He might be different."

"Fine," she muttered, knowing that Clara's persistence would eventually wear her down. "I've gotta go. I'm at my client's house. Talk to you tomorrow, ok?"

She turned her car off, ending her conversation with Clara. She paused, looking at herself in the mirror to get ready. Her green eyes flashed as they gazed into her reflection. *Yup...my great dating history can only get better, right?*

Without answering, she opened her door and pulled her massage table out, walking with confidence and ease up the sidewalk to face her noon client. She brushed the thought of her upcoming interview and Todd Wenzley out of her mind. She needed to focus and discover what her client might be harboring in her body. Most of all, she had to concentrate on making sure that whatever energy pattern she found and removed in this session did not attach to her. Nothing felt ickier than an entity catching a ride.

Chapter Two

Harmony rifled through her closet for the third time, trying to find the right outfit for her job interview. Her eclectic, bohemian tastes did not carry a large variety of professional office wear. *Oh, this is so frustrating! I need more clothes!*

She kept sifting through her thick closet, finally settling for a black pencil skirt that hung a few inches above her knee and a rose pink camisole which highlighted her creamy skin. She paired a black fitted jacket to accentuate her trim waist and accessorized with a simple smoky quartz pendant and silver earrings. Turning around, she studied her appearance and smiled. She liked this urban professional look. It seemed to express calm, cool collectedness.

She studied her wild mane and sighed. It was a curse to have such thick curls and a blessing to have them arranged so artfully. She decided against binding her long hair, opting to wear it freely instead. This would have to do.

Noting the time, she quickly applied her make-up, keeping it simple, with just a little eyeliner and mascara. Harmony painted her full lips a deep maroon and puckered, giving herself a kiss in the mirror. She was ready.

Her alarm went off, signaling that it was 10:10 a.m. She needed to hurry. Traffic in Austin, Texas was unpredictable – most of the time. Jetting out of her apartment, she walked quickly to her car. She hated being late, and felt nervous to boot. Her mind reviewed some of the potential questions that Clara had shared with her. Pulling out of her apartment, she began driving onto the oncoming traffic, aware of the busyness of the early morning.

She was so wrapped up in her thoughts that she barely felt the bump behind her. *Did someone just hit me?*

She pulled over and stopped, glancing quickly at the clock. 10:25. *Oh man....this is so not what I need.*

Looking up at her rearview mirror, she could see a large white Toyota Tacoma pulling up behind her. Exasperated, she threw her door open and climbed out, trying to be as graceful as possible in her black skirt and high heels. She walked behind her Forerunner, trying to assess the damage the truck may have caused. She saw nothing, not even a scratch or a bump.

Turning, she watched the driver exit out of his truck. Her breath caught in her throat when she saw him. He was...beautiful. Tall, muscular, confident and breath-taking. She blinked her eyes several times, worried he was a hallucination.

"I'm sorry," he began. "I didn't see you. I got too close. Are you ok?"

"I...yes...I'm ok," she stammered. He made her feel even more nervous than she already did. There was something about him that she couldn't take her eyes off. Perhaps it was his bright blue eyes or his rugged good looks or the raw masculinity that he exuded. He walked past her and examined her bumper, touching the frame. She was fascinated by his movements, even more, by her reaction to him. She looked around for some kind of distraction so that her ogling wasn't obvious.

"Your car seems ok. Are you sure that you're not hurt?" he strode over to her, his eyes filled with concern.

"I'm ok, really! And I'm running late. I have to go."

"Wait," he said, pulling his wallet out. "This is my card. My name's Tristan Alexander. If you feel anything – whiplash, pain, swelling – call me. I'll take care of it."

He held his card out to her. As she reached for it, their fingers touched, eliciting a small shock in her hand. The contact triggered something electric and their eyes widened simultaneously. Neither spoke for a beat, staring at one another, feeling the current intensify.

"And your name is?" Tristan asked. He gazed down into her green eyes. She hesitated.

"My name is Harmony. Harmony Mendelson." She turned towards her car and reached into her purse, bringing a business card out. She pressed it into his hand, feeling a strange sensation run through her fingertips again.

"Harmony," he murmured. "Please let me know if anything comes up – especially if you need my insurance info."

He extended his hand to shake hers. Grasping his, a surge of heat flowed between them. *What is it with this guy?*

She forced herself to look away and drop his hand. Walking towards her car felt like a supreme effort but she knew that time was quickly flying by. Starting it up again, she pulled away, aware that Tristan was watching her drive. *Oh my! He's super foxy!*

She smiled at him before weaving back into the traffic. It led her to the flowing highway and onward towards her interview. Taking a deep, grounding breath, she forced herself to drag her attention from Tristan Alexander to her upcoming meeting.

Focus! She told herself. *Focus on the job – not the guy!*

It took less time that she had anticipated to reach NET Media. It was located right in the heart of downtown Austin, nestled in the high offices of the Frost Bank Building, the third largest skyscraper in the city. She found herself reciting an age-old mantra her guardian had taught her: *I AM the Light of God. All that is before me is made of love.* She kept repeating it to herself as she walked into the glass-lined building, her confidence rising as the elevator took her up to the top floor.

When the doors opened, she was struck by the opulence of the NET Media Headquarters. An attractive blond receptionist greeted her coolly at the front desk and indicated for her to have a seat. Harmony appraised her surroundings, taking in the multiple awards that were displayed along the dark mahogany walls. Large, modern, Italian leather couches perched on beautiful Persian rugs. Oval glass tables in front of them held crystal vases full of fresh flowers. The scent of tulips and irises mingled in the air. Large Impressionist paintings, probably originals, accessorized another wall, giving an air of culture and style. Everything resounded with the crisp, clean energy of wealth and success.

"Ms. Mendelson," the receptionist addressed her. "Ms. Cary is ready to see you. Right this way, please." She turned towards the ceiling-height African mahogany doors and pushed them open. Harmony followed her as they threaded through a series of suites and office cubicles, finally reaching the conference room in the back. An impressive oval table which could easily seat twenty greeted her, but she was alone.

"Please, have a seat. Ms. Carey will be here soon."

Harmony didn't have to wait long before the doors opened again and a graceful woman in her early fifties entered. She had short blond hair, cut at a fashionable bob, and a stylishly tailored Chanel suit. Attractive and professional, she smiled courteously at Harmony, extending her hand to greet her.

"Harmony, my name is Lydia Carey. I'm the Wellness Director for NET Media Enterprises. Please – have a seat."

Lydia began her interview in a brisk and efficient manner, asking Harmony about her working history and the types of clients that she dealt with. She also probed her on the types of massage that she offered and other techniques that enhanced her practice. She often referred back to Harmony's resume and grilled her with more questions. Harmony could feel her nervousness abate, answering with confidence and ease.

"Why would you like to work here at NET Media?" Lydia asked.

Because my best friend works here. "Well," she began, "I support companies that believe in the health and wellness of their employees. The fact that you have a wellness department is impressive."

"What's your true motivation?"

"I like my freedom. This job position allows me to have the flexibility to still see my own clients and yet serve this company. It's a nice balance."

"We do attempt to work with our employees, Harmony, but we do not stand for tardiness, frequent call-ins, and inconsistency. Do you have a problem with this?"

"No, ma'am."

Lydia smiled. "Well then, I will be sending your information to our Vice President for review. You will, of course, have to do two massages before getting hired so we can assess your competency. Will that be a problem?"

"No, ma'am."

Lydia stood up, signaling the end of their interview. Harmony rose with her. She shook Harmony's hand firmly. "I'll be in touch in the next few days to let you know what we decide. Until then - thank you for coming." Walking smartly out of the room, Harmony was left alone to gather her belongings and make her way back to the front. She held her breath until she reached the elevators of the great front reception. Once inside, she sagged against the wall with a sigh of relief. *I'm so glad that's done!*

As if knowing her interview was completed, her cell phone rang. Clara again.

"Hey," she answered, her voice flat.

"How'd it go?"

"I'm not sure. She seemed a little cold and detached."

"Yeah – she was like that for me too. Then I had to give her and the VP a massage, and she seemed a lot better after that."

"You're kidding! I have to give that woman a massage?"

"Only if you want the job."

"I want the job."

"You'll be fine! Don't worry! Hey – are you ready for dinner and drinks?"

"Sure. I'll be there in thirty minutes."

"I'm totally positive that you're in."

"Well, I'm glad one of us is."

"And if you're super lucky, Todd Wenzley will be the man of your dreams!"

"We'll see," Harmony replied softly, her thoughts drifting to her earlier accident.

"Ok see you soon!" Her call with Clara ended. Too quickly, her interview at NET Media was out of her mind, replaced by something much more delicious. She tried to remember the details of how Tristan looked, but all she could remember was the electric tingle of his touch when he'd handed her his business card.

Oh well. Snap out of it! He's probably taken. A super-babe like that probably has women crawling all over him. Grrr.....

Chapter Three

Harmony waited patiently for Clara, Mike and Todd to arrive at the already full G'raj Mahal on Rainey Street. The converted food trailer served rich, creamy and sinfully decadent Indian cuisine. Housed in a trendy neighborhood and flanked by swanky bars, the eatery tended to bring a lot of young middle-aged people who wanted something filling and delicious before a serious night of drinking.

"Harmony!" She turned to see pretty, petite Clara waiving to her as they entered the restaurant. Clara looked like the All-American cheerleader, a perfect girl-next-door. Her blond curly hair framed a delicate face, accentuating large blue eyes.

Following in her company was Mike, her equally good-looking boyfriend, and another stranger. He looked a little on the conservative, law-abiding side. Harmony assessed him quickly, noting his clean-cut and gentle demeanor. *He seems harmless enough. Hopefully he has some intelligence and a sense of humor.*

Clara gave her a warm hug, enveloping her in jasmine and rose. Mike came next, stiffly introducing his co-worker, Todd Wenzley. Todd awkwardly shook Harmony's hand, mumbling something about how nice it was to meet her.

"Let me get us a table!" Clara gushed.

"It might be a wait," Harmony said.

"Nope! I see us getting seated in fifteen minutes. Tops!" she turned around and headed to the hostess, flashing a bright and irresistible smile.

"I don't how she does it." Mike shook his head, amused. He turned to look at Harmony. "How was your interview?"

She shrugged. "I guess it was ok. I feel like the Wellness Director is a little conservative."

"It's that kind of company. They run a super tight ship – the brothers."

"The brothers?"

"Yeah," Todd interjected. "Nicholas and Eduardo Torres. They started NET Media eight years ago, and they've been crazy successful ever since!"

"Really?"

"They've got the advertising and digital media down to a science. It's like people want to buy whatever they promote. They're that good!"

Their conversation was momentarily interrupted as Clara indicated for them to follow her.

Damn, how does she do that? Harmony wondered. Seated comfortably around a white metal table, they perused the menu in silence. A server came by for their orders, and they resumed their conversation.

"So, you must really like working at NET Media," Harmony offered. Todd and Mike nodded enthusiastically.

"I've been there for five years now in the graphic design department," Todd started. "And they've given me a lot of creative freedom."

"Freedom, you say? I like that word."

"See, Harmony?" Clara chimed in. "You're going to love working there! Their massage rooms are totally dreamy!"

"I use it," Todd interjected. Harmony turned to look at him, gazing into his brown eyes. He was a handsome man with dark brown hair and a closely trimmed beard. Narrowing her eyes slightly, she looked closer into his energetic field. Everything looked clear until she spied a round, olive-green mass at his abdomen. It sat like a heavy blob, not moving and dull in vibration. It rolled around lazily, occasionally forming undulating waves. She felt a rising sense of unease and began to pull away. It was enough. She didn't need to see anymore to know what her instincts relayed.

Todd, Mike and Clara bantered about NET Media as Harmony listened in. Suddenly, a large party of eight walked through the door. She froze. One of those people was Tristan Alexander. She watched him hug the other men and women before strolling through the restaurant. They walked right by their table, towards a private seated area in the back, laughter and jokes trailing behind them.

Oh My God! What is he doing here? Errant thoughts of the handsome stranger ran through her mind. She stole a glance at him as he passed. He was gorgeous, his tan skin contrasting against the white shirt tucked neatly in his dark blue jeans. His shaggy blond hair fell carelessly around his face, giving him a wild, untamed look.

She felt a ripple of excitement. Just seeing him again made her tremble inside. *Damn, he is fine!*

"Hey!" Clara interrupted her thoughts. "Todd was asking you how long you've been a therapist. Are you on this planet right now?"

"I'm sorry," she mumbled. "I got distracted by something." She struggled to pull herself back together and tried to focus on her group's conversation. Turning her attention to Todd, she politely answered his questions, all the while wondering which of the women she saw in the group was with Tristan. That thought was both unnerving and nauseating.

Their food arrived quickly and soon took up the space of their conversation. Harmony ate, trying to be present in the conversation between Mike, Todd and Clara, but her mind was somewhere else. She didn't feel at that moment that she had much to share.

Clara noticed and leaned forward. "What's going on?" she whispered. "You're acting like you're not even here!"

"I know. I'm sorry. I've just got a lot on my mind – you know – with the interview and stuff." *And the car accident. And Tristan. And how hot he is.*

"Well, come back," Clara pleaded. "I think Todd really likes you."

Harmony looked up, forcing a smile as she met Todd's curious gaze. His eyes lit up with her attention. *Oh no! He thinks this is a good sign. Dangit!*

As soon as they finished their dinner, they left G'raj Mahal and returned to Rainey Street. It was already filling up with people celebrating their Friday night. They headed across the street to Clive Bar, a dark, sensually lit bar with a large spacious outdoor patio. Mike headed to the bar to place their orders. Normally, Harmony didn't drink, but tonight she was going to celebrate.

Mike returned with four drinks in hand, doling out the tasty concoctions. She gratefully sipped the sweet, tart margarita, surprised at the bite of the tequila. It was strong. Mike and Clara were huddled in a private conversation, leaving her to contend with Todd and his hopeful doe eyes. *Oh boy...*

"Did you like the food?" he prodded.

"It was good."

"How's your drink?" She took a long slow sip. Or three. *This is going to be a long night...*

"It's good."

"Umm...seen any good movies recently?"

She suddenly stood up. The small talk was grating on her. "Excuse me, I'll be right back. Ladies' room," she mumbled, turning away from his curious gaze.

No sooner had she swung the door open to the main bar than she found herself standing smack dab in front of Tristan. He looked amused, taking in her flushed, flustered face with a grin.

"It's you!" he exclaimed.

"Hi..." her voice was breathy. *I hope I don't smell like a margarita.*

"You're the one I bumped into this morning."

She smiled. "Yeah – that's me. I'm...really surprised to see you...again."

"What are the chances?"

"Indeed."

He leaned against the bar, studying her. The world around her seemed to fade as she looked at him.

"It seems like we may have started off on the wrong foot." His voice was husky, sending shivers up her spine.

"How so?"

"I don't normally drive so recklessly. I really hope that you're ok."

"Really…I'm fine. Besides, if I do have any pain – I have access to a lot of body workers who can help me out."

"Well, I do feel a little guilty that I may be the cause of some of that discomfort."

Her green eyes locked into his blue, and something inside her quivered. *Why do I feel like a schoolgirl around this man?*

"Guilt won't serve you in the long run." She replied softly, looking deeply into his eyes. He was mesmerizing.

"How perceptive you are. Still…I'd like to make it up to you."

She was quiet, assessing him and his relaxed frame. All she could see was a column of gold light that ran up and down his spine. *Strange….I've never seen that before. It feels really strong. And sexy.*

"Well?" he asked suggestively. "How can I make it up to you?"

She smiled, extending her field of energy around him. "I'm not sure. What do you have in mind?"

"How about dinner? That's good start, right?"

"Sure - I'm a big fan of food."

The door swung open. Todd stared at Tristan and Harmony in shock. With a disgusted shake of his head, he turned around and walked back to their table, pouting as he sat next to Mike.

"Boyfriend?" Tristan asked, cocking his head.

"Hardly. Just an acquaintance I met tonight."

"Well good fortune must be smiling on me then."

She smiled shyly, blushing at his words. "For us to meet twice in one day must be a sign."

"It's a good sign then. Besides, you can't go against the Universe when so many events align."

He held out his hand. She took it timidly. That electric shock of coursed through her again, making her arm and shoulder tingle. She could see a similar pathway creeping up his arm. *He must feel it too!*

"So how about tomorrow - dinner?"

Tomorrow?! Damn it! Of all days! It had to be tomorrow!

That was the day that she had signed up to work as a massage therapist of a metaphysical fair. There would be many potential clients trying her style of massage. It was too lucrative to pass up. And....she was broke. She also needed to make her rent in two weeks, and she was short and feeling the financial pressure.

"Darn – I'm already booked. I'm working at a Metaphysical Fair tomorrow. It's an all-day thing."

"Are you doing massage?"

She nodded. "I don't know if you're into that kind of thing, but there are a lot of other vendors there too. People from the Green, Eco-Sustainability world."

"Well perhaps I can come visit you and get a session."

Harmony quickly drew in a deep breath. The idea of touching Tristan and feeling his sinewy muscles move under her fingers made her giddy. She felt herself blush from head to toe, feeling like her thoughts were maddeningly apparent to him.

"If you come for a session tomorrow, I can guarantee that I'll make your muscles melt under my fingertips." *Holy cow! Is that the alcohol talking?*

He raised an eyebrow, surprised at her boldness. "How can I turn that down?"

Her eyes dropped coyly. "You're not supposed to." *OMG! Did I just say that?*

"You're intriguing! I'll give you that. Let me see what I can do."

"Consider that the first step to making it up to me."

All of a sudden, the door burst open again - this time, Clara was walking towards her. She looked furious. She quickly took stock of Tristan and their hands together and whipped her head to glare at Harmony.

"We're leaving. Are you coming?"

Harmony was bewildered. *What did I do wrong?* Turning once again to face Tristan, she dropped her hand and gave him a sweet smile.

"Perhaps tomorrow then."

"Perhaps," he smiled in return, stepping back to give her the space to return to her party. She turned to Clara, who grabbed her arm and dragged her to the bathroom.

"What the hell, Harmony?" she fumed once they were inside. "What are you doing?"

"What do you mean?"

"You're supposed to be on a date with Todd and you're holding some other guy's hand at the bar?"

"It's not what you think, Clara."

"It's freaking rude! Todd is super pissed!"

Harmony pouted. "He has no right to be. He doesn't own me."

"But you're on a date! Who was that guy anyway?"

Harmony couldn't hide her smile. "That was Tristan Alexander. He hit me with his truck this morning. He was simply apologizing."

Clara was incredulous. "Apologizing? That guy looked like he wanted to rip your clothes off!"

"Clara! Stop it! It wasn't like that at all!"

"Well maybe you couldn't see it, but I could, and the vibes between you two felt superhot! It made me blush! No wonder Todd was mad. You certainly didn't put those vibes towards him!"

"Can you blame me? I mean – there's no chemistry there. Did you see him compared to Tristan? Oh my God! Tristan's totally foxy and well...Todd's not."

Clara softened. "Well...we've gotta go. Todd's throwing a really lame attitude now. Mike wants to leave and call it a night."

"I'm with you on that!"

They both exited the bathroom. Scanning the bar, Harmony felt a little disappointed. No sign of Tristan. She sighed. Forcing a friendly smile on her face, she prepared to appease Todd's sullenness. Knowing the night was almost over was a huge relief.

Tristan watched Harmony and her friends leave from the dark shadows of his truck. She dodged Todd's paws for her hand, and he grinned, amused by it. He enjoyed watching her. His eyes lingered on every detail. Her wild mane framed a beautifully sculpted face set with emerald eyes and full red lips. Her breasts were round and full and her legs were long and toned.

It was more than her good looks that caught his attention. It was the way she could see right through him – into him that caught him off guard. The way her eyes registered surprise when she looked into his body and energy field betrayed her gift. *How am I going to get into that beautiful head of hers?*

It was lucky that he'd run into his old permaculture friends as they were about to have dinner. Perfect timing; better still, she didn't seem the least bit interested in the wanna-be date following her around. *So, what does interest you?*

There was no way he was going to pass up that opportunity to see her tomorrow. The very idea aroused him– a sensation he'd forbidden himself in a long time. *A massage with a woman like that? I'd have to be mentally insane to pass that up!*

He smiled at his errant thought, watching her pull away in her Gold Forerunner. He was looking forward to tomorrow.

Chapter Four

Metaphysical fairs in Austin were a common event, drawing practitioners and healers from all walks of life. It seemed that there was always some kind of spiritual, alternative or energetic gathering that brought people together. Harmony enjoyed the cornucopia of modalities, and she never knew what kind of people she would run into.

She walked into the drab hotel lobby, noting the different practitioners ambling through with their Tupperware bins full of eclectic tools. In the large conference room, she could see therapists, healers, and readers of all kinds setting up their tables - sprinkling them with crystals and laying out their books, CD's and promotions.

Still, there were a few kooky practitioners, too slick and arrogant for their own good. They used savvy marketing techniques that had long lines of people waiting outside the door, beside themselves with excitement to get a session. Harmony avoided them for a good reason. She didn't quite trust what they offered.

The hustle and bustle of energy, voices and collective movement transformed the ordinary grey-carpeted hotel meeting room into a circus of activity. An unspoken truce hung lightly in the air as readers regarded one another with competitive curiosity. Vendors of metaphysical art and new age books arranged and re-arranged their display in an attempt to draw the curious newbies to their tables. Multi-level marketing health nuts advertised and promoted their 'best thing product to cure anything.'

She sighed. She never quite understood what drew someone to a practitioner. Perhaps it was karma, curiosity or a feeling. She just knew that there was only one that she visited regularly: Katrina Von Straff.

Katrina was not from Texas or even the United States. She was an Eastern European gypsy, and looked the part. Her black mane, thick Hungarian accent, and crystal ball gave her the facade of a tarot card illustration. The ball was for show; her charisma and vibrancy were real.

Harmony smiled at the memory of their first meeting and gracefully glided up to Katrina's table. She flashed a wide, welcoming smile.

"Good morning, Katrina," she said happily. "How're you feeling today?"

Katrina opened her eyes from her meditative state. She had been resting her hands on the crystal ball, as if to keep them warm.

"Dah-ling Harmony!" She gushed sweetly. "It's going to be a wonderful day. I feel like the forces are strong today in the Universe, and the energies are ripe for falling in love."

Harmony laughed. "Oh no Katrina! Not again! You said that three months ago, and I spent all those months dateless, no phone calls—and men looked at me like I had a horn on my head."

"You don't?"

"No! And it's not nice to tell people that they do. It gives them a complex. So what's the word - am I going to fall in love today?" *Please let it be a yes!*

Katrina looked intently in her crystal ball. "The future is unclear on that one."

"Perhaps if you shake it, it will say, "Try again later.""

"Really dah-ling, you'll have to come back later. I'm just not warmed up right now. I still haven't got my kundalini past my belly-button."

Harmony smiled as she walked away. "Of course. No worries! I trust that what happens is supposed to happen."

Katrina's eyes narrowed as she stared at Harmony. "I would give him a chance, honey." she whispered. "He's different."

Their eyes locked in silent communication as Katrina psychically passed information between them. Harmony smiled and sighed, shaking her head in amusement. *Surely, she can't be talking about Tristan. It's too soon.*

She turned away from Katrina and began walking back to her table, brushing the thought of her semi-reading aside. More people were beginning to arrive, and she needed to man her chair and massage table. She arrived at her booth to find three people already waiting in line for a massage. She smiled at their familiarity. Returning clients. She always liked to re-connect to her clients at the fair. She hugged each of them in turn and began to work on her first session.

Harmony loved bodywork, relishing in the feel of muscles and the fascia that lifted them up like a glacier stuck on a mountain. She enjoyed the sensation of stiff tissues relaxing and loosening under her fingers. Her strong hands inevitably found the areas of blockages and pressure. With sure fingers, she kneaded the tension out of the body. She also practiced moving the balls of stagnant energy out of the muscles and releasing them outside of the client.

She was careful where she chose to release that energy. Her experienced awareness had witnessed people's energy changing when they walked through a field of negativity. It stuck on like glue. And sometimes, that stockiness carried heavy vibrations, dark entities, or worse. Some people called it being an empath. She called it disturbing and gross, being reminded of her early childhood and feeling "left-overs" all over her grandmother's home.

Her day was busy, moving with an effortless flow, as people, new and established, came to visit her. She knew that by the end of the day, she would not only have rent paid, but extra to perhaps buy herself an indulgent present. She barely gave herself a break, only taking twenty minutes for lunch and quick trips to the bathroom. She had already worked on ten people by the time 4:00 pm came. Names were quickly signed off her list as the line dwindled. She only had an hour left before she could close down. Her body felt fatigued and heavy.

"Finally," a voice behind her stopped her in her tracks. Her heart thudded in her chest. "Do you have time to do one more session?"

OMG! He's here! She turned around slowly, a smile growing on her face. Her glowing green eyes met the ocean blue depths of Tristan's. His smile made tiny crinkles form around his eyes. She felt a warm flush grow in her abdomen at his close proximity.

"That depends. Are you on my list or did you cut in line?"

"What list?"

He looked around. It was just the two of them. Her list had indeed been cut short. "I guess I just got pushed to the front of the line."

Harmony blushed and looked down. She didn't feel so tired all of a sudden, a flash of energy and excitement rushing into her body. She looked up again, smiling shyly. "Would you prefer the chair or the table?"

He cocked his head to the side, his hair partially covering his eyes, and shrugged. "What's best for you?"

A string of naughty thoughts ran like a freight train through her head. *Control yourself! You're supposed to be a professional!* "I guess it depends on what you want me to work on."

Tristan headed to the table and sat down. "How about my lower back? I've been doing a lot of travelling recently. It feels kinda stiff and sore."

Harmony found herself being drawn irresistibly closer to him. She could feel the energy growing between them. It was strong and magnetic, and she was acutely aware of his presence, smell and warmth.

"How about laying on your stomach? We can get started there," she gently suggested.

Tristan smiled, making her catch her breath. His eyes darkened as he took in her appearance from head to toe. She turned crimson under his scrutiny.

How am I going to be able to concentrate when he looks at me like that? Focus, focus, focus! She quickly turned around, prepping her hands with lotion and rubbing them to warm them up. She was glad that her back was turned.

She would have blushed even more had she seen how his eyes passed over the round, firm curve of her buttocks. She took a deep breath to calm and center herself.

When she turned back around, she found Tristan lying face down, his head nestled in the cradle. Her eyes perused the length of his fit, muscle-bound body. She knew that she would have to exert extra strength to relax this stiffness that she could see bulging from his trapezius and latissimus dorsi.

"You're going to feel a little coldness with my hands," she whispered softly in his ear. "But it'll warm up."

"It's already pretty hot in here," Tristan replied back, his voice muffled by the cradle.

Oh my! That's for damn sure! With long, slow and firm strokes, she began to knead his muscles, reveling in how the tautness of his body responded to her touch. She could feel him initially stiffen, unconsciously contracting his muscles.

"Relax," she whispered soothingly. This time, she could feel him take a deep breath and bring the oxygenated vitality to his muscles.

Harmony concentrated on finding the balls of stuck energy. She rolled them around in her hands like dough, pulling them out and throwing them up, towards the ceiling. The more she worked on loosening his muscles, the more he relaxed. They didn't speak, and she was grateful for that silence. It allowed her to admire him.

She knew by the way his muscles and torso were shaped that he did a lot of physical exercise with his solid biceps and triceps, taut back, and trim athletic waist. In a sculpted form, he would have been the perfect model for Michaelangelo's David.

Working her way down, she eased into a rhythmic movement, getting in deeper touch with his body. Tristan had become deeply relaxed, his breathing even. When she began to manipulate the muscles of his lower back and the ridges of his vertebrae, he sighed in pleasure.

She felt herself being drawn to pull any vestiges of stress and tension out of his lower chakras. Peeking into his first power center in his pelvis, she pulled energetic debris and recalibrated it to its full speed and clarity. She did the same for the second, third and fourth power centers as well. These were some of her favorite places to work. Many people stored tension and trauma from their early development in this part of the body yet were unaware of the past programs that they carried.

Her laser focus on massaging his body made time disappear. As she worked deeper, she was able to psychically and holographically tap into his energy field, noting the golden column of light that shined like a beacon up his spine. A star tetrahedron floated up and down the column, spinning clockwise as it moved up and then counterclockwise as it came down.

The golden beam of light began to move, forming a vortex of energy like a tornado. Strange shapes, formulas and images ran through the vortex. He emanated power, control, and strength. She was curious and fascinated by what she saw. She had never seen anything like it in anyone's body.

Her timer began beeping, startling her out of her concentration. It was hard to believe that forty-five minutes had passed. It felt like seconds when she had first touched him, energetically connecting them together. Looking around, she could see that the fair was over. Practitioners were breaking down their tables and display and leaving in droves from the conference room.

She leaned over Tristan's ear. "We're all done now."

He turned over, languid and unhurried. His blue eyes opened to meet hers with a twinkle. He looked younger and more relaxed, smiling at her with genuine pleasure and satisfaction. She felt her knees weaken.

"You were right," he sighed. "You can relax me deeper than I ever thought possible."

Harmony smiled and blushed at the same time. *What is the deal? Does he have access to my blush button?*

"Thank you," she murmured. "You were a willing participant. That helps."

Tristan sat up and pulled on his shirt. "So how about letting me take you out to dinner as my way of saying thanks?"

Harmony smiled as she began to put her supplies away. Her stomach rumbled in protest, reminding her that she had not eaten throughout the day. "I would like that. I'm totally famished."

Tristan stood up and reached out to touch her arm, sparking a bolt of fire-engine red energy between them. She stopped and met his eyes. They drank each other in, acutely aware that it was only them in the room.

Harmony's cheeks flushed crimson as she gazed into Tristan's eyes. Her breath caught in her throat, making it impossible to speak. *Whoa! What is that?!*

"Thank you for that great session. I guess I really needed that."

Harmony smiled. "I'm glad that you came."

Tristan pulled out some money, handing her more than she expected to receive. She began to pull out only what she needed and automatically handed the rest to him. He refused, closing her hand over the large wad of cash.

"You deserve it. You're really good. And you're worth it."

Dammit! Now her face was really red. She looked up at him, her eyes bright. "You know, we could get out of here quicker if you help me."

Before she could even finish her sentence, he was already loading himself up with her massage table, chair and bags. She laughed and picked up her purse, heading towards the elevator.

Chapter Five

Harmony drove to Suzi's Chinese Kitchen, aware that Tristan was following behind her. She could feel the energy that he directed towards her as she wove skillfully through traffic. Knowing that she would be sharing a private booth with him very soon filled that lower area of her stomach with butterflies. *I can't believe we're having dinner! This has got to be my lucky day!*

There was something about him that was different from the guys she normally attracted. His captivating good looks, self-confident decisiveness and raw masculinity was wrapped in a package that was delicious and intriguing.

She noted the admiring glances that he received from women around him and wondered if she was beautiful or attractive enough for him. That thought made her feel unsettled inside. *Don't overthink this. Just try – and I mean - try - to be in the flow with him. Don't eff it up!*

She hated that her subconscious was more right than her doubtful mind at times. As she pulled into the parking lot, a *ding* from her smart phone caught her attention. A new email. She turned her car off and reached for her phone, opening the email with curiosity.

From: Lydia Carey, Wellness Director NET Media
Date: Saturday, March 16, 2013 – 6:30 p.m.
Subject: Second Interview
To: Harmony Mendelson

Dear Harmony,

Thank you for coming to our office to interview for the Per Diem Massage Therapist position in our Wellness Department. After extensively reviewing your resume, we would like to offer you a second interview. You will have the opportunity to demonstrate your abilities to two of our executive staff: I and Eduardo Torres,

VP of NET Media. As we are eager to fill this position, we'd like for you to come in on Sunday, March 17, at 10:00 a.m. The massage studios are usually booked during the weekends. We have arranged for your two massages at 10:00 and 10:40.

Please respond as soon as possible so we can arrange our schedules accordingly.

Best Regards,
Lydia Carey
Executive Wellness Director
NET Media

A huge smile blossomed on Harmony's face as she quickly typed back her reply, confirming her appointment for the following day. *YES! This totally rocks*!
She opened the door to find Tristan standing beside her car, watching as she emerged with his steady gaze.
"Guess what?" her voice was brimming with excitement.
He grinned in response. "What?"
"I just got offered a second interview with NET Media!"
His smile slipped, a dark shadow crossing his eyes. "Congratulations."
"Yeah! I'm totally excited! It's in their wellness department. Clara hooked me up with a job interview, and I can't believe I'm going back for the next step!"
He was quiet as they walked towards the door. They were greeted by a pair of Asian women in silk robes, who glided through the crowded restaurant and led them to a private booth in the back.
She felt his hand touch the small of her back, leading her in front of him. That touch sent shockwaves up and down her spine. Heat radiated from his fingertips as it rested against her shirt, causing her to shiver. *Why does his touch do that to me?*

As they perused the menu, she could feel his gaze burning into her. She looked up, catching her breath at the intensity of his blue eyes. He watched her with amusement, his full lips curved in a smile as she avoided the urge to blatantly stare at him. The waitress came to take their order, giving her a moment of reprieve from his smirk.

"So you obviously know what I do," she began. "What do you do?"

He smiled and leaned back, his eyes never leaving her. "You could say my job is in human resources."

"Hiring and Firing?"

"Not quite."

"Consulting?"

"Closer."

"You're being rather evasive."

"I'm a tracker." His eyes narrowed. She felt that flutter in her belly grow stronger.

Whoa! "What do you track?"

"People."

Harmony stared at him. Thoughts thundered like a freight train through her mind. The accident. Clive Bar. The metaphysical fair. Dinner. *Was it all just a coincidence?*

"So are you working right now?" she asked, her eyes bravely meeting his.

"It's half and half. Half work, half pleasure."

"Are you tracking me?" The words came out like a half-whisper.

"Partly. A big part of me is simply enjoying the company of a very beautiful and intriguing woman."

She flushed at his direct compliment. "Why?"

"Because I like to look at you. And I like the way I feel when I'm around you," he purred.

She was silent and surprised at his admission, forcing herself to hold her tongue as their waitress delivered and set their steaming plates in front of them. Tristan smiled and began to eat, never taking his eyes off her.

Scarlet heat crept across her cheeks, and her eyes flew down to her hands. She was wringing them nervously. This was not how she thought her night was going to go.

When she looked up again, she felt a shift in the air as a charged electrical energy pulsated between them, bringing them closer together in awareness of each other's presence. The restaurant, conversations, and the aroma of food – it all disappeared.

"Do you feel that?" he rasped deeply. A shiver of fire rose up her spine. She nodded, spellbound. He held her gaze, igniting her inside with a spark of arousal. She could see it in his eyes. He wanted her.

"Why are you tracking me?" she asked softly.

"Because I find you pretty damn irresistible. Now eat! I know you're starving."

"You sure know how to distract a lady," she smiled. "But really…I want to know why you came looking for me."

Tristan waited until Harmony began to eat her meal and then continued. "You've got some very unique abilities that I would like to help you develop."

"You're referring to my…"

"Ability to see into the body and move energetic blocks, entities and other creepy crawlies."

"Oh…" The secret was out. *Great! And I thought I would only attract normal guys.*

"Why do you want to help me develop those abilities?"

"Because I would like to invite you to join a very special underground organization called The Tribe of Light."

"What is that?" She asked between mouthfuls of food.

"We're an international collective of Light and Energy workers. We work with the Earth and her people. We are the stewards, the peacekeepers, the warriors of light."

"You know, that sounds a little out there."

A wry smile crept across his handsome face. "You don't know how many times I've heard that statement."

"So explain it to me then."

"The Tribe of Light is made up of four elemental groups that represent the foundation of our organization: Air Traders, Earth Keepers, Water Bearers, and Fire Starters. Each group have special gifts that represent that element. From psychic abilities and shape shifting to manipulating electricity and the forces of nature, our organization was created to bring balance to the Earth."

"This sounds like a sci-fi movie."

Tristan smirked and continued to speak. "We've fought for the freedom of people's conscious and spiritual evolution for thousands of years. We've been coming towards the apex of our revolution in the past ten years."

"You make it sound like you're at war. Are you?"

"On some level - yes. But our weapons are much more subtle than the military's. We use the gifts that we were born with to fight. Psychic mind games, energetic attacks, elemental and mind control."

"You're kidding! How does the public not know about this?"

His gaze was serious. "I'm not kidding, Harmony. We ferociously fight to keep our organization a secret. We've survived throughout these years in anonymity because we are the hidden forces of Light. Our world has always been shrouded to protect its members."

"You know this sounds right up the conspiracy theory lines, right?"

"I know. That's why I'm asking you to trust me. Our mission is simple. We help Lightworkers discover who they are, what they can do, and recruit them to join our side and our fight against the dark forces, The Corona."

Her eyes narrowed as she listened. "Who is The Corona?"

His voice dropped a few tones lower as if sharing a private secret. "The Corona is an organization that has been in power since the time of the Medici in Rome. They were created to protect the religious and political leaders of that time. Since then, they've grown in power and use psychic and energetic warfare and mind control to carry out the plans of the old paradigm of world domination."

A cold shiver ran through her as she wrapped her arms around herself instinctively.

"The Corona wants Lightworkers and Energyworkers as much as we do. They use these people to help manipulate the rest of society so they can preserve their current power, prestige and income. They are your politicians, corporate giants and elite leaders."

"That's twisted! How do you stop them?"

"We try to get to the Lightworkers first so that they're trained and armed to defend themselves. Some follow the light. Others go towards the path of money, fame and riches. The balance is shifting, though. People are waking up, changing how they look at the world. The Corona is feeling that shift, and it's making them desperate."

Harmony could feel her palms heat up and a bead of sweat trickle down her spine. She didn't want to ask but knew it was inevitable. "What does this have to do with me?"

"They want you as much as we do. As much as I do." Just when she thought she'd gotten it under control, he made her blush again.

"Why? I'm just a massage therapist."

He leaned back to study her, allowing her words to hang in the air. "You make it sound insignificant because you consider yourself just a body worker. Do you not know who you are?"

Her eyes blazed with indignation. *What the hell are you talking about? Of course I know who I am!* "I suppose you're going to tell me you know?"

"Harmony….they want you because you're half-light and half-dark."

She looked away, feeling the sting of his answer. "Half what? You've got a lot of nerve, Tristan. You don't know anything about me."

He leaned forward and gazed intently at her. She felt his piercing stare and looked up, her pained eyes catching his. "I know more about you than you realize."

Her brows knitted together in a frown. She did not like her privacy invaded at all.

"Look...I'm sorry." Tristan continued. "I know this might be difficult for you, but I need you to listen and tell me what you do know. There will be others looking for you soon, and I need to know how to protect you."

"Protect me?" she sputtered. "Protect me from what?"

"From them. They're relentless. Once The Corona sets their eyes on someone, they don't give up. And right now – you're the main target."

Geez! What am I getting myself into? Her eyes narrowed as she assessed him. "How do I know I can trust you?"

"What kind of chance are you willing to take?" He shifted in his chair, reaching out to touch her hand. That skin to skin contact made her jump, shocked as a liquefying heat started to pool in her pelvis. She wanted nothing more than to launch herself at him and lose herself in the feel of his mouth. *Stop thinking about sex!* She reprimanded herself.

He drank in her softly parted full lips and her flashing green eyes. He took her hand firmly. She felt heat spread from her center and travel up her spine, igniting points of light along the way. She felt lightheaded and weak. *God, I want him to kiss me so bad!*

As if reading her private thoughts, he brought her hand up to his lips, planting a soft kiss on her palm. His lips seared her skin; a sigh escaped from her, and her tension melted away.

"Tristan," she whispered. "What are you doing to me?"

"Same thing you're doing to me."

"What's that?"

"Pushing past my comfort zone."

"Oh!" she gasped, as his tongue traced over her index finger.

"You make me forget why I'm here," his voice was husky and deep. "I'm throwing all the rules out the window."

"There are…rules?"

"There are always rules of engagement," he murmured seductively against her skin. She felt the heat reach her chest. Her heart filled with warmth and brightness even as lust exploded in her cells.

"Maybe some rules are meant to be broken," she suggested, not knowing what she was referring to. "Or bent…"

"Consider this the first of many…" And he abruptly reached across their table and clasped the nape of her neck, drawing her close. She felt the gap between them disappear as she met him half-way, her lips open – waiting, ready, turned-on.

He kissed her with slow, gentle pressure that soon turned more demanding and insistent as he traced the outline of her lips. She could feel him drawing deep into her well of desire, invoking all her senses to wake up and shout. She felt a growing ache between her legs as his tongue speared into her mouth, touching and licking her, setting her internal world on fire.

She kissed back with abandon, moaning against his lips as her breathing became ragged and shallow. He pulled away first, placing his forehead against hers, his eyes closed.

"I want you to say yes to me." His voice was raspy and husky, sending chills up her arms.

"I don't know what I'm saying yes to."

"I want you to join me in the Tribe of Light."

She pulled away, looking into his cerulean eyes. *Damn! Where did this man come from?* "I don't know, Tristan. This is all too new. Everything is happening too fast right now. I need to think about it."

Releasing his hold on her neck, he settled calmly back in his seat. "I should warn you now. I don't give up so easily. 'No' is not an option with you."

"What happens if I say yes?" Her question was hesitant.

"Then I will unravel your world and bring you to the highest heights of pleasure, awareness and consciousness you've ever known."

She gaped at him. "And if I say no?"

"*No* is not an option," he snapped. His eyes were lit with a glint of determination and resolve. She drew back, studying him with mixed emotions. She wasn't used to having someone dictate her world.

He stood up abruptly, flagging their waitress, and handed her his credit card. "We have to go. Make this quick. Please."

Harmony was fascinated at how quickly his mood changed. From a suave, sensual seducer to a cold, commanding masculine power. Had she met her match?

She grabbed her purse and stood. He reached over and brought her closer, molding her to the musculature of his fit body. Her curves seemed to melt effortlessly against his – as if made for his body – like Radha for Krishna, Isis for Osiris, and Magdalene for Yeshua. That realization flooded her with a high vibration of awareness.

He really wasn't like any of the others. And she knew why he was finally here. *So now you've found me. What now?*

"Don't look at me like that," he muttered under his breath. "Or so help me God, I'm going to take you on top of this table!"

What?! Have you no shame? "You wouldn't dare!"

"Don't tempt me," he growled softly, pushing her back against the edge and pressing on her until she felt herself sit. She was trapped between the wooden top and the evidence of his arousal. Curious eyes from around the restaurant turned their direction, his bold move screaming loudly in the crowded room.

"Ok, ok!" she placated, looking down and blushing furiously. *Holy hell! He's going to get us arrested!*

He pulled away, leaving her gasping and reeling in shock as he deftly retrieved his credit card from their embarrassed waitress's hand. He signed the receipt, not taking his gaze off her once. With a smooth move, he grabbed her hand and led her towards the door. Ignoring the flurried display of good-byes from their Asian hostesses, he led her towards her car in brooding silence.

At the car, he turned her to face him, standing close. Too close. She could barely breathe. When she did – all she smelled was his masculine scent mixed with musk and amber. It was a heady and aphrodisiacal combination.

"What is it going to take for you to say yes?" he murmured against her temple. Her heartbeat quickened. Every part of her wanted to say *yes*, but she wasn't sure quite fully what she was agreeing to.

"I need time, Tristan. And more information before I decide."

"We don't have much time, Harmony."

"I don't know that. You're the one that is setting up some kind of time constraint, and as far as I'm concerned, I don't see it. I need time to get to know you. To trust you. I mean…I just met you."

His hand ran through his glorious blond mane, easing the frustration and pressure that he felt inside. "Ok, I get that. Just don't discount what I'm about to show you."

"What are you talking about?"

"Harmony, my gifts are also unique. I'm an Earth Keeper, and like the Earth – I hold impressions of moments in time in my DNA. I show people flashes of their past, present and future possibilities. This is how I know – I was meant to find you."

She stepped away from him, her eyes wide with questions. He raised his right and touched her cheek. She reveled in the tenderness of that touch. "Here….tell me what you see," he murmured.

Harmony gasped as a flood of images tumbled through her mind. The scattered pictures were jumbled, slowly turning, until they began to morph into a scene.

A Roman soldier in brass battle regalia and a red velvet cloak looked down into the face of his Beloved, an elegant woman in a white and gold tunic. A blue stola covered her elegant shoulders, and her eyes were emeralds ringed with dark khol. She beckoned him to kiss her upturned, full lips. As he bent to taste her, tears of love and pain fell from her eyes. She strained towards him

– her love wrapping and protecting him as he prepared to go to battle...

This scene vaporized as another came into view...

A young woman, clad in a dark green cloak, walked through the dense forest. She met in secrecy with a group of similarly clad women around a full moon-lit clearing. It was Beltane, and the hunt for the lovers would begin at the sound of the horn. A ringing call echoed through the night. The young woman bolted, hearing the sound of heavy thudded feet. She glanced around, relieved to find a cave hidden by an expanse of trees. She crawled in, expecting to find it empty, shocked instead by the bright, hungry blue eyes that met her. Her cloak fell away as she gave in to the onslaught of kisses and fire that consumed her....

One again, the scene vanished as another swirled into her mind...

A small family picnicked in the verdant grass of a beautiful French park. The father was handsome and debonair, with flashing blue eyes and a boisterous laugh that echoed around his children's squeals of delight. The mother was a beautiful woman whose soft green eyes overflowed with love at the sight of her son and daughter playing with their father. The young parents gazed at one another, sharing a look of tenderness and great love. The husband reached towards his wife, kissing her gently, all the while being tugged in multiple directions by little hands that wanted his attention....

Harmony pulled away, her eyes wide with awe. "What was that? What did you just show me?"

Tristan's hand moved from her face down to her arm, holding her hand in his. "That was us."

"Us?" her voice was incredulous. "You mean –"

"From past lives."

"But how can you be sure?"

"I don't control what shows up, Harmony. These are imprints from a higher source. They contain messages for the person who receives them."

"What's the message?"

He pulled her close. "The message is that we were meant to find each other. That's why I'm here. I came to you to help trigger you to remember."

Shock pervaded through her body, assaulting all common sense and logic. *This doesn't make sense! It's too soon!* The visions. His admission. Her body reacting so intimately and familiarly towards him. She felt a deep recognition tugging somewhere in her, but she couldn't point her finger to it. *Why me?*

"Don't you see?" he asked softly, his finger caressing her cheek. "This is not a coincidence."

"Tristan – this is a lot to take in all at once. I need a moment to get my head on straight."

"Ok, I can give you that. What are you doing tomorrow?"

Whoa! Change of direction here! "Tomorrow? I have my second interview at NET Media in the morning and then I'm free in the afternoon."

"On a Sunday?" his tone was suspicious.

"That's what the email said. Why?"

"I want to take you somewhere afterwards."

"Really? Where?"

"I can't tell you. It's a surprise. Trust me – you'll love it."

"And if I say no?" she teased.

He brought her closer to him, making her catch her breath as he grasped her chin and lifted it up. "No is not an option." he whispered.

His lips descended on her, assaulting her senses with his raw masculinity. She drank him in, granting his probing tongue access into her mouth. He caught her lower lip in his, sucking on its fullness. She groaned at his gentle tugs, his hard body rippling with energy as they kissed. It ignited a boiling hot core in her center.   Something in her snapped, like a rubber band pulled too tightly. She could feel it. She could remember. She could taste the essence of it in their kiss.

Chapter Six

Harmony opened her eyes as the sound of music filtered out of her alarm clock. 8:00 a.m. She groaned, relishing the luxurious stretch of her body. She touched her lips, delighting in the memory of Tristan's kisses claiming her, urging her to respond to his touch. Her mind was filled with the three scenes he'd imprinted on her. The nature of their connection shocked her. *How can I be sure?*

She sat up, staring at her comfortable, familiar surroundings. Her cream down comforter was rumpled, a contrast to the tidiness of her room. Crystals adorned her shelves and images of powerful female deities covered the walls. Rose and lavender wafted in the air, creating a feminine relaxed feel to her room.

It was her sacred space - a place that she called home. Even in the sanctity of her room, she still felt Tristan all around her. He elicited a feeling so strange and foreign yet familiar. She couldn't place it but it tugged at her cellular memory.

Moving gracefully out of bed, she walked over to her yoga mat. Standing upright and firm, she reached above her head as if to grasp the sun, and began to move through a series of poses. The asanas awakened her energetic centers, grounding and preparing her for her day ahead. She forced herself to focus on her breathing, allowing its vitality to travel though her body, coaxing and stretching the muscles. It was a comforting, steady practice that cleared her mind and sharpened her thoughts. She would need that to focus if she wanted to land this job at NET Media.

A buzzing from her nightstand interrupted her reverie. She stood with fluid grace and walked towards her cell phone. There were three text messages: Tristan, Clara, and Todd Wenzley. She quickly opened her messages, viewing Tristan's first. A smile spread on her face.

Good morning. Greatly enjoyed our dinner last night. You're a tasty dessert. Can't wait to see you later!

She quickly replied: **Waking up with thoughts of you! Big smile on my face ☺. Can't wait to see you too!**

She hit send and looked at her next message from Clara: **Good luck on the interview! Call me later! Can't wait to hear about it!**

She quickly replied: **Thanks! I'll call you later and fill you in! So much to tell you!**

After hitting send, she eyed Todd's message with a wary eye: **So nice to meet you! Would LOVE to have dinner again. Just tell me when.**

She gulped. *Oh Todd! You don't stand a chance. Sorry.* Better to be direct. She quickly responded: **Nice to meet you too. I'm pretty busy right now. I think it's better for us to be friends.**

With a sigh, she hit send. It was futile, she knew. She didn't want friendship or anything more with Todd. How could she? Since meeting Tristan, he occupied her thoughts, and she didn't want any distractions.

She turned towards her small white altar in the corner of her room. She opened the doors gently, greeted by the scent of sage and copal. This was her sacred time to connect to Spirit before she prepared herself for her day. Kneeling down, she stared at the figurines of Mother Mary, Isis, Kuan Yin and the Angels. They were her Guides. Her anchor. Her foundation.

She bent her head to murmur a few words of prayer, giving thanks for her blessings, as she connected from her heart. A peaceful calm enveloped her, setting her mind at ease. She surrendered to the vortex of energy and light that flooded over her.

Her mind drifted to the first time Emily taught her how to pray. Emily had shared that she and Harmony came from a long lineage of women who served the Mother Goddess, the Creatrix. Her lineage was composed of priestesses, Queens, healers, mothers and leaders who carried the vibration of the Divine Mother in their DNA.

Emily taught her well and she used the mantras and mudras to cover herself in a veil of protection. It was the grounding force that kept her from losing her mind when the images of creepy creatures inside people's bodies began to emerge.

A beeping sound interrupted her and she looked at the clock. 8:45 a.m. She needed to hurry. Even though it was Sunday and traffic would be light, she wanted to give herself ample time to prepare for the Wellness Director and the VP of NET Media.

Ok...here goes nothing. I hope this will be worth it.

~~~~~

The massage rooms at NET Media were resplendent in rich dark blues, soothing greens, and creamy pale yellows. Transcendental, meditative music filtered into the room, emitted from Boss speakers tucked discreetly in the corners. Lavender, ylang ylang and bergamot infused the air giving the room a relaxing and soft feeling. The hanging paper lanterns cast a muted golden light. Harmony felt at home. This was her world.

She ran her hand across the thick fleece blanket that covered the padded massage table, sighing at the softness of the cotton. Reaching underneath the table, she turned the warmer on.

A soft knock at the door indicated that Lydia Carey had arrived. Harmony greeted her, pleasantly surprised to see her in jeans and a t-shirt. Her blond bob was tucked under a baseball cap. Without the constraints and formality of the suit, Lydia looked much younger and more carefree.

"Thank you for coming on such short notice," She began. "I can go ahead first. Mr. Torres won't be here until around 10:30."

"That's fine." Harmony smiled. "I'll leave you to get ready for your session. Please get undressed and place your face in the cradle when you're ready. I'll be back in a few minutes."

She walked out of the massage room to give Lydia some privacy. Outside the room, the Wellness Department greeted her, stocked with every kind of exercise equipment a gym could possibly need. She viewed the class schedule and noticed the company offered Pilates, Yoga and Dance classes. *Hmm..great perks! I might like working here afterall.*

She turned back to the door and slowly opened the handle. "Are you ready?" she called out softly.

She was rewarded with a muffled "yes" from a prone Lydia. Easing gracefully into the room, she came up to Lydia's right side and took a deep grounding breath, centering herself and applying her shield. Saying a silent prayer of gratitude, she placed her right hand on the top of Lydia's neck and her left on her sacrum, feeling the energy running up and down her spine. Her eyes were closed as she connected to the field that was known as Lydia Carey.

Once she felt complete in her assessment and connection, she turned and rubbed warm lotion over her hands. Using a series of long, slow effleurage strokes, she kneaded the muscles of her back, moving from her neck down to her tailbone. Lydia's sigh of pleasure indicated that the pressure was perfect. She continued to work on her back, first on the right, and then on the left. She could sense Lydia letting go and beginning to relax.

Her intention was to move down to her legs next, but a movement caught her eye and caused her to pause momentarily. With a narrowed gaze, she allowed herself to psychically look into Lydia's body and noted a dark blue column appearing in her spine. It was long and tubular starting from her coccyx to the tips of her cervical vertebrae. It was filled with strange, worm-like creatures that undulated to the meditative music. Their hypnotic movements were slow and languorous, drawing her closer.

Harmony gulped and closed her eyes, shaking her head to break free from the trance. *Gross! What the hell is that? People really carry some crazy stuff in their bodies!*

She forced her to continue, applying pressure as she moved down Lydia's back to her legs. Even as she used her fingers to knead out knots, her knuckles to ease out stiffness, and her elbows to dig in deeper, she could not ignore what she saw. She immediately strengthened the force field around her, not wanting any of the worms to attach on her.

Continuing to massage her legs, she completed one and then the other. They had only fifteen minutes left. She asked Lydia to turn around and face the front. With eyes respectfully averted, she held the blanket up to help Lydia. All too soon, she began to massage her neck, occiput, and shoulders, eventually moving down both arms. She kneaded and stretched the muscles along the way. Harmony gently rolled her side to side, back and forth, using a technique that kept the muscles loose. The timer dinged. It was 10:30 a.m. Harmony eased the massage and stood next to Lydia's right side.

"Please take your time getting dressed. I'll wait for you outside." She murmured close to Lydia's ear. She couldn't wait to get outside of the room and take a deep cleansing breath. Removing the image of the tubular worms out of her mind was her first priority.

Moving carefully around the table, she slipped out of the room, not wanting to disturb Lydia's descent back to Earth. After quietly closing the door, she heaved a sigh of relief. And then froze. She could feel someone's eyes on her back, and she slowly turned around.

She was struck by a pair of amber eyes housed in an achingly handsome, flawless face and radiating from a powerhouse of a man. He seemed to peer deep into her soul, invoking something inside that shivered down her spine. She turned around to face the door again, trying to steady herself. *Oh my God! Who is that?!*

"Hi." His firm, deep voice reached across the expanse between them.

She turned around again and stared. It was impossible not to marvel at his thick dark lashes, straight, chiseled nose, strong cheekbones, and finely etched lips. He reached out to shake her hand.

"I'm Eduardo Torres – your 10:40."

She blushed. *This is the VP?!*

A smile crept across her face. Taking his outstretched hand in hers, she shook it firmly, feeling a strange, searing heat as they touched.

"I'm...I'm Harmony Mendelson," she murmured, firmly meeting his gaze.

For a suspended moment in time, they stood gazing at one another. She looked away and gestured to the rest of the gym studio. "You have a really nice department here."

His smile eased their tension. "Thank you. We believe in keeping our employees happy and healthy. How are you doing, by the way?"

His question caught her off-guard. "I'm well, thank you. And thank you for the opportunity to demonstrate my abilities."

"I look forward to it." His voice was soft and raspy, eliciting a strange fluttering sensation within her. The door opened and Lydia came out, looking revitalized and refreshed.

"Thank you, Harmony," she said. "That was a great massage! I'll let you prepare the table for your next session. I'd like to speak to Mr. Torres a moment, if you don't mind."

"Of course," she muttered, grateful to excuse herself from the intense stare of Eduardo Torres. She entered the safe, muted haven of the massage room. A nervous tension raged inside of her. Was it attraction or something else? *Why did I respond like that? It was just a handshake!*

Shaking her head to clear her thoughts, she began to strip the table, dumping the old linens into a bamboo basket in the corner of the room. She opened a cabinet to find more neatly pressed flannel cotton sheets. She chose a pale blue fitted sheet and placed it over the massage table. Fully aware that she would be massaging Eduardo Torres in a few minutes, she could barely concentrate.

Harmony finished, and forced herself to be still and ground. She began to breathe in a cycle that Emily had taught her and found herself regaining equilibrium and peace. When the knock came and the door opened, Harmony was at ease.

She smiled, welcoming Eduardo to the room. He came in with ease, commanding the space with his powerful build and muscular frame. He wore fitted black jeans, a black pin-striped jacket, and a white button-down shirt. He shrugged out of his jacket and placed it over a chair.

"I'll leave you to get ready, sir," she said softly. "I will be back in a few minutes when you're done. If you don't mind lying on your stomach, we can get started on your back."

Once again, his amber eyes pierced into her, and her stomach was full of butterflies. "I look forward to your body work."

She nodded in agreement and stepped out the door. There was no one else in the department. Harmony paced back and forth, stretching her body restlessly. After a few minutes, she knocked and opened the door, relieved to find him lying prone on the table.

"Are you ready?" she asked softly.

"Yes."

Walking over to his right side, she closed her eyes and silently repeated a mantra of protection before laying her right hand over his occiput and her left over his sacrum. A searing heat once again flashed against her palms. Her eyes closed as she energetically assessed his body.

He had a similar column of dark blue energy in his spinal cord, but unlike Lydia's, which housed strange creatures, his was outlined in silver and it radiated like a thermonuclear device. She could not see into the column itself, but felt the presence of a heavy energetic wave running through her as their contact continued. The heat beneath stayed constant as she touched him.

With supreme effort, she pulled away to put lotion on her hands. Eduardo emitted such a heated vibration that she was sure the lotion would melt and run like butter over his muscular body. As Harmony turned around to face him, she was struck by his beauty. Sculpted like an athlete, his build was muscular and strong and his skin was olive-toned and smooth. If milk chocolate had a form, it would have been Eduardo Torres.

She placed her shaking hands on his upper shoulders, kneading the muscles with smooth, firm effleurage strokes. As she worked on his shoulders, he began to relax, breathing deeply with each passing moment. Encouraged, she continued to move down his back, using petrissage and effleurage strokes to ease the knotted muscles along his spine. She worked on both sides of him, reveling in how easily his body succumbed to her work. She kneaded downward towards his strong legs, offering him reflexology when she reached his feet. He remained silent and still as she worked on him.

She completed her work on his left leg smoothly and quickly. They were twenty minutes into his massage.

"Would you like to turn over so I can work on your front?" she asked gently.

"Absolutely. This will give me a chance to look at you," he replied. She lifted his covers and averted her eyes. When he was settled on his back, she replaced the cover and tucked it securely around his sides. His eyes were open, watching her with a panther's gaze.

His eyes! I've never seen that color! It's beautiful! Damn....he's beautiful! Harmony scolded herself and managed a smile, feeling his eyes burn into her. Lotioning her hands, she worked on his shoulders and neck. Her hands rubbed strong circles over his firm pectorals and his sides, careful to avoid his abdomen. Initially, she didn't make contact with people's abdomen unless they gave her permission. This area generally made people feel uncomfortable and vulnerable.

She glanced down and found his heated gaze fixed on her face. His intense focus was chilling and exciting at the same time. *I really wish he wouldn't look at me like that.*

"Do I make you nervous?" he asked softly.

"A little."

"Why?"

"I feel like you're trying to see through me – into me. It's a little unnerving."

He gave a small laugh, it eased his features immediately. "I seem to have that effect on people. I would have to blame it on the eyes."

"Your eyes are beautiful."

"Well, they're made for appreciating great beauty."

Harmony was speechless. *What am I supposed to say? This guy is too much.*

"Umm...thank you," she whispered, focusing on massaging his arms, hands and fingertips.

"Would you be willing to massage my scalp? I know we're almost done. I could really use a nice head massage."

"Of course." She began to work on his scalp, enjoying the feel of his dark, ink-jet black hair between her fingers. His sigh urged her to continue as she gently pressed on his cranium, massaging with her fingers to stimulate blood flow around his head. As she continued to work on his head, she could feel a warm heat creep up her fingers. Her eyes closed as she allowed this heat to languidly move through her, connecting her to him as she worked on the planes and suture lines of his skull.

When she opened her eyes, she found Eduardo staring at her again. This time, his eyes had taken a more orange hue, making him look strangely carnal and savage. She was unable to break his gaze as she rubbed his temple and his occiput.

The alarm chimed, indicating their time was up. The spell broke as she stepped away.

"Our time is finished," she said in a husky voice.

He sighed and stretched his arms. "That was quite delightful, Harmony. Thank you."

"You're welcome." She blushed at his compliment. "I will wait for you outside once you're dressed."

"Of course."

Harmony opened the massage door and slipped out. The change in the air was welcome as she took a deep breath. Inside the massage room, every breath she inhaled was charged with Eduardo Torres. It took all her concentration to stay centered and not fall under the hypnotic spell of that powerful, attractive man. No wonder he was successful in his business. He had an aura of authority and charisma that drew you in and asked you to succumb. *He even smells like danger! And sex!*

She walked over to the window, looking out at the expanse of the city below her. The view was phenomenal. Tiny pointillist people scurried in order around the cars zigzagging through the streets. They were so distant from the power in the office, the intoxicating atmosphere at NET Media. *Would this become my world too if I decide to join them?*

"Pretty spectacular, isn't it?" Eduardo's voice startled her. He appeared next to her, looking refreshed and relaxed as he gazed out the window.

"It's quite impressive."

He took in her flushed face and calm demeanor. His eyes narrowed as they travelled down her body, noting the visible rise and fall of her chest and her shapely legs. "Would you like a tour of the office?"

"Sure." He placed his hand on her elbow and led her out of the Wellness department. The contact of his skin shocked her again as she felt that searing heat travel through her. *Why does he make me jump like that? What is that?*

"I see you feel it, too."

"Feel what?" She asked shakily.

"That pull – between us."

He did NOT just say that! "Well...people do radiate energy and vibration. Perhaps that is what's happening."

"I don't think so," he murmured. Abruptly, he changed the subject, discoursing on NET Media, their history, and the kind of clientele they served. Eduardo led her around the main office, peppered with cubicles and smaller executive suites, and finally brought her to the studio where they filmed TV ads and interviews.

"Our film department is located at our East side office. We have our own studio and crew. There's also a massage office for both staff and clients' needs. You may get pulled to work there sometimes."

"I was under the impression that I might have the opportunity to float around to different offices. How many are there?"

"There are three in the city, and we also have four locations in other parts of the country: San Francisco, New York, Washington D.C, and Miami. That option to travel is available if you decide you want to be part of our elite team. "

"Elite team? You have massage therapists travel to other locations? Why don't you just hire out at these locations?"

His scrutinizing eyes bore down on her. "We are very selective of the people we hire. Our therapists are as important as the executives and accountants. We look for skill and talent rather than availability. That's why you were given an interview." She remained silent, their eyes not breaking contact. "Your ability to grow in this company and travel to other locations is self-determined. It's up to you."

"I have a choice?" she asked, shocked.

"You always have a choice, Harmony," he responded. "Remember that."

She nodded, grateful for that option. "Thank you for that insight. My freedom is very important to me."

"But of course. We would not ask you to give up anything that was of value to you. On another matter...just so I might appease my curiosity...what did you see inside of Ms. Carey?"

Her eyes narrowed and a defensive shield slid over her. "I'm...I'm sorry. I don't quite know what you mean."

A smile grew on his face, crinkling the skin around his eyes. He looked younger and more carefree, but it was only on the surface. His eyes glinted with determination and awareness. "I know that question must seem like a shock to you. But I know what your gifts are."

She froze and looked away from him. *Shit! There goes my job!* "How do you know?"

"Because I can see into people's thoughts?"

"What?!" *Oh no!*

"Don't be alarmed. It's not every thought that I can read." His smirk expressed approval of the ones he'd caught. "It's only the ones that have a certain vibration. When you came out of the room, your thoughts were about what was inside of Ms. Carey. So are you going to tell me?"

"I…I saw a blue column of light in her spine," she stammered.

"And?"

"And it was filled with these strange looking creatures that looked like worms."

"I see."

"Are you going to tell her?"

"Oh no! This will be our little secret. You see, I think we'll have great use for someone of your talents in our company. As a matter of fact," he leaned in closer to her, "I think we'd make a pretty good team."

She felt immediately on guard, stiffening at the proximity of his body. "How so?" Her voice wavered.

"Well…if you can work on our 'special clients' and share with me what you see inside, perhaps we can help them be more amenable to our suggestions. You know, come to an understanding that benefits everyone involved in the project."

"So you mean…mind control?"

"I don't like the use of that word. It implies that someone doesn't exercise their free will."

"But isn't that what you're asking me to do?"

"I'm asking you to help our clients relax and get them in the frame of mind that will ensure greater success for their campaigns and ours. I just want you to share the resistance that our clients and staff face when it comes to working together as a team. You will, of course, be generously compensated."

She was silent, thinking about his words. This did not sound like the typical massage gig that Clara had signed her up for. As a matter of fact, every part of her wanted to turn around and run. But she was desperate. Her financial situation was rocky and she was tired of having to hustle for clients every month.

"So what do you think, Harmony. Would you like to work here?" Eduardo's voice was soft and tempting.

Her green eyes met his amber and stared deeply into them. If she decided to work here, she would have to be careful. Very careful.

"I would like to work here, Mr. Torres. Just so you know and that we are clear…I wouldn't want to do anything that makes me question my integrity and truth."

"Of course." His eyebrow lifted in surprise.

"And if a client should arise that causes me great discomfort, I would like the option of passing on that session."

"Sure. We have other therapists who can take your place if need be."

"Then I accept. It would be my pleasure to work here at NET Media."

A huge smile ignited his face. "Great! I'm glad you accepted. Your conditions are not unreasonable. I very much look forward to working with you, Harmony. And believe me….you will find your experience here educational and, I'm sure…quite exciting."

She wasn't sure what to make of his last sentence. She nodded. "Thank you. I'm sure it will be enlightening."

"I will see you Monday, then, for orientation."

"Yes. Of course."

"Don't worry about the massage room. The cleaners are coming to the office today. They will take care of everything."

He led her back to the wellness department to collect her belongings. This time, he made no motion to touch her. She carefully guarded her thoughts.

"Thank you again, Mr. Torres, for this opportunity."

"Please, Harmony, call me Eduardo. You're part of the family now."

"Thank you….Eduardo." With their good-byes said, she returned to the massage room and quickly grabbed her purse. She headed towards the elevator, pausing briefly to check her phone. There was a message from Tristan.

The door opened and she slipped in. Harmony leaned against the side, grateful that she was finally done with her massages and away from Eduardo Torres. As the silver doors were closing, Eduardo stepped through the doors fluidly. Clearly, he was ready to leave too.

"Busy day?" he asked casually. She quickly put her phone away, wanting to keep her message and her mind private.

"I think so. I'm stepping into a 'surprise' when I get out of here."

"That could be good," he responded.

"That's what I'm hoping."

"Of course, if you have a brother like I do, surprises are usually expensive, and someone gets hurt," he continued.

"You're lucky. At least you had a sibling growing up. I just had a crotchety grandmother whose idea of a surprise was slipping bacon in a ham and cheese sandwich. I mean....what's the surprise? You're still eating pork!"

He laughed, and she was struck at how easy the vibe between them felt – now that she wasn't touching him. She relaxed. He shared some of the antics he and his brother had gotten in to growing up, and Harmony laughed along. They were still giggling when the door opened to the ground floor. His eyes were golden with merriment and hers twinkled in amusement. As they stepped off the elevator together, they were greeted by a statuesque blonde beauty. Her frosty blue eyes glinted daggers at the sight of the two them laughing.

"It took you long enough," her cold voice snaked out and wedged between their laughter, promptly ending it. "Where the hell have you been?"

"Mariska," Eduardo murmured, leaning in to give her a kiss on the cheek. "May I present Harmony Mendelson. She's our newest therapist in the Wellness Department."

Harmony felt an arctic blast as Mariska's blue eyes assessed her from head to foot. She met her gaze squarely, her emerald eyes flashing. Harmony searched her energy. Mariska, too, had a blue column of light in her spine. This one was turbulent, with green blobs of jealousy floating around like a lava lamp.

"It's nice to meet you," she responded politely.

Instead of answering her, Mariska purposefully ignored the greeting and turned towards Eduardo, slithering closer to him. "Are you ready to go? I have a surprise for you."

"I hope it's good," he answered. He looked at Harmony knowingly and extended his hand. "Thank you again for coming to see me and Ms. Carey. We'll be expecting you tomorrow. Lydia will be in touch."

She accepted his hand, shaking it and ignoring the heat. "Thank you, sir, for the opportunity."

She headed for the door, opening it towards the outside traffic. She was grateful to escape Eduardo and Mariska. They seemed like the perfect pair: a powerful, hot man to melt an ice witch. She felt a buzzing in her purse: Tristan. This time, she answered it.

Chapter Seven

"Hi, Tristan," Harmony answered warmly.

"Hi, lovely." His relief at hearing her voice was audible. "How was your interview?"

"Good. They offered me the job."

"And you said?"

"I said yes."

Silence followed her answer. The pedestrian traffic hummed as Harmony waited for Tristan to respond. She could sense the tension building between them.

"Tristan...say something. Please."

"I guess congratulations are in order. Where do you want me to pick you up?"

She breathed a sigh of relief. "I'm downtown in front of The Frost Bank Building."

"I'll be there in five minutes."

Their conversation was short, and she had a feeling she was in trouble. It didn't alleviate the unease Eduardo had brought in her. *I wonder how much of my thoughts he's seen.*

It was disconcerting to think that her boss could pry into her private world without her permission. No matter how sexy and alluring he seemed, his intrusion was still not welcomed. She would have to shield herself more effectively if she wanted to work there.

All of a sudden, Harmony felt a lift in the wind, goose bumps rippling down her harms. She felt him before she saw him. As she turned, her emerald eyes locked into Tristan's. He sauntered towards her, muscular thighs flexing like a predatory cat's. He was a broad-shouldered vision of heaven, cased in a tight white t-shirt and fitted blue jeans. She was transfixed – all thoughts of Eduardo, the massages and her morning instantly erased from her mind. She saw only him.

Wow! He looks incredible! Good enough to eat!

"Hey beautiful!" He greeted her with a smile, enveloping her in a crushing hug. Her arms automatically reached up to wind around his neck, allowing her to press herself even closer. This was where she wanted to be. He dipped his head, softly her temple with his lips. She could feel herself humming with their connection, tantalized by his spark.

"I'm glad to see you," she spoke softly, a smile dancing on her lips.

"Missed me already?" he teased. "It's only been a night."

"A night. A year. A century. It doesn't matter. I'm glad you're here."

"I hope so." His smile widened causing her heart to flutter and beat rapidly.

"So what is this grand surprise you've got planned?" Curiosity dripped out of her voice.

"I'm keeping you in the dark. I don't want to ruin it!" He clasped her hand and started to lead her away.

"What about my car?"

"Leave it. I'll bring you back later."

She followed happily. *He could have told me we were backpacking to Hades naked, and I would have said yes!*

As they walked towards his white Tacoma truck, Tristan squeezed her hand and then stopped. It was as if he had run smack dab into a brick wall.

"Shit!" He swore under his breath. "He can see into your mind?" A venomous edge came out of his voice, and she cringed.

"What?"

"Eduardo Torres. He could see what you were thinking today."

"Oh God! Not you too!" she groaned. *Why can't people stay out of my head?* "Please don't tell me you can read my mind too."

"No, I can't," he responded flatly. "But when I held your hand, I saw the imprint of your interview. I saw him admit to reading your mind and offering you the job. Dammit, Harmony! You can't work there!"

"What do you mean I can't work there?" she immediately let go of his hand and whirled around to face him. "Who are you to tell me that?"

He ran a hand through his blond hair, sighing in frustration. "Harmony…this is a bad idea. The Torres brothers are notorious. They're as dark as you can get."

Her arms rose up and defensively folded themselves in front of her, giving her some space from the attraction that drove them together. "I don't see what the problem is, Tristan. I want this job. I need it right now."

"Look if its money you want, I can help you." His brisk response increased her irritation.

"No! I don't want your money! I can do this on my own."

"You're putting yourself in danger."

"What danger? This is just a massage job. And I need the work."

"Let me help you," he demanded insistently.

"No!" Her voice was stubborn. "I need to do this on my own."

"God, you're being impossible!"

"And you're being a bossy control freak!"

They glared at one another. Heated anger swept between them as they stood their ground, oblivious to the passersby who watched in curious interest. Tristan quickly stepped towards her, drawing her in to a passionately brutal kiss. She parried with a thrust of her tongue into his parted lips, holding her own as she answered his invitation to submit. She wouldn't. She couldn't fold. She licked and bit his lower lip, eliciting a groan as she sucked it between her teeth. He pulled her firm buttocks towards him, pressing his growing erection against her thighs. A soft moan involuntarily escaped her lips.

"Give it up," he growled between kisses.

"No," she snapped, kissing him back.

Still they continued to kiss, ravaging one another until they were breathless with desire. In the midst of a busy sidewalk, pedestrians passed them, averting their eyes at the overtly public display. Tristan pulled away, wrapping his arms around her and nuzzling her temple. She sighed, trying to calm the raging inferno that burned in her veins. She wanted him, and it made her ache inside with longing.

"God, woman! What am I going to do with you?"

"I've got a few ideas," she murmured against his neck, pressing her lips against his skin and biting gently.

"Your negotiation skills are quite impressive."

"You should see my make-up skills."

He chuckled, gazing down to look into her mischievous green eyes. "Are we going to test that theory?"

"It depends. Are you going to show me your surprise?"

"Alas, madam! Your perseverance will be worth the wait." He took her hand and continued walking. And that was it. Their first fight was quickly diffused by the torrential exchange of lip-locking. Harmony followed Tristan to his truck, careful to keep any more discussions away from NET Media.

Tristan started his Tacoma and began weaving through traffic, pulling them away from the cloistered frenzy of the downtown. As they headed west, the trees became fuller and the landscape shifted to residential homes and small businesses. Concrete roads weaved around the gentle incline of hills, transforming the rush of the city into a quieter pace. Soon they entered into silence and nature.

He drove further west towards Spicewood Springs. Tristan was lost in thought – his mission running rampant through his mind.

He didn't like her proximity to the Torres brothers. It touched a nerve that triggered anger, protectiveness and possessiveness. And yet he knew he couldn't interfere with her decision. She would have to see for herself what kind of men she was dealing with. But would he be able to stop her if she decided not to join The Tribe of Light? He wrestled with the dilemma, feeling a frisson of anxiety run through him.

Many people were asleep. The ones who awakened all took part in the conscious evolution of the planet and her people, positioning themselves in key grid lines throughout the Earth, their light a beacon for others to follow. His assignments had taken him to the jungles of Brazil, the mountains of Nepal, the tropics of The Philippines and the desserts of Egypt. He had crawled through hell and tunneled into madness looking for Lightworkers of the world. None of those previous missions ever felt as dangerous as Harmony Mendelson.

He turned his head to study her as they drove in comfortable silence. Her full, pouty lips could spit fire and kiss with abandon; while her green eyes enticed him to go deeper into the boudoir of her soul. The scent and color of her skin was like a drug, intoxicating him whenever she was close.

Gaining her trust was paramount to her saying yes to joining the Tribe of Light. Once she agreed, then they could return back to Terra Quattro and he could continue living his life like normal.

But what is normal now? His eyes narrowed at the question. He didn't realize that his life was impacted irrevocably by the appearance of Harmony Mendelson. She brought a piece of that puzzle that had kept him incomplete.

With her around, he felt like he a part of him returned to his center. An opportunity came alive that she could be his. That realization hit him like a freight train. Perhaps now he could finally stop punishing himself for the wrongful death of his wife. He reached over and squeezed her hand. Turning her head towards him, she flashed him a beautiful smile.

"Where are we going?" she asked, her voice a lilting melody.

"You'll see. It's a very special place. I've never taken anyone there." He enjoyed her curious anticipation.

"I suppose I couldn't use my womanly wiles to get it out of you?" she teased.

You could try, and I'm sure I'd like it very much. He smiled. "No. We're almost there. Hold your horses."

She pouted. As he squeezed her again, a scene came into his mind, knowing that she would view it as well.

A desert caravan travelled through the Sahara, encircling itself to protect from the growing sandstorm. A man dressed in Bedouin garb hugged the woman closely to his chest, covering them both from the stinging sand. They hid inside of the caravan, hearing the roar of the wind around them and feeling helpless in its fury. His lips sought hers, drawing her fear out as she shook like the gale of the storm. Their passion for one another was barely contained. Here in the searing heat and blinding wind, he could not get enough of her. He tasted the saltiness of her tears, his hand sliding under her layered garb to gently cup her breast and squeeze. She let out a moan of pleasure and desire.

Harmony gasped at the vision as Tristan smiled.

Harmony held her breath as a flood of sensations washed over her body, reignited by the kiss she witnessed in the imprint Tristan had left her. *Again! How many times have we been lovers?*

Suddenly, her train of thought broke. She gaped at the massive wrought iron gate before them. Tristan punched a series of numbers on an inconspicuous keypad, and the gate opened. The top of the gate held a large series of circles woven together to form the Flower of Life symbol with the words *Sacra Tellus* inscribed inside. Centered inside the sacred symbol of the Flower of Life was another image – The Eye of Horus. She felt a firm, squeezing sensation against her chest. Moving her right hand, she could feel the edge of it. *What is this?* The crushing weight made her feel panicked and ready to bolt from his car.

"Do you feel that?" Tristan asked, watching her palpate the invisible barrier.

"Yes...what is that?"

"It's a force field that surrounds this place. It's supposed to keep outsiders away. The closer you get, the stronger the pressure is. Most people can't even get past the gate."

"How can I stand it? I feel like it's pushing on my chest and throat. I can hardly breathe."

"Here, put this on," Tristan handed her a pendant, a quartz star-tetrahedron crystal that hung delicately on a silver chain. The moment Harmony clasped the chain around her neck, the pressure eased immediately. She took a deep grateful breath.

"Oh that's better! What is this?" She toyed with the pendant.

"It's a merkaba crystal. Consider it a hall pass to get to the principal's office," he teased. She didn't know how the pendant worked, but she could feel it negate the stifling pressure and she was glad for it.

They wound through the hilly estate, curving around oak and ash trees. Her gaze took in the small cabins that dotted the land. They passed under a heavily treed archway to reveal a sprawling Spanish-styled mansion with terracotta tiles and sandstone adobe walls.

"Welcome to Sacra Tellus or Sacred Earth." Tristan's voice was soft. "This is one of the residences of the Tribe of Light."

"It's beautiful!" Harmony's eyes widened as she took in the vast estate.

Tristan killed the engine of his Tacoma and gracefully jumped out. He opened her door and reached for her hand, assisting her out of his truck. He led her to the front door and deftly placed his thumb on a scanner, spoke into a voice decoder, and looked through a retina scanner, before it opened, welcoming both of them in.

"Tight security?" She mused.

"It's necessary," He responded brusquely before ushering her into the vast home.

Classic furnishings filled the enormous foyer with Greek statues and a large marble fountain. He gave her a tour, showing the sitting and formal living room, both artfully decorated in a modern, yet timeless style.

"This is quite impressive." She admired the large island kitchen with its sleek stainless steel appliances. It was the kind of kitchen that she dreamed about cooking in. "So who lives here?"

"No one really lives here. We have a house and groundskeeper that manage the upkeep. It's a training facility for new Lightworkers and Initiates. It gives them a temporary place to call home until they're invited to go to the Tribe's main location. Some people have had to wait for a while, so they try to keep it stocked with the latest in fashion and entertainment."

"Are you staying here?" She asked softly.

He smiled at her question. "For a while. At least until I can convince you to come with me."

She remained quiet. *What if I say no? Will he disappear as quickly as he reappeared?*

He held his hand out to her, inviting her to join him. "There's more. Come."

He led her outside, past the manicured lawns and a large garden full of organic vegetables and fruit. Harmony was mesmerized. The whole scene looked like paradise or a fairy tale. *I wonder what kind of rabbit hole I've dropped into?*

He gave her a tour of the spectacular grounds, still holding her hand and pulling her forward. They reached the edge of the greenery to stand in front of a small man-made pond.

He pointed to a building made of glass that stood in the middle of an island, surrounded by crystals that were taller than the average sized man. They were the biggest crystals Harmony had ever seen: Clear Quartz, Amethyst, Citrine, and Aurolite. They stood like 8 foot tall behemoths, radiating a field of vibrant energy.

"This is why you're here," Tristan pointed towards the glass structure. "I wanted to personally bring you to this place. It's time you know more about who you are and what you're capable of doing."

"What is that building?"

"It's called The Chrysalis. It helps Lightworkers protect themselves while they're in the process of developing their power."

Harmony looked around, bewildered at how they would reach the floating island. There were no boats or canoes around. "So how do we get there?"

Smiling, Tristan raised her hand to his lips, brushing lightly and causing a red heat to flare up inside. "We swim there."

Harmony looked down into the water. It was so clear she could see the bottom. There were numerous coiled metallic springs encased in pyramids and surrounded by crystals of different shapes and sizes. But did they really have to swim there? It was at least the length of an Olympic sized pool.

"Why do we have to swim? Can't we just take a canoe or a kayak?"

He smiled gently, sensing her trepidation. "We have to swim. This water is charged with orgonite coils at the bottom, and the crystals are programmed to clean your field. When you enter that house, you're light and clear. If not, you'll get sick."

"Ok, fine. I'll swim." Her curiosity was getting the best of her. "What do I have to do?"

"Change into your suit." he indicated towards a bathhouse near the pond. "And I'll meet you here in five minutes."

She nodded, swallowing her nervousness. Turning wordlessly, she walked towards the bathhouse. Being here in this opulent spread made her feel strange, like she was being watched. As she passed through the wooden door, she noticed the cameras set up in the rafters. It increased her discomfort and apprehension. She could understand needing security for such wealth and luxury, but she wondered who was behind those lenses.

Ducking into a stall, away from the probing lens, she changed into her two-piece bathing suit. She hadn't been sure what to pack, but her aquamarine suit showcased her fit figure, full breasts, and curved derriere. She stepped out, taking one last look at herself in the mirror. Her green eyes were bright and excited, and her cheeks bloomed red. Her thoughts were filled with the movie of her day. *First Eduardo, then Tristan, and now all of this! Did I fall into a fantasy?!?*

She walked out towards the pond, finding Tristan basking in the sunlight. Seeing him so open and exposed made her feel sensuous and hungry to touch him. She longed to feel his lips on her, to draw that fire out even more. She drank in his tall, muscular frame, the light dusting of hair on his broad chest. His firm abs rippled with every movement and his skin glowed golden in the light. He looked like a sun god in human form.

He turned to look at her, feeling her eyes on his body. The electric pulse between them charged and grew, drawing them both together. His eyes leisurely moved up and down her body, smiling in appreciation at her beauty.

"You look beautiful." His smile deepened. "That color really suits you."

"Thank you," she murmured, blushing hotly. "You look pretty damn good yourself."

His smile tugged at her heart. Oh what she wouldn't give to know more about him, find out what exactly was in his head when he looked at her. Her excitement at his proximity swelled.

"Are you ready?" he asked, bringing her closer to him.

She nodded nervously. "I'm not the strongest swimmer."

"That's ok. We'll go slowly. Just remember to breathe and trust that nothing is going to hurt you, ok?"

Tristan took a deep breath and plunged in head first, emerging a few feet away. He paddled around on his back, watching her with a relaxed grin on his face. She waded up to the level of her thighs, allowing her body to acclimate to the cool water. The temperature was warmer than she expected. With a sigh of resolution, she took a deep breath and plunged in, allowing her system to register the shock of the cool water. She emerged a few feet from Tristan, her arms and legs keeping her buoyant.

"This feels heavenly." her voice was soft as she swam closer to him. He brought her close, kissing her sensuously on the lips.

"I know. I could stay here all day. But we've got to go. We need to reach The Chrysalis while the sun is still high in the sky."

They began to swim at an unhurried pace towards the center island. Harmony could feel the charged particles in the water encasing her body, her skin absorbing them. A ripple of light ran from her crown to the tip of her toes. As she continued swimming, images of her morning, Eduardo Torres, Tristan, and Clara rose in her mind.

Previous days and long-forgotten memories followed them insistently.   It was hard to concentrate on swimming when her body felt like it was expanding and contracting at the same time. *Why am I thinking this stuff? I don't want to get lost in childhood memory lane right now.*

Tristan swam close to her, patiently going at her pace. "Don't fight it, Harmony. Let the thoughts come and give it to the water. That's what it's supposed to do. Pull out all the vibrations and energies that are cluttering your mind."

"But some of those memories are important."

"It's not pulling out the memories. It's negating their energetic effect. Sometimes our filters are clouded by our experience. This water is super charged to help you reach equilibrium."

The floating island came quickly within their reach. Tristan arrived first, climbing up the ladder and onto the deck to wait for her. She followed a few minutes later, coming up to the waiting ladder. Reaching up to his offered arm, he pulled her up out of the water and onto his soaking, hard chest. Their contact sparked a pulsating energy.

"You did great," he reached over to a bench and grabbed two large towels to wrap around them. He dried himself first, then turned and patted the water from her skin. She closed her eyes and gave herself over to his ministrations. His gentle treatment belied a great deal of strength and self-control.

As they walked towards the glass house, she could see that they were standing on top of a medicine wheel, and that the four monolithic crystals stood in the four directions: Clear Quartz to the East, Amethyst to the South, Citrine to the West, and Aurolite to the North.

Her eyes appraised each gigantic crystal with great admiration and respect. The clear quartz was so pure; it appeared almost invisible in its clarity. The rich purple hues of the amethyst emitted royalty and serenity. The golden citrine sparkled like a sun captured in stone form, and the layered purples and greys of the Aurolite reflected the earth's passage through time.

She could feel a radiant energy surrounding the house as she walked closer. The clear panes of glass glittered flawlessly. Sunlight streamed through the building, reflecting in rainbow arcs all around them. The roof, a golden pyramid, gave the building a mystical, other-worldly feel.

Tristan opened the glass door, beckoning her to follow. As she came to the threshold, she felt a gigantic blast of energy slam into her. It felt like the space between the molecules of her body opened a fraction of a centimeter – large enough to let a high vibration of light pierce through her shell. There was no fear, only fascination that filled her as she looked into the inviting world of The Chrysalis.

Chapter Eight

The glass walls of The Chrysalis gave an air of fragility but Harmony suspected otherwise. As she entered through the doorway, a rolling wave of light scanned her from the top of her head to her feet. It came from an instrument panel, tucked secretly against the door frame. She was suspended in place until she felt a clarity wash over her. She turned a questioning eye towards Tristan.

"Energetic scanner," he answered. "It's checking your field for any Corona programming."

Her eyes widened dubiously. "Really?"

"There are technologies in this property that would blow your mind. This energy scanner is a tool that The Tribe of Light has been developing for years. We have it in all our structures and vehicles."

"Why don't more people know about this?"

"Because human beings and those that control them are irresponsible and selfish."

She nodded, taking in the luxurious surroundings. It felt like she had dropped into a chapter of Arabian Nights. Plush pillows artfully rested atop low, thickly cushioned couches. They were arranged in a diamond formation on top of thick, colorful Persian rugs. Octagonal tables, inlaid with abalone and gemstones, held decanters of water and juice. A small spread of cheese, fruits and other delicacies waited for them.

"Please, have a seat," Tristan invited as he settled down on a large, white cushion.

She smiled, reminded of the earlier imprint in the Bedouin tent. Her gaze was drawn to the golden ceiling which blazed with the brilliant sunshine. She could see fine etchings of formulas and equations on the ceiling, and wondered vaguely what they meant. Tetrahedrons, icosahedrons, dodecahedrons, spheres, and Mobius strips were suspended like mobiles from the ceiling, twirling and radiating their own vibrational energy. They hung on nearly invisible strings, seeming to float in midair.

"This is a beautiful place," she murmured, taking a tasty morsel into her mouth. She settled into a cushion across from Tristan's.

"Yes – The Chrysalis is magnificent. It was created for a purpose greater than aesthetics. It helps strengthen your power centers and increases your energy field every time you use it. Plus, it blocks out the dark forces that attempt to get in."

"Is that why I'm here?" she asked, her eyes searching his face.

"It's one of many. If you choose to work at NET Media, you're going to have to use The Chrysalis at least once or twice a week to stop their programming."

"What if I don't have time?"

"You're going to make time."

"That's awfully presumptive of you."

"Harmony," Tristan's voice was serious. "There's nothing I won't presume about you and their intentions toward you. You're too valuable to The Tribe to not take things seriously."

"What about you? Am I just another assignment?"

He was quiet, shocked at how abruptly she caught him off-guard. "No," he finally replied, shedding a light on his armor. "You started out as an assignment, and now…"

"Now what?" she pressed.

"Now I want something more."

Her gaze softened. "What do you want, Tristan?"

"I'm not sure. I just know that this assignment – that you – mean more to me than any before."

She left her cushion and went to him, her arms wrapping around him. "There's so much more of you I want to know about. I know we just met, but I can't deny this pull that I feel towards you. It kind of scares me."

"I know. I feel it too. That's why we're here. I want to share with you some techniques that will hopefully help us alleviate this burning we have for each other."

"Techniques, huh?" Harmony teased him.

"Not those kind…yet," he murmured. "I have to be sure that you're ready."

"Ready for what?"

"Tantra."

"What's tantra?"

"Tantra is an ancient Indian Vedic practice that spreads the light of knowledge through yoga, sound, and the spiritual art of love. When you mindfully create a circuit of energy within yourself and another, you expand your abilities to heal, tune in to your power and generate strength."

"So we're meditating?"

"Today we are. I'd like to introduce you to the White Tantric practice first so that you can energetically shield yourself even more when you go into NET Media. Through white tantra, you can clear and heal any blocked energies with your breath, mantras and mudras. When you're ready, we can take it to the next step and practice the Red Tantra."

"What's Red Tantra?"

"It's the sexual practice of elevating your energy fields, directing that flow of current and cultivating your power. You will really understand how to control your skills and develop it even more."

"Can't we just skip to that?" she teased him, running her fingers up her arms, eliciting a spark of heat.

"Soon enough, my impatient paduan." He took her fingers and kissed them chastely. "But first, we must get started. The light of day weakens with each passing minute."

"Ok," Harmony pouted as she arranged the pillow to face Tristan. It was hard to concentrate as she faced his bare chest, muscular arms and impossibly handsome face. "You do realize how difficult this is to focus when you're sitting there in front of me?"

"Don't push me." his voice was husky and inviting. "You're sitting there, practically spilling out of that tiny top, and I'm doing everything in my power not to rip it off you."

"Ooooh - a challenge. I love it," she smirked.

"Exactly. Let's get started. The sooner we finish, the sooner we can celebrate."

"Ok," She smiled, taking a deep breath. "I'm ready."

"Close your eyes. That's the first and start breathing. Just listen to my voice and follow along."

Harmony closed her eyes, basking in the sun light that covered The Chrysalis. She could feel the heat rising in her under Tristan's penetrating gaze. A tingling sensation hummed in her pelvis, bringing awareness of her desires.

"What I want you to do is visualize a fireball of energy forming at the base of your spine. With your mind, direct it up to your power centers. What do you see?"

With eyes closed, she began to see a white snake with silver scales begin to coil and uncoil in a rhythmic dance, pulsating with a vibrant energy while emerging from the bright red fireball. "I see a white snake unwrapping and moving."

"Good. Intend for it to move up to your first power center. See it coil around a blood-red sphere. Do you see it?"

She nodded, feeling a warm heat growing in her root, spreading like a thick, velvet cloak. Her center of pleasure began to quiver as she witnessed the silver-white snake writhing up towards an orange sphere, wrapping around this center located in the heart of her womb, her uterus. She felt like she was falling into a tangerine flavored sea, igniting her senses. She wanted nothing more than to feel Tristan's lips roaming all over her. Shifting restlessly in her seat, she felt herself open and invite him deeper.

"Focus, Harmony." He whispered, feeling her imprinted thoughts on him and acutely aware of his growing erection. "Keep going. Bring that snake higher."

She took a deep breath and turned her attention inward, watching the white snake uncoil around her second power center and move towards a ball that radiated like the sun in her solar plexus. The snake enveloped the golden sphere, shining a bright ray of light around her, burning her with its intensity. She sighed as she felt a growing wetness between her legs.

A sensuously deep ache began to blossom inside as she watched the snake move upward towards her heart, wrapping itself around her fourth power center. A spiraling pink light began to form in the center, soothing the aching tension in her chest. She felt a soft hiss escape her lips as she focused on the white snake moving towards the fifth power center in her throat.

A turquoise sphere appeared, spinning in a clockwise direction that made her open her mouth and sigh. It was like diving into a Caribbean sea, weightless and buoyant, as the waves of ecstasy rolled majestically around her. A soft moan escaped her lips as she felt her nipples tingle and harden. The snake continued upward towards her third eye, her sixth power center, filling it with an amethyst fountain of light that unlocked her pineal gland.

As her pineal gland continued to unfold, she saw the opening of a library – her library of knowledge. She gasped as she was given a sneak peak of her soul's blueprint. A current of excitement rippled through her as she felt her body becoming more aroused.

Hungry for more, the snake unwound around her sixth power center and headed for the top of her head – her crown – her seventh power center. There the white snake wound around a silver-white ball that absorbed it, emitting rays of spectacular light around her. The top of her crown opened and she began to shake as downloads of information and energy began to rain down on her. It was like plugging directly into the Source of All – the Great Creator.

Her body began to expand and dilate as formulas, mathematical equations, sacred geometrical symbols and helical sequences enveloped her. Her eyes rolled back as the barrage of information began replacing and altering sequences in her DNA. She shook her head, releasing old information. As she clutched Tristan's hands, he felt the imprints of her download.

Slowly, the downloads faded, allowing her to break free of the hypnotic hold. She opened her eyes, dazed and dizzy. She caught Tristan watching her intensely and she smiled weakly. He raised a hand to caress her face.

"Wow!" was all she could say. "I've never experienced that before."

"I know," Tristan smiled at her reaction. "Welcome to The Chrysalis. It rocks your world every time. How are you feeling?"

She rubbed her temples, feeling the energy radiating through her spine, making her feel tipsy as if she'd been drinking. "I feel kind of drunk."

"Too drunk to do that again and this time, circulate that energy with me?"

Her eyes widened. "I think I can do it."

He leaned forward, capturing her lips in his. She barely registered the touch, still disoriented from the infusion of information.

"You really amaze me, you know that?" he whispered, his finger tracing her jawline.

"Yeah?"

"That amount of energy that you were able to capture and absorb usually makes most people pass out."

"Well, I feel like passing out right now."

"You won't. I won't let you. I will push you to the extremes though."

She laughed shakily. "And this is white tantra? Geez...what's going to happen when you do red tantra on me?"

"I hope I don't turn you into an insatiable monster," he teased.

"Stop challenging me. Haven't you figured it out yet? I won't back down."

"Good. I need a feisty woman by my side."

"Consider that job filled," she whispered, planting a branding kiss on his lips.

"It was filled the moment I saw you."

She blinked at his admission, a red flush of surprise coloring her cheeks. "Ok, let's do this. I'm ready to get my other training started."

He laughed and reached for her hands. Facing each other, they smiled and held one another's eyes. She could feel herself swirling deeper into his blue pools. They mesmerized her as he whispered the words to awaken the white snake at the root of her power center.

This time, the movement was more fluid and easy to circulate. She could feel him breathing in a relaxed rhythm that helped her to focus on moving the energy between them. With her third eye open, she was able to see the white snakes of light moving between them, wrapping around each power centers and then reaching the crown. Instead of being absorbed at the top, the white snakes reached above their heads. They entwined and then dove down their spines, filling their vertebrae with a blinding light that bound the holographic strands of their spiritual and sexual DNA together.

He breathed the circular pattern around them, imprinting them both with images and sensations, filling them to overflowing with information. Her body began to wind tighter and tighter, ignited by sensuality and excitement. A fine sheen of sweat glistened on her brow.

Tristan continued the cyclical breathing. After nine cycles, the white snakes met above their heads, twisting upwards to explode into a bright spectrum of light. Energetic downloads of sacred formulas and symbols, Flower of Life geometries, and high frequencies poured into them. A series of images flashed quickly – a Chinese couple holding hands, a Native American warrior entering his family home, a French artist painting a beautiful woman, a King and Queen holding court...

Harmony knew these had to be imprints of other lifetimes. She felt passionately alive. The vibrations rose to a fever pitch inside of them as they began to shake with orgasmic release, groaning and moaning in pleasure. Surfing on a tunnel of liquid light, they rose higher and higher as the dam of limitations broke free. Together, they walked a pathway, unhindered, unbroken – whole and complete.

Minutes passed as their breathing settled. When Harmony opened her eyes, Tristan was staring at her, a smile etched on his face. It took a moment for her to get her bearings in order as The

Chrysalis came into view. The sunlight through the panes was not as intense, casting a golden yellow glow into the room.

"Welcome back, beautiful," Tristan greeted her, leaning forward to kiss her gently on the lips. She welcomed the contact, feeling a change inside of herself. *What is that?*

"How do you feel?" he asked.

"Charged. That's the only way I can describe it."

"Yes, baby. That's exactly how I feel." He examined her eyes. They looked like the color of lush green grass after a rainstorm. "You really are quite a powerhouse."

"Really? I don't even know how to explain everything I felt and saw."

He nodded. "When the downloads came, I had no idea it was going to pour out histories like that."

"What does it mean?"

"It means that a lifetime isn't enough to love you."

She was speechless as her gaze locked with his. She could feel him inside of her, under her skin, in her cellular matrix. "So what is enough?"

He smiled. "I don't know what's enough. I just know that I keep coming back to find you."

She got up from her cushion and went to him. His arms wrapped around her, and she settled in his lap. His nuzzled her temple, feeling the heat radiating from her. Harmony felt safer than she ever had.

"Tristan," she began. "I know that this might not be the right time to say this."

"Say it. You can tell me anything."

"A part of me is scared to let you in. This experience here in The Chrysalis makes me feel like we're bound to each other somehow. But you have to know something. With my past history, men tend to leave. I don't know how I'll feel if you do that too."

He turned her head to face him. "Harmony, after all these imprints you've received, do you think that I could leave you now?"

"I don't know. People change. Things happen."

"Well then we change with the circumstances. I'm not letting you go."

"What about my job?"

"We'll deal with it. When you're ready, we'll leave. Until then, we've got to stay, and I'll keep training you."

"And when do we get to practice the Red Tantra?" she hinted, looking up into his blue eyes. They twinkled with a sensual merriment.

"Oh my impatient student," he teased. "Let's get you integrated first before I blow your circuitry with all that sex."

"Oh Tristan," she sighed with longing. "You can blow my circuitry any time you want."

He smiled, bending down to kiss her lips, groaning softly as she kissed him back. Their tongues twisted together, their first and second power centers awakening in response.

"Soon, my love, we'll start training soon," he whispered against her lips. "Trust me. You'll need time to integrate this energy. Things are going to come up."

"And what if it's too much?"

"Don't worry, I'll help you. That's why I'm here."

They wrapped around each other contentedly. Harmony smiled, feeling adored in the circle of his arms. Soon, a pink light replaced the warm golden stream through the windows.

"It's time to go." He finally spoke after a few minutes, breaking their revelry. "We still have to get your car, and I want you to be well rested for tomorrow."

She searched his face with a touch of apprehension. "Call me crazy, but I don't want to leave our bubble. This feels too good to be true."

"Don't worry. It's not popping any time soon."

He stood up first, reaching for her and pulling her close. Smiling, she embraced him again, seeing a vibrant column of golden-rod yellow light inside of his body. It radiated power and strength. He reached for her hand and led her outside of The Chrysalis. As they got to the edge of the platform, Tristan turned to Harmony.

"You know this is just the beginning."

"The beginning of what?"

"The beginning of us. The beginning of your transformation into a Lightworker."

"And if I say no?" she teased him lightly.

"No is not an option." He responded and dove straight into the water, turning back to give her an inviting smile. "Come on!"

With a shake of her head, Harmony smiled to herself. *Good thing you're hot, because it makes your stubborn behavior easier to deal with.* And she dove into the warm, clear pond, swimming towards him and their distant reality.

Chapter Nine

The pale, faint pink light of dawn peaked through Harmony's curtains, waking her to the rising sun in the distance. Turning her head, she saw the time on the alarm clock: 6:30 a.m.

She stretched her body, aware of a current of energy that ran through her. She felt vibrant and awake, her thoughts running to the day before with Tristan at The Chrysalis. Her lips still felt his touch and her skin tingled with his closeness. *Did I dream that?*

She wasn't sure these days which was reality and which part was magic. Being around Tristan created a wondrous connection to a world that was veiled by the illusion of the mundane. Since his arrival, her ability to see clearly into people's bodies was becoming more astute. She shuddered, remembering what she had seen in Lydia and Eduardo. *I hope I don't regret this decision.*

With a sigh, she picked up her phone. There was one person she knew that would be awake at this time, and would not be surprised at her phone call: Emily Morgan.

"Hello, dear heart." Emily's cheerful greeting immediately dispelled her anxiety. "I was wondering when you were going to call."

"Oh, Ms. Emily!" Harmony gushed. "Good morning! I'm so sorry that I'm calling so early. So many things have happened. I have so much to tell you."

"Of course, my dear. You knew I would be up anyway. Trust me when I say this is not an imposition. I've missed your voice." Emily's gentle laughter reached across the divide. "When are you coming? I know it's time. I've been waiting for you."

Harmony was flustered. Emily's strong, fine-tuned psychic nature always caught her off guard. There was not much she could hide from this woman.

"So you know, then."

The momentary silence created a heavy weight in their conversation. She could feel a shift immediately as her discomfort returned.

"Of course I do," Emily answered, her voice noticeably cooler. "And I don't like it. You've gotten yourself involved with both sides, and it feels like you're playing with fire."

"Ms. Emily, please," Harmony stammered. "I need to understand what's going on. Why are The Corona and Tribe of Light after me? I'm not sure what to do."

"Harmony, this is very difficult for me. I've seen your world unfolding, and as much I detest your connection to Tristan Alexander, I'm even more dismayed by your decision to work at NET Media. I realize that this is not my life to live. I can still dislike it greatly though."

"I need some answers. I need to make sense of what I'm doing and why Tristan is in my life right now. What happened between you two?"

Silence sat between them for a long while, and Harmony thought they had lost connection until Emily finally spoke. "My daughter, Serena, was married to Tristan for about six months. He was initially her student, and her decision to marry him came because she wanted to avoid the love affair that was going on between her and a powerful Dark Energy warrior, Nico Torres. Tristan was her shield and she used him to get away. He knew that, but he didn't care because he was loyal to her and The Tribe. He should have stayed away and not interfered."

Harmony remained quiet, willing Emily to continue speaking. She had never mentioned anything about her mysterious daughter or her death. All this was new to her. Surprise filtered through her awareness. *And she was married to Tristan too? Geez!*

"I tried to counsel Serena, but she was always a headstrong and stubborn woman. I told her to leave both of these men, but she wouldn't. In a lot of ways, you remind me of her."

Harmony was speechless. This was a side of Emily that she had never seen before. She had always viewed her Guardian as infallible, strong and independent. To discover that she had a daughter caused a tidal wave of emotion to overcome her.

Emily continued. "Serena's loyalties to the Tribe of Light were strong. But she couldn't stop loving Nico either, no matter how hard she tried or how evil he was towards her. She fought her feelings towards him by marrying Tristan, and it drove Nico to the extremes of violent behavior. He began to psychically and energetically attack her. He was relentless. And eventually, she didn't have the strength or the reserves to fight him back."

"Why couldn't he just leave her alone? She was married!"

A bitter laugh erupted from Emily. "Men like Nico Torres do not honor rules of behavior. He was never going to leave her alone. As unfortunate as it was, they had a soul match."

"A soul match?"

"Yes, dear. It's a bond that's formed when two people discover their kismet and karmic connection. It's one of the reasons human beings come back on this plane of existence. They're looking for their soul match."

"Well, if Serena and Nico were a soul match, why would she marry Tristan?"

Emily sighed. "People sometimes fight their soul matches if it goes against the greater agenda. That's what Nico represented to Serena: her enemy. She hated that he was a Corona, and that she had to choose between him and The Tribe. She couldn't turn her back on her lineage, her family or herself. Neither could he."

"What does Tristan have to do with any of this?"

"Tristan's headstrong and stubborn nature pursued her, even though she was madly in love with Nico. He just couldn't let it go. And when she was at a juncture of choosing between Nico and her place in the Tribe, it just about killed her. Tristan was her scapegoat."

Harmony absorbed all this information. "So she married Tristan even though she loved Nico?"

"Yes, dear," she continued. "Nico swore to destroy their marriage, even if it meant killing her. His revenge was brutal and awful. There was not much she could do to protect herself." Her voice broke, filled with sorrow. "And there was not much we, as a family or a Tribe, could do to help her."

Harmony could feel the relief mixed with pain in her voice. "Ms. Emily, if Serena chose Tristan over Nico, why do you dislike him so much?"

"Because, my dear," she growled. "He interfered with their soul match. When a Lightworker knows there is a soul match between two people, he knows not to intercede. He didn't listen, despite all the warnings from the Council and me. He was as much responsible for her death as she was. And now...he's back and in your life. I don't know if I can handle losing another daughter."

"Oh, Ms. Emily...please...no one could take me away from you. You're the only family I have." Harmony sobbed, her heart clenched. "But...I've never felt this way about anyone before. I really...I really like him."

"I know that, dear heart," her voice was heavy. "And I can't interfere...he's your soul match."

Harmony was shocked. "Really?" her voice whispered. "He's my soul match?"

"Yes, potentially. There is only one that comes along in each lifetime. But your blood line has given you two possible options. Tristan is one of them."

"And the other?"

"The other has not openly revealed himself yet."

"What does this mean?"

"I don't know, darling. I truly have not been able to see clearly what your path with these two potential men are. I must warn you though...if you go down this path with either soul match, it may be painful. You will experience your root chakra dysfunction to the maximum: fear, abandonment, insecurity and self-doubt. It will be one of many tests that you will undergo for your soul match to come to fruition."

"What should I do?" Harmony's voice held a trace of panic. "Tristan asked me to leave and go to The Tribe but I'm not sure yet. I just started this job at NET Media, and I feel like the opportunity is too good to pass up."

"Choose wisely. It is not my place to interfere. But you do need more training if you're going to work at NET Media. You and Tristan must come to visit me soon."

"How soon?"

"This weekend," she said firmly. "It's time you and Tristan learn more about why you were brought together. If you choose to take this path with him, I must help you prepare. There is still much more about the Tribe's tradition that you need to understand to help you raise your vibrations to meet his."

"Ok, we'll be there. I promise."

"Good. It will be a full moon. It's the best time to enter the Sphere of Light. Its construction is now complete. And Harmony…" Emily added. "Know that I'm doing this because I love you. My feelings for Tristan are still contained in a vessel of anger and blame. I have worked on it for years. But so help me God, if he does anything to hurt you…"

"Yes, Ms. Emily. I understand."

"No dear," Emily's voice dropped another few degrees to sub-zero. "You don't understand. Not yet anyway. But I will reveal that to you soon. Until then, I love you."

And then the line went dead, leaving Harmony both pensive and confused. *What was really going on between Emily and Tristan? And am I going to be able to make them both happy in the end with whatever I choose?*

Turning to look at the time, she realized that she had only an hour to get ready before her first day at NET Media. She wanted to make sure she gave herself plenty of time to shield and protect herself before she entered that cold, corporate world again.

~~~~~~

Harmony entered the NET Media office at 10:00 a.m., pleasantly surprised at the transformation of the media ad agency on a busy Monday morning. The reception room was filled with elegantly suited men and women, all holding some sort of smart phone, tablet or laptop. She gave her name to the detached blond receptionist, Tabitha.

Tabitha ushered Harmony to an office that held a handful of new employees, waiting patiently for their orientation to start. Harmony was grateful for the sea of expectant faces. She was glad that she wasn't the only one who felt butterflies in her stomach

Within minutes, Lydia Carey entered the room, commanding everyone's attention with her sharp, direct presence. She was a different woman from their previous interaction, dressed in a grey power suit, radiating authority and respect. After a perfunctory greeting, she began to review the company's policy and procedures in a cool and confident voice.

Harmony felt the austerity of corporate power reeking all around her. It was a world so different and foreign to her upbringing. Her grandmother had been so strict and controlling, providing such a contrast to Emily's gentle and loving nature. And now she was sitting in this office, listening to an impartial voice drone about the importance of working as a team and contributing to the company's success. *What in the world am I doing here?*

Rent! Bills! Life! Take care of it! The voice in her head reminded her. She consciously brought her attention back to the room and her seat. She felt fidgety and restless. *Stop it! You're here because you chose this. So deal with it!*

With great effort, she forced herself to look impassive. This would have to be like second nature if she truly wanted to work in this office. She began taking deep breaths, willing herself to be still in her chair despite her great desire to take off running. Lydia continued to talk about NET Media, finally concluding the exciting presentation on benefits and retirement packages.

As they broke free for a break, Lydia motioned for Harmony to follow her. They slipped out of the office and headed down the hallway towards the Wellness Department.

"I'd like to discuss your availability, Harmony," she began. "We have a busy week coming up. There's an advertising trade show happening this week and there will be a lot of traffic coming through the office. We need to get you booked so you can start working on some of our clients."

"I was under the impression I would only be working on staff."

Lydia appraised her with a steely look. "I was given direct orders from Eduardo himself that you're working on clients only and high-level execs. Clearly, you must have made quite an impression."

Harmony remained quiet, pretending to look as clueless as she felt. *I made an impression all right.*

Secretly, she was relieved that work was readily available. She was in need of an increase in her financial stability, and Clara, who had already been working there for three weeks, had boasted of a remarkably generous paycheck. It sounded like such a sweet relief from having to travel to different client's homes.

"Let's go over the days and times that you're available and the locations you'll be needed at." They headed over to Lydia's office, an impressive room with a broad view of the city. Lydia pulled the scheduler on her computer screen, indicating for Harmony to sit down. As she printed the schedule and the locations, Harmony took a look around.

Lydia's office had a softer feminine touch in comparison to the cold, modern décor of the company. She had fresh flowers and pictures of her friends resting on her desk. Engaged and happy, she seemed like a different person in the images than the detached robot who ran the department.

After reviewing the dates and time slots available, Harmony agreed to work on Wednesday and Thursdays only. She preferred to work part-time, leaving her schedule open for her private clients. Lydia quickly penciled her in and stood up to shake her hand.

"I'll see you here at 9:00 a.m. on Wednesday. I've already got the Kirasaki executives scheduled for that morning. You'll have the General Motors VP in the afternoon. Sound good?"

Harmony nodded, shaking her hand to seal the deal. It was done. Officially on their schedule, she was now part of the NET Media team. Looking at her new schedule, she could see that she was scheduled for 6 massages in two days. She knew the money would be good. She was looking forward to the work.

Her phone buzzed in her purse, effectively ending their meeting and orientation. She quickly said her good-byes to Lydia and headed towards the elevator. A text message from Tristan greeted her: **Ready for lunch? I'd love to see you & take you out!**

She quickly replied: **Heading out the door now. Meet you at the corner of Congress and 4th St.**

She walked through the Wellness Department, heading towards the elevator, before a voice halted her in mid-step.

"Leaving already?" Eduardo's voice was seductively soft, causing her spine to stiffen in recognition. She slowly turned around, her green eyes catching his amber gaze. There it was. The crackle of electricity rose up quickly between them. She could see his gaze darken as he drank her in.

"I'm done for the day. Thankfully, the orientation was quick and painless."

"And you start when?" he asked, walking up to her to stand next to the elevator door.

"Wednesday."

"That seems a long ways away." His gaze pierced into her, examining, curious and hot. She felt a flame of red heat burst inside, making her look away so that she could avoid his probing eyes.

"It'll be here before you know it." The ding of the elevator prompted her to move forward quickly. It was empty and she hoped fervently that Eduardo wasn't planning on following her. She was wrong.

He stepped in with fluid grace, casually standing next to her with his hand in his pocket. He looked cool, calm and controlled, studying her with an impassive look. She forced herself to face forward, trying to ignore the pull between them.

"I still make you nervous," his voice was low, making her tingle.

"A little."

"That's good. You do the same to me."

"I can't fathom why."

He reached out, placing his hand at the small of her back. That intimate contact made her jump as she felt heat coursing between them. She could detect a sharp intake of his breath as he caressed her back. She locked down her thoughts, willing herself to think of nothing.

"Why are you hiding from me?" He prodded softly. "What don't you want me to see?"

She turned her head, facing him with flashing green eyes. "Why are you looking into my mind?"

"I'm curiously drawn to you, Harmony. I was the moment I first saw you step out of that massage room."

Harmony was quiet, her breath slow and deep. She had to focus on keeping her shield up. Eduardo's charm and energy was intense and magnetic. "I can't do anything about that. Maybe it's all in *your* mind."

"Hardly." His raspy voice elicited goose bumps to rise in her arms. The air between them was charged with a heady energy of primal attraction. "I know you feel something. I can see it. Sense it. So why are covering your thoughts?"

She turned to face him, stepping back and forcing him to drop his hand, severing their connection. "Because I'm a private person. I don't share well with others."

"As am I. But this thing between us," he gestured between them. "It's not like anything I've ever experienced before."

"Pheromones. It must be a chemical reaction to something I'm wearing. It'll pass." she brushed him off lightly.

He closed the gap between them, caging her inside of his arms against the corner of the elevator. The intensity of the air between them was thick and laced with hunger and rawness. He bent low, his lips hovering inches from hers. She could feel his breath on her face, weakening her knees.

"This is more than just chemistry. You'll see." His voice was husky and promising.

The door chimed their arrival to the ground floor, and Eduardo immediately released her, leaving her breathless and sagging against the wall for support. People filed in and she pushed her way out towards the front door, seeking refuge in the morning sun.

How am I supposed to work here when I feel cornered by him everywhere I turn?

She barely had time to register her thoughts as Tristan met her at the corner of Congress and 4th St. His blue eyes narrowed as he took in her frown.

"What happened?" His voice was brisk and tense.

"Nothing...I just ran into Eduardo in the elevator."

"And?"

"It's nothing, Tristan. He just makes me nervous, that's all."

He ran a hand through his thick, blond hair. "Harmony, I've got a bad feeling about this. This job is not worth it. You don't need to be around those scumbags. There's got to be another way."

Harmony slipped her hand through his, squeezing him in an attempt to pacify his anger. "It's ok. You just have to trust me that I'm doing the right thing. I want this job, and I don't want it to come between us."

Tristan released a frustrated sigh. "This really tests my self-control. I'm not used to having to wait, and I definitely don't like sharing."

She wrapped her arms around his waist, forcing him to look down at her. "You're not sharing me with anything or anyone. I'm here, and I'm not going anywhere."

"Good," he replied, bending down to place a chaste kiss against her lips, igniting that desire that woke so easily at his slightest touch. "We're going back to The Chrysalis. I can feel your shield is up, but it's not strong enough yet. We've got some work to do."

"What kind of work?"

"We've got to continue your training and shield work."

"More mind-blowing work?" She teased him, her frown disappearing and replaced by a playful light in her eyes.

He smiled. "Oh baby, I haven't even begun to blow your mind yet."

Harmony smiled at his words. All thoughts of Eduardo Torres disappeared from her mind as she and Tristan walked away from her soon-to-be-corporate-world. She gazed up at him, awestruck that such a handsome, powerful, and mystical man could be in her life. He made her feel like she was the only one that mattered. That seemed enough for now.

But a nagging thought disrupted her equanimity. *What am I supposed to do with both of these men?*

Chapter Ten

Harmony and Tristan drove to Sacre Tellus in silence, both absorbed in their own thoughts. Stealing a furtive glance at Tristan, she wondered if there were other motives that brought him into Austin, other than her. Her knotted, worried fingers betrayed her anxiety. *How can I feel attracted to both men at the same time?*

Both men were powerful, determined and wanted her. She could barely think straight, let alone keep fighting her body's natural urges to give in. *What if neither of them wants me in the end? Am I always going to end up alone?*

Her eyes appraised Tristan, admiring his classic profile and the confident way that he controlled himself.

"What's on your mind?" Tristan's deep voice brought her back to the present.

She quickly guarded her thoughts. "I was wondering why you feel it's so important to teach me more about shielding right now. Aren't I doing enough?"

His brow furrowed momentarily. "There are a lot of levels to shielding. What you're doing would work fine if you weren't around people like Eduardo Torres. He can poke holes through your defenses easily and go deeper than you may want."

"How do you know that?"

"Because I can penetrate it too easily. And I pick up on the imprints he leaves behind."

"Oh, that's creepy. You should both just stay out of my head."

"I will. Once I know that you're safe."

"Tristan – it feels very violating to know that you and Eduardo keep tapping into my private thoughts and feelings without my consent. It makes me want to pull back."

"I know you don't like it, but I have to know what to do in order to protect you."

"Protect me from what? I need some answers, Tristan. What is Eduardo looking for that makes you feel that way?"

"He's looking for information."

"Information about what?"

"He knows I'm here, and he wants to know why The Tribe sent me to find you. He wants to know what you might be holding inside that is valuable."

"You're being cryptic. There's nothing inside that's valuable."

"That's where you're wrong, Harmony." He looked somber. "Your value to The Tribe and to The Corona is very high. You hold a specific genetic code in your hologenetic field that we need. This code is important to the success of the Revolution."

"That's the most ridiculous thing I've ever heard of."

"That's because you don't know about it. Emily Morgan may not have ever told you about it – on purpose. You've kept it safe and hidden all these years – totally unaware. But The Corona knows you've got this is in your DNA, and that's why Eduardo is digging."

"I'm still confused. This code…what does it mean?"

"This code has everything to do with your abilities. You haven't been forthright in sharing what you can do."

"You know what I can do, Tristan." Her voice was soft. "I just see creepy crawlies in people's bodies. That's not enough to make me special."

"You're holding back, Harmony. I can tell you're lying. It changes the vibrations in the air. You've gotta work on that."

Her arms crossed defensively in front of her. "What do you want from me, then?"

"I want to know what you can really do. That's the only way I can help you."

She was quiet, quaking at the thought of letting him inside.

"You have to trust me, Harmony. I'm on your side."

"Until when?" She shot back, her voice tight and filled with anguish. "Until you get what you need from me? And then you'll leave, too?"

Tristan turned to gaze at her, his blue eyes piercing and assessing her – taking in her fragile vulnerability. "That's it, isn't it? You're scared that I'll leave if you let me in."

She looked out the window, refusing to meet his eyes, feeling the truthful sting of his words touch her aching heart. "Everyone always leaves."

He reached out to grasp her hand, squeezing and imparting his warmth on her cold fingers. "I'm not leaving. I've been running for a long time, and for the first time, I feel like I've come home. It's because of you that I feel that way."

Tears began to well up in her eyes, threatening to break free from her self-control. "I want to believe you, Tristan, but I don't know. If I open up and you hurt me, I don't know how I can take it. What I feel for you…it aches inside. And it scares me how fast I've fallen."

"Well that makes the two of us then. I'm in agony every time I separate from you or when you walk into NET Media. I feel like my hold on you is tenuous, and that any minute they could take you away from me. That drives me to a really dark place, and I feel like there's nothing I wouldn't do to protect you."

Harmony felt a warm glow spread through her, melting the ice wall around her heart. He meant it. She could feel it. How could she fully love him if she didn't trust him? They would have nothing to build on if she didn't let him in. Taking a deep breath, she began to speak.

"Emily Morgan showed up in my life when I was twelve. She was my saving grace, literally. She adopted me from my grandmother, who made it publicly clear that she didn't want anything to do with me. It was a really rough time."

Her voice was ragged, raw with emotion. Tristan squeezed her hand in encouragement. "I didn't know what was happening to me. I could see into people's bodies and discovered this whole other world filled with strange creatures, beings and shapes that were invisible to the human eye."

Her gaze was fixated on the blurry scenery, seeing nothing, remembering the dark moments of her youth. "It was really scary, especially when these things realized that you could see them. That's when they would attack." Her voice quivered with fear and trepidation.

"Wow!"

"Emily quickly realized what was happening, and she trained me to control my fears so that I could fight back. That was when I discovered that I could control, affect, and remove these creatures." Harmony paused, closing her eyes tightly.

" I could reach into people's genetic matrix and find that sequence that created the problem and change it. People were being transformed. Immediately. I was doing it to protect myself, and I didn't want anyone to know, but word spread. People all over the world were coming to find us for help."

"What did you do?"

"Emily and I helped them. Miracles happened. Word spread. "

Her voice became subdued as she looked out the window. Memories flooded her mind, allowing Tristan to get imprints of her experience. He understood. The pressure that she carried as a child was heavy.

"Everything was good for a while. Then the darkness came. I was fifteen years old. That was when the dreams and psychic invasions started happening. It was summertime, and I was out at the pool with some of my girlfriends. I didn't see the car come up to the curb, but all of a sudden, there was a group of four men, dressed in black suits surrounding our circle. That was when they grabbed me and took me away."

The sharp intake of Tristan's breath hissed with violent fury. He saw the imprint and a shudder of anger reverberated through him. She could see him tensing with rage.

"Go on," he said encouragingly.

"They stuck me in a cold room, blindfolded, bound and gagged. I don't know how long I stayed there because time didn't exist in that darkness. It just felt really long and scary. They would drag me out of the room and lay me on a table a few times a day. I had no idea what was happening. I could feel them injecting things into me, and sometimes it burned like fire and other times it was just pure pain. It felt like I was being cut open and my insides were being ripped apart."

Tristan's sympathetic groan of pain made the tears spill out. A sob erupted from her chest. "I don't know what happened afterwards because I passed out from the fear. I just remember opening my eyes and seeing Emily Morgan kneeling in front of me and offering me water to drink. I wasn't in the cell anymore. Somehow…I was at home, but I wasn't the same person after that."

A heavy silence hung between them. "Emily told me a little bit of how they found me and saved me from all that torture. I had only been gone for two days, but it felt like forever. She told me that they had tried to do psychic surgery on me, but they couldn't get past the shield that I had protecting my energy field."

A bitter laugh escaped her. "My whole body hurt all over like I'd been beaten up, but she kept assuring me that they didn't do anything like implants or programming. I wasn't sure. I was screwed up for a while after that. Acting out – misbehaving – getting into trouble. That's when we moved. Emily took me away from that little town in Alpine, and we moved to Austin with the intention of blending in and being invisible."

"Well you can forget that. The Corona knows that you're here." Tristan's voice was flat and hard.

"Well even if they find me, I won't use my abilities."

"You may not have a choice. You've got to control your fears and learn how to defend yourself. Quickly. I don't want what happened to you to happen again. We're in the middle of spiritual warfare. You cannot second guess what to do."

She let the implications of his words hang in the air. She could not deny that he was right. "I don't ever want to repeat that awful situation. I'm prepare to do whatever."

"I can help you," He responded simply.

Harmony kept quiet, letting his offer sink in. "Ok," She finally responded after a few moments of silent struggle. "So what do you suggest I do?"

"I want to train you to move without hesitation into someone's body and influence what you see. You need to control your fears and master these creatures and programs. They're weaker than you. You can make them do what you want – or buy yourself time so that you can get away."

"How are you going to do that, Tristan? I don't even know that I'm capable of doing that."

"Well I do. We're going to build such a complex shield around you that no one will ever hurt you like that again."

"How?"

"Through sacred sex."

Her eyes widened in innocence. "Really? You've got to be kidding me."

"We're going to transform your body into the ultimate vehicle of light."

"Using sex? You know, that sounds kinda hot." She murmured softly. *Sacred sex? I think I like this kind of training!*

"Oh you haven't even begun to fathom just how hot it's going to be. There will be no one else for you when I get done with you."

"Is that a promise or a threat?"

He smiled, a determined look flashing in his blue eyes, melting her resistance. "Both."

~~~~~~

When they arrived at Sacre Tellus, Harmony could feel the invisible force field press on her again. It abated when Tristan placed the crystal star tetrahedron pendant around her neck, relieving her of the suffocating feeling. Driving forward, Tristan brought her towards the sprawling mansion. She gazed appreciatively at the stylish stucco, artfully manicured foliage, and Romanesque fountain.

Tristan got out and quickly opened her door, pulling her against him to place a passionate and heated kiss against her waiting lips. She could feel herself open to his luscious attack, sucking on his lower lip. She bit gently as he ground his hips against her.

"What's that for?" She asked breathlessly.

"A teaser."

"You're the tease!" She responded, laughing as his blue eyes darkened.

"Enough!" He growled, pulling away from her. "Let's get to The Chrysalis. I don't know how much longer I can wait to make love to you."

"That's the best suggestion you've made all day. But Tristan...I'm starving!"

"Of course! I've got to feed you before training. I apologize." He laughed, pulling her towards the door. "There's a spread waiting for us in the kitchen. I had them arrange it so it'd be ready when we got here."

"You're a man after my own heart," she smiled teasingly, following him into the grand house. A large feast of grape leaves, falafels and other Mediterranean goodies greeted them. She heard her stomach grumbling in protest. Tristan smiled, handing her a plate filled with delectable selections. He took her hand and led her to the outdoor patio, tending to her in a gentle and protective manner. A spark of pleasure ignited as he served Harmony as she ate.

They ate quickly, sharing small talk, barely able to take their eyes off one another. She could feel a heated tension between them, growing with each passing minute. He watched her eat like a predator assessing its prey, causing shivers of anticipation to run down her spine.

"I'm done." She pushed the plate away, careful to not overeat, knowing that she would have to swim the orgonite rich pond to The Chrysalis.

"Good. Let's go!" He grabbed her hand and pulled her out the door. His impatience caused a smile to grow on Harmony's face. Knowing he wanted her as much as she wanted him sweetened the anticipation.

Walking quickly through the grounds, they reached the pond's edge in a matter of minutes. He pulled his shirt off and began unbuttoning his pants. Harmony froze. *I don't have my suit!*

"What's wrong?" Tristan asked as his boxer briefs slid down his thighs, freeing his ready erection. Her jaw dropped. He was beautiful, smooth and ready for her.

"I...I don't have my suit. And..."she stuttered, feeling shy and unable to focus her words clearly. "I...can't think with you being so...aroused."

He turned and walked towards her, displaying his full nudity with confidence and sensual pride. He moved like a large cat, with graceful stealth and ease. She felt her blood boiling in her ears as a wave of desire coursed through her, triggering a cascade of wetness and lust inside.

"I think you need help." He murmured as he lifted the hem of her t-shirt and swiftly pulled it above her head. His hands deftly removed her bra, trailing over her breasts lightly. Her nipples stiffened and swelled with need. His hands trailed down her abdomen, pausing briefly at the top of her black yoga pants. With a swift and easy move, he pulled her pants and panties off, bending down to nuzzle her soft opening with his nose. Breathing deeply, he inhaled her musky female scent, growling with pleasure at how ready she was for him.

"Oh Tristan," she moaned.

He stood up quickly, pulling her into a heady embrace as their lips met, sucking and inviting. She could feel his erection pressing between her legs, rubbing her wetness, creating havoc in her body.

"You. Me. The Chrysalis. Now." His voice was thick and urgent. He slipped his tongue into her mouth, raising her to a frenzy of need and want. She gripped his tight, firm buttocks, drawing him closer as she ground her hips against his. He groaned, crushing her closer to him, forcing her to bend to his will.

"Come on." He pulled apart from her and led her towards the pond. They both eased into the warm water, swimming towards The Chrysalis with even, hurried strokes. She could feel her body aching to touch him again. She pushed herself a little harder, wanting to reach the glass building that held the key to her release.

Harmony reached The Chrysalis first, climbing up the ladder and absorbing the heat of the sun over her aching, wet body. She suspected that Tristan lagged behind purposefully so he could watch her emerge from the water first. She rewarded him by slowly turning around, arching her spine as she flipped her hair back, wringing the excess water out. Her eyes met his as her hands moved from her head to her body, wiping the dew from her skin, breasts, stomach and legs.

An audible growl came from him as he hoisted himself up onto the platform. She was riveted to his impressively large erection, which stood proudly against his leg. Her mouth watered at the thought of tasting him and running her tongue up and down his slick manhood. Feeling a bolt of hunger explode between her legs, she glided towards him, ready and waiting. He smiled, his brilliant blue eyes darkening as they drank in her luscious, wet body.

He brought her close to him while his hand stole up her side, caressing her as it made contact with her breasts. He cupped and massaged them as a moan of raw pleasure escaped her lips. He kissed her again, their tongues exploring one another, delving into a sea of delight and sweet torment. Harmony could feel herself opening as their kisses turned fierce.

"You keep kissing me like that, woman, and we're not going to make it inside."

She nuzzled his neck, while biting licking a hot trail across his skin. "Make me stop."

"I'm going to make you come so much; you're going to be begging me to stop."

Her eyes widened at his boldness. "Promises, Tristan? I might not make it back to work on Wednesday."

"That's my plan," he grinned, nipping her earlobe, causing her to shiver. "Clear your schedule tomorrow. You're mine."

"What about my clients?"

"Reschedule." He swept her up in his arms, walking towards The Chrysalis and pushing the door open with his foot. His gaze was hot, burning her with the need to be possessed by him. The energy of the room crackled as he laid her down on the cushioned bed. Their eyes were locked in an intense exchange of desire for union. It had been too damn much – all the waiting, the seduction, the attraction. Harmony wanted to feel him inside of her – longing to connect as intimately as the imprints had shown her. She reached for him, bringing him down towards her, but he pulled back.

"Oh not yet, love," his whispered roughly. "First, you have to learn how to surrender."

"What? Don't make me wait! I want you so much!"

"I want you, too. But first, I need you to completely open – surrender your resistance to letting me in. I want you to let go and allow me to show you all the levels of pleasure that your body is capable of."

"Yes," Her voice was breathless. Her eyes devoured him, her need pulsating like liquid fire. She couldn't think – only feel the wanton urge to wrap herself around him, be consumed by that maddening heat that threatened to burn all her resolve away. It was futile. Her body was on auto-pilot on a course to catapult and release.

"Don't think. Just trust me and feel your body. That's all you have to do."

Tristan pulled a dark, red silk scarf out and wrapped it over Harmony's eyes. The cool silk against her flushed face heightened her ardor.

"I want to show you something." his voice was thick, inviting her to sharpen her senses. "I want to show you how to make a serpent rise up from your groin."

"Back to the serpent again?" Her voice was touched with confusion. "Didn't I just do this?"

"Yes," Tristan smiled. "But this is different."

"In what way?"

He traced her jaw with his finger, sending shards of sensations to course through her face. "Today we're going to initiate you into red tantra."

"Finally!" She whispered. "It's about damn time!"

His hands wrapped gently in her hair, bringing her face close to his. His mouth rained hot, sensuous kisses all over her face. She felt herself melt as she succumbed to his kisses. "This is what red tantra is all about. We're going to amplify the energy that's in you and move it around your body and mind. That red serpent is the sexual energy that I want you to control. But first, I want you to visualize a fire-engine red dragon that's coiled at your root chakra, your power center."

"Ok, I got it." She wasn't sure where he was going with this.

"I want you to intentionally visualize that red serpentine dragon uncoiling from your pelvis and move it up to your stomach, then your heart, up to your throat, and then to the middle of your forehead."

"Why?" The desire in her was growing. She felt her body tingling, aching for his touch.

"Because we're going to wake you up, baby," He whispered in her mouth. She fell back into the heady, erotic kisses that he planted all over her body, moving lower towards her sacred spot. She couldn't help writhing as the growing pleasure cascaded like a waterfall all through her.

"Oh Tristan," she whispered, as his mouth found the center of her sexual pleasure. "What you do to me...oh!"

"See it." He whispered, his tongue darting down to taste her again. "See that red dragon uncoiling in your body."

Harmony saw a starburst of light blaze up in her pelvis, increasing the temperature of her desire. A red, fiery-eyed dragon began undulating and uncoiling at the root of her body, slowly twisting and unraveling its majestic frame. As if awakening, the dragon writhed in ecstasy, moving to a rhythm of a sacred dance. Tristan's tongue dipped into her pussy, tasting and pushing deeply into her. She sighed, her hips lifting up towards his mouth.

She could see the red dragon wiggling around her first power center. It ignited the sphere with a velvet maroon glow, filling her with a red heat. Hypnotically, it began to dance up to her second power center, igniting it with a bright orange light, causing her sex to open up as Tristan began to lick her clitoris. She moaned as she felt the velvety softness of his tongue caressed the folds of her lips, grazing her clitoris with his teeth, sending shivers of ecstasy through her.

Harmony felt her body awaken...

The red dragon continued its journey to her third power center, lighting her solar plexus with the vibrant golden ray of the Sun, warming and increasing her temperature. He inserted two fingers smoothly into her pulsating, wet velvet underground. She moved helplessly, grounding her hips to the bed. She wanted him so badly. She could feel herself heating up as the dragon moved upward towards her heart, attracted to her fourth power center. It sparked a pink glow, tinged with red highlights, emanating desire and love.

Harmony felt her heart expand...

Tristan continued his onslaught as his mouth sucked her wildly and his fingers continued to invoke and push her closer to her orgasm. She thrashed and groaned, her hands clutching his hair, holding him passionately against her unfolding pleasure.

She could see the red dragon writhing towards her fifth power center, unearthing a magnificent turquoise blue, as sounds of anticipation and agony erupted from her lips. She had never wanted anyone so badly. Tristan pushed in three fingers, driving her mad with his tongue on her clitoris. He sucked her deeply, sensuously, hungrily. She was close, feeling herself on the edge. The red dragon unfurled and moved upward to the center of her forehead, her Third Eye. Upon arrival, the dragon began to coil around a sacred goblet, the keeper of knowledge of her sacred power - her Pineal Gland.

Harmony gasped, feeling her mind open......seeing and feeling all the dimensions of..... LOVE.

She screamed as her orgasm struck, searing her body as it erupted, shaking her to the core. She shuddered violently as Tristan continued sucking and licking her pussy in her release, leaving her limp, languid and barely able to move. Her breath was ragged, mirroring the tumultuous crash of emotions and energy running through her veins.

Tristan continued his sensual onslaught, leaving her trembling sex and moving up to her abdomen. He suckled and licked at her breasts, catching her lips in his. She could taste her own saltiness, triggering a flame of arousal inside of her. Oh my God! That was amazing!

"Do it again," Tristan whispered in her ear. "I want to be inside you when we do his together." He paused briefly, sheathing himself with a condom. He entered her with slow, sensuous pleasure. Harmony gasped. He slid in and out of her, filling her and triggering the sensitive spots inside to light up and open. Their movements synchronized as pure sensation burst all over them.

"See the dragon again." his voice was thick with lust, making her broil. He was so hot for her, holding back his pleasure to make sure she could fully reach hers.

Oh my God, she thought. *How can I focus on this dragon when this feels so freakin' good!?!*

She brought her attention to her heart center, inviting the dragon to move up as it shot up from her root, to her throat, to her forehead. Her body tingled all over again. Tristan's breath was hot and heavy as he continued to pleasure her, driving his will into her body. He ravished and pushed her to the edge again. She envisioned the dragon coming up to her forehead, circling around and around, inviting his body to respond. He groaned in her mouth, feeling his momentum building.

"Again," he whispered into her ear. "Do it again. Don't stop."

Harmony was hypnotized by the rhythm of their bodies moving in and out. Tristan dove deeper and deeper, making her rise higher and higher. Surrendering to carnal pleasure, she allowed the dragon energy to move from her root area to her forehead in an automatic cycle, building concentrated pleasure, waiting to explode. And it did.

Harmony's hips lifted in mid-air. She was set ablaze as waves and waves of orgasmic energy rolled through her. As the dragon moved freely up and down, her body climaxed. Tristan pushed her harder and harder to the edge of the precipice, until they both exploded in a liberating sea of light and ecstasy, calling each other's name in their orgasmic release.

Chapter Eleven

Tristan removed the silk blindfold from Harmony's eyes, momentarily blinding her with the golden light that streamed in from the glass walls of The Chrysalis. It took a few seconds for her eyes to focus, her mind still reeling from two earth-shattering orgasms. A delicious ease settled over her as she turned towards Tristan. Her heart squeezed tightly in her chest as he dazzled her with his beautiful smile and tender look. He ran his fingertips down her cheek, bending down to kiss her parted lips. A soft sigh escaped as she felt her body tremble at this touch.

"Wow!" She sighed, relishing the feeling of her body possessed and loved by him.

"My thoughts exactly." His deep voice warmed her even further. He brought her closer to his side, nestling her against his still-hot chest. In their post-coital glow, her desire for him flickered as she wiggled her buttocks suggestively closer to his groin. His semi-hardness stiffened again.

"You've got me completely undone," she murmured. Harmony planted soft kisses on his hand, licking and nipping as she said. "I've never made love like that before."

He leaned in to kiss a sensitive spot behind her ear, causing shivers to run down her spine. He inhaled deeply, their scent intermingled with sex. He continued to kiss the back of her neck, biting and growling gently. She arched her back and whispered his name. His hand slid around to cup her breasts, fondling and tugging at her nipples until she was breathless and moaning with unrestrained desire.

"I want you again." He growled against her ear, his tongue licking the outer shell and sparking sensations that made her skin tingle. She could feel the hardness of his desire pressing behind her as he slipped it between her legs. The folds of her lips were wet as they slid against his hard masculinity, allowing his tip to touch her sensitive and highly charged clitoris.

A sigh escaped her lips as she reached down to cup his firm erection, squeezing and massaging him with skilled fingers. He hardened even further, his moves becoming more urgent and forceful. She could feel the power that he wielded in his body, and how he was keeping it in check during their lovemaking. But she wanted more. She wanted him to be as open and raw as she felt.

"Show me more, Tristan. I want you to unlock my body to what it can do." She whispered, encouraging him to delve deeper into the layers of her sexual energy field.

"Lay back." He commanded, turning her so that she was on the bottom. "I want you to focus on channeling this red root energy up and down your spine. When I tell you to take it to your crown, do it and then send it over to me."

"Yes..." She sighed. Her body woke up to his touch, activating that root chakra energy of desire from its slumber. She was ready again for him.

He gazed at her, his blue eyes darkened with need. "You are so beautiful, baby. I knew it would be this way between us."

Bending down, he claimed her lips, kissing her fiercely and possessively running his tongue down her throat to her , claiming her. She felt herself surrender, her breathing shallow and heated. His mouth closed over her nipple, sucking passionately while grazing them with his teeth. His other hand squeezed and plumped her full mound, pulling against the tender peak as a liquid fire of red light coursed up and down her spine. Her temperature rose again, building to a fever pitch.

"Focus. See that red light energy moving up and down....move it faster."

The bolt of red light raced up and down her spine, building her kundalini, as his tongue moved down to her wet and ready sex. He bent down to taste her juicy pussy, and she arched her back and offered her center of pleasure to his will. She could feel her spine burning like fire as the red energy moved from the base of her spine up to her forehead, looping around like a circuit.

He inserted his rock-hard erection an inch inside of her. She could see a pulsating light at the tip of his cock as he entered her. That light of his crown grew in intensity as it rippled through her and connected to the light at the base of her pelvis, spreading its heat and fire up and down her spine. It was almost unbearable, his fullness taking over her body, spreading her wide as she squeezed him all the way to his root. He grunted with delight, pushing in deeper, until he was touching her cervix, stimulating her nerves to higher levels of sensitivity and pleasure.

He took both her legs and pressed them against his chest, moving in synchronicity with her body's rising desire. He drove her higher and higher as the circuit of red, heated energy moved through them. She could feel herself shaking as her orgasm wound up.

"Now, push that light to your crown and send it to me."

Harmony could barely register his words as she began to crest, her body overcome with light as it erupted in orgasmic waves. With supreme effort, she pushed the bolt of red lightning up to her crown and sent it to him, feeling it surge in his body and then loop around to re-enter her again.

The red rush sent her overboard, gasping his name in her release as she surrendered, the flow of vibrant light circulating between their bodies. Tristan stiffened and then began to shake, jetting his hot seed inside of her. He followed that radiant river of light as he thrust with abandon into her, groaning as he reached his release.

~~~~~

Harmony awoke from her nap, finding herself alone in The Chrysalis. Tristan was nowhere to be found. Her body was relaxed, yet sore in all the right places. A smile of secret knowing crept on her face as she assessed the rumpled bed sheets, evidence of their afternoon of hedonistically high vibrational pleasure. The essence of hot, passionate sex still lingered in the air, making The Chrysalis charged with vibrant Earth energy. She stretched luxuriously and crawled out of bed. Her lithe and toned body moved with the ease of someone who'd just had their mind and body properly blown away.

She eyed the beautiful setting of The Chrysalis. In white and gold, the large king-sized bed fit perfectly in the glass house of sacred sex. Green, vibrant plants radiated freshness and clarity, enhancing the pure and life affirming energy. The chamber, with its gold pyramid roof, was the setting for a dream come true – making love to a man who could only be a fantasy. And yet…he was here and the door was wide open.

Don't run, she reminded herself. It was too easy in the past to run when something emotionally challenging faced her. But how could she run from someone who made her feel like this? How could she turn around and walk away from Tristan when she felt like she had met her match, the other half of her whole?

And then there was Eduardo. How could she feel that strong attraction for him too? It was an attraction as equally raw as she felt for Tristan. Yet it was an attraction separate and detached from Tristan.

What the hell am I getting myself into? Questions stacked layers of confusion and indecision in front of her and she shook her head in an attempt to think clearly. It conflicted and pained her, realizing that she might have to choose between one of them one day. It was new, too much right now. *Look who you're with. Right now. That's all that matters.*

She brought her mind and body back to the present. Grabbing a robe off a nearby hook, she wrapped herself and walked out of The Chrysalis, curious as to where Tristan had gone. Her searching gaze found him standing on the other side of the pond, partially wrapped in a towel, and talking to an older gentleman with snow white hair and a regal air. As if sensing her presence, both men turned to look at her, freezing her in place with their piercing gaze. Tristan lifted his hand to wave at her, but Harmony's eyes were riveted to the older man, who was looking directly into her emerald eyes.

She shivered, feeling a strange sensation of recognition, but unsure of its source. He broke away from her gaze and turned towards Tristan, whispering a few words and gesturing with his hands. After a few minutes, he turned back to look at Harmony.

Then he promptly walked away from both of them, heading towards the main house and leaving them alone.

Tristan turned towards her, dropping his towel and exposing his virile and beautifully sculpted frame. He eased into the water, his muscles flexing and relaxing as he swam towards her and The Chrysalis. Harmony watched in fascination as Tristan made short work of the distance between them, his tanned body slicing through the water. Seeing him swim so effortlessly, radiating power, stirred carnal feelings in her depths, causing her to redden. *Wasn't it enough that they had just had sex twice in the last few hours?*

She could feel herself getting wet, wanting him to take her again. *Oh my God! I feel like I can't get enough of this beautiful man!"*

He hoisted himself up onto the deck, dripping wet. She met him half-way with a plush towel, ready to dry his fit body. The thought of touching him again aroused her and she forced herself to look away from blatantly staring at his hard erection. *Damn! It's got to be a crime to look that good!*

"Hey beautiful," he greeted her, bending down to plant a wet kiss on her soft lips.

"Hey lover," she murmured back, returning his kiss.

"I didn't want to wake you up. You looked so peaceful sleeping."

"That's ok. Who was that man you were talking to? He looks familiar to me."

"Peter Drugell. He's a member of The Tribe of Light and the current leader of the Air Traders."

"I've seen his face before but I can't place from where I'd seen it."

"He came to deliver a message."

"What is it?"

Tristan shifted uncomfortably on his feet. He gazed at her with narrowed eyes, hiding his emotions. She looked at him, assessing the energy inside of his body. She saw the golden column of light shining brightly with a small black rivulet of energy, barely perceptible, streaking into the column. *He's afraid of something.*

"What are you worried about?" she asked quietly.

"What make you think I'm worried?"

"When people worry, they get these black rivers of energy that seep into their field. You didn't have that before you talked to Peter Drugell. What are you hiding from me?"

He pulled her towards the edge of the deck to sit down. Their toes grazed the top of the water, creating circles that expanded and touched each other. They sat in complete silence, Tristan searching for the right words to say.

"Peter came to warn me that a group of The Corona Elite are coming to Austin this upcoming week. There's a big media tradeshow that's happening and apparently, they're unveiling something. We're not sure what that is. It must be big if they're flying in their elite members."

"How does that affect me?" She was baffled.

"The Tribe knows that you're working at NET Media. They want you to find out what The Corona is up to. Whatever the Torres brothers are doing must be important if their elite are coming in during this time. The Tribe wants you to pick up whatever information you can. That's all."

Harmony was quiet, allowing the information to sink in. She didn't know what to look for. It was already stressful enough having to be around Eduardo Torres's magnetic, sexually charged presence. *I'm just a freaking massage therapist! I don't know what the hell I'm supposed to be looking for!*

Tristan felt her resistance as he reached for her hand. "I don't like the idea of you having to spy for The Tribe. It makes me sick. Hell....even you working at NET Media makes my blood boil."

"Why, Tristan? I mean....if The Tribe needs my help...why shouldn't I step up and do it? I already work there."

He turned to face her, a look of agonized fury blazing in his eyes. "You know why I hate you working there? Nicholas Torres killed Serena Morgan. He's Eduardo's brother and the President of

NET Media. It's bloody hell for me to have you be so close to those bastards. And I know what Eduardo wants, and it's driving me to a really dark place."

"What does he want?"

"You!"

Harmony pulled back, her eyes wide as she searched his face. "You've got to me kidding me. That's ridiculous."

"No. I'm not kidding. I've seen and felt it in the imprints he's left on you. I'll be damned if I lose another woman I care about to The Corona."

"Tristan." She pulled his hand close to her heart. "You won't lose me. I'm here. For you."

"I don't know, Harmony. Sometimes I wonder if this dream is going to disappear, and I'll be back in my nightmare again. This time with you…"

He turned to look at her, his blue eyes stormy with unsaid emotions. She could feel his turbulence inside.

"This time with you has brought feelings I didn't know I could feel," he whispered. "I don't know what I'd do if something happened to you."

She moved closer to him until his arm was around her. They sat like this in silence, both absorbed in the magnitude of having found one another.

"I feel the same way about you, too," she spoke softly. "I never thought I would know what it felt like to love someone and have them love you back so completely. You make me feel something I've never felt before."

He hugged her closer, shrouding her in a protectively possessive way that made her heart melt. She felt herself falling deeper into a trance in love with him. There was no shaking him now.

"Listen," he began. "You don't have to take this job at NET Media. That's an option for you. But more importantly – you have to exercise your choice of what you want. If you decide you want to stay, then I need to teach you some shielding techniques. We need to fortify you if you're going to be there."

"Ok. And what's my other option?"

"We leave. Tonight. To the Tribe."

"I can't just leave, Tristan. This is my life, and I'm trying to build something."

"Fine. We'll buy you some time to get your life in order. But when I say we go – don't fight with me about it again." His voice was firm and commanding.

"How can you just come into my life, tell me what to do, and expect me to give everything up? I'm trying to establish myself – be independent and sustainable." Her voice was tight and defensive.

"You're not thinking big enough. There's more for you than this little town." Tristan's voice was stubborn, inflaming her irritation.

"More? You mean to take up this war with you?"

"Exactly."

"Listen, Tristan, this war the Tribe has with the Corona does not involve me. And yet, here I am. How the hell did I get swept up in this?"

"Harmony, that's why I'm here. Our world is changing. Fast. Things are happening at quantum levels and triggering an evolution. Which side you choose makes a difference in the balance of our collective conscience."

"Great…no pressure," she shot back sarcastically.

"Don't fear or question it too much. Have faith that you're being guided."

She turned to gaze at him, taking in the seriousness of his eyes. "If you say it like that, then I'm choosing to stay at NET Media."

"I fear that may come with a price."

"It may," she replied, after a pause. "But I feel like I have to see this through."

"Why?"

"I don't know. I can't even formulate the words. I just feel like I have to be there."

Tristan looked away, concentrating on the water as he continued. "You're a stubborn, head-strong woman. I knew this assignment was going to be more complicated than the others."

She studied his brooding face. Fear wrapped its insidious head around her heart, clutching it with an ache. "Do you regret it?" Her voice came out as a whisper. "Do you regret coming to find me?"

His head snapped to face her, his eyes blazing. "No! You're one decision I definitely do not regret."

"Then why did you say it like that?"

"Because I knew that once I saw you, met you, felt you – there would be no turning back. I felt that flicker of recognition the first moment I saw your face."

A small smile etched her lips, easing the strangling unease. "I want to help you, Tristan. Do whatever it takes to make it easier for us to be together."

"Are you ready for this?"

"Ready for what?" Her voice was tinged with curiosity. *What did he have planned for her now?*

"I want you to think of yourself as a carrier. You're going to absorb and carry the information on some of the clients you work on and place that imprint in a cell inside of your body. That cell will be fortified, locked, and shielded, so that only I will be able to access that and get the information The Tribe needs."

"What if The Corona finds out what I'm doing?"

"You have to guard your thoughts and feelings fastidiously. You cannot leak out that I'm in your life, that you work for The Tribe, or that you know Emily Morgan."

"That's a lot of pressure to keep a lid on things."

"You can handle it. You wouldn't be sitting here with me if we didn't feel like you were capable of carrying this missive through. We just have to prepare you to layer yourself with enough shields to deflect their probing curiosity. I have just the way."

"Really? And what do you have in mind?"

"We're going to build you an armor of light, and program it so that you can use your willpower and intention to deflect any negative energy put towards you. You will be able to project it into a person's body and cut any holds they may try to put on you."

"Wow! That sounds really far out, you know that?"

"Welcome to my world of far out. Our reality is the fantasy that most people aspire to live in. We just manifest it into existence." Tristan grinned, his eyes lightening to the color of the ocean after a rainstorm.

"So when do we start?"

"Today. We'll begin building the physical and emotional shield of armor. Tomorrow – your schedule needs to be cleared so we can program the rest. Are you in?"

Excitement leaped through her blood as she thought of the energetic and metaphysical work. Never had an adventure into the land of the psyche seemed so inviting and alluring.

"I'm in!" Her voice was firm and confident.

"Good. Let's begin!"

He stood up and took her hand, leading her back to The Chrysalis. Her breath caught in her throat at the anticipation of going back to the sexually charged room. He smiled at her eagerness, and together they stepped through the threshold hand in hand.

He motioned for her to sit on a cushion on the floor. While she prepared herself, settling comfortably, he walked to the side of the glass wall and flicked on a clear panel, almost invisible against its surroundings. He flicked on a few switches and typed in a series of numbers and letters. All of a sudden, she heard a whirring sound and looked up.

A golden ring began to descend above their head, turning in a clockwise direction. Inside of the circle, a series of numbers, letters, shapes and formulas ran across, as if on a screen. Her fascination increased as light came out of the ring, spiraling around them in a vortex that covered where she sat.

As the light entered her body, she felt a tingling sensation, her pulse accelerating and her breath catching in her throat. It was as if someone had dipped her in a hot bath making her skin burn and then settle with the heat.

"Don't panic." He said as he took a seat in front of her. "And don't fight it."

"What is this?"

"This is called The Ring of Light. It's a tool created by The Tribe to synchronize your biorhythms and open up your genetic codes to plug you into the Tribal grid. You're flooded with high frequencies of light and formulas to alter your body's ability to manipulate its surroundings – internally and externally."

"What does that mean?"

"That means – if you're around The Corona, you can alter your body's biorhythm to make it look like you're one of them. Lightworkers and Dark Warriors have different energies and rhythms. Blend in and they won't suspect you. Stick out like you do now, and they will find you and…"

"And what?"

"Let's not go there," he snapped. "Just focus. I'm going to sit with you and go through the breathing cycle to open up your channels. Trust me?"

Her emerald eyes flashed and met his. "With all my heart."

He nodded and took her hand. "Good. Concentrate on my voice. Follow what I ask you to do with your mind. And most importantly, open your cellular memory bank to absorb the light frequencies."

"Ok. I'm ready."

She could feel the vibrating light all around her, charging her skin and infiltrating through her body as she breathed. It felt like she was swimming in a sea of golden liquid, her mind seeing a multitude of shapes, numbers, and colors, blending in at light speed.

"Bring your attention from your mind to your heart. Now focus on my words as you send a beam of light from your heart down to the center of the Earth. Bring that light back to your heart and send it up to the Creator. Feel that light connect through you and run through your spine."

Harmony could feel her body awaken. A bright column of golden light formed from her coccyx to the top of her head. A double helix appeared, turning in a clockwise direction, as the energy moved and up down her body. She could feel a force emanate from the column and spread through her body until it was outside of her, outlining her in a golden light.

"Now see that light outside of you growing stronger in color, intensity, and vibration. It is being programmed with instructions and downloads. Feel the difference between light and dark. And breathe. Continue to breathe, and bring that energy up and down your spine."

Harmony took a deep, cleansing breath, allowing her body to radiate with oxygenated blood. She could feel the difference between the light and dark. The light felt warm, like the sun during a warm, spring day, whereas the dark felt cold, as if blasted with icy, frigid air. The difference between the two invaded her senses. She would have to remember to keep these two separate, willing herself to be in the dark when it was necessary.

She felt a pressure in her head as she continued to breathe. Her eyes closed as the Ring of Light delivered pulsating frequencies, attuning attuned her body to the activations occurring in her DNA. It was subtle, but she could see her column of golden light growing stronger and more vibrant. She continued to breathe, feeling her chest rise and fall in a cycle that matched the movement of fluid in her spine.

The images that infiltrated her mind stunned her. She saw a golden sphere, encoded with numbers and letters, superimposed with the five platonic solids: the tetrahedron, hexahedron, octahedron, dodecahedron and the icosahedron. The shapes stacked and turned, blending into a three-dimensional model. Finally, the Metatron's cube emerged. She gasped, her body turning on as if a key was inserted into a lock.

"See it?" Tristan asked. "Now use your willpower and mind. Take Metatron's cube and run that up and down your body."

She followed him, feeling herself expand exponentially as it was covered in the sacred light of Metatron's cube. She could feel the golden armor outside of her strengthening and thickening. She felt herself shifting, separating from the physicality of her body and tuning into the microcosmic molecules that were held together by the fusion of energy and light. She witnessed the expansion of her DNA as it absorbed the Metatron's cube.

The clockwise vortex of energy began to spin at an infuriatingly fast pace. Her breath sped and her heart pounded. Every part of her felt like she was preparing to jump into hyperspace, tingling, vibrating, tensing and relaxing.

"Hold on," Tristan's voice encouraged her. "You're almost complete. Keep breathing. This acceleration will be over soon."

And like the orgasmic energy of sexual union, her body erupted in a burst of light. She shook with spiraling waves of ecstasy. They rolled through her, moving from the top of her head, down her spine, to her toes, which curled with the delicious sensation of bliss. She moaned as her body continued to absorb the high energy, replacing resistance and tension with light and pleasure. A final sigh of rapture escaped her parted lips, causing her shoulders to relax and her head to fall back in surrender. After a few minutes, she lifted her head, opened her eyes to look at Tristan. Her emerald green eyes met his ocean blue gaze. And what she saw made her speechless. He loved her.

Chapter Twelve

Harmony gazed at Tristan, still buzzing and reeling from her experience with the Ring of Light. Everything was quieter in The Chrysalis as dusk fell across the land. The soft pink, purple and orange hues turned the glass structure into a kaleidoscope. Harmony allowed the integration to continue in her body. She felt different, magnified and charged. Even her skin seemed to emit a golden glow.

"I want you to stay with me tonight," Tristan whispered, his hand caressing the small of her back.

She smiled and moved closer to him, her full, luscious body fitting perfectly with his. "I'd like that."

"This seems too good to be true," he murmured, nuzzling her hair.

"Why do you say it like that?"

"I guess I always thought that people in our line of work wouldn't get to have the happy lives like everyone else. It seemed like our sacrifice to serve was our cross to bear."

She rose up on an elbow to look at him. He seemed so vulnerable and open. "It doesn't have to be that way for us, Tristan. We can still have our happy-ever-after."

His eyes met hers, searching. "I want to believe it, but I have this feeling inside that makes me uneasy. I'm not sure why."

She laid her head on his chest, trying to find comfort in their connection as she drew lazy circles around his chest. "I know what you mean. I guess there are too many variables right now that make it unclear."

He clasped her tightly, as if trying to penetrate his very essence into her. "Just understand something, Harmony. Everything I'm doing is so that you and I can be together. It may not make sense to you sometimes, but I'm asking you to trust me and know that you have my heart."

She stilled, her hand frozen in its movement. *I have his heart! Oh My God! Did he just say that?* "Tristan-"

"You don't have to say anything right now. Just know that I won't let you go. Ever."

His words pierced her to the core. For years, she'd longed to hear someone tell her that she was that valuable and important.

She sat up, pulling her hair away from her face. Her eyes shone bright with emotion. "Good. I'm glad that we have that clear. I won't be letting you go either."

She bent down to kiss him. They lost themselves in the heady embrace. With a groan of surrender, she relaxed and let go as Tristan re-ignited the flame of desire between them, filling her cravings for him and their union.

~~~~~

Harmony awoke with Tristan sleeping soundly beside her. They had moved out of The Chrysalis the night before and into his large bedroom in Sacre Tellus.

She laid on her pillow, keeping her breathing quiet so that she wouldn't wake him. Taking the rare opportunity to study him, she delighted in his full lips, parted slightly, and his blond thick hair carelessly strewn around his face. He was like a Roman god with his strong, straight nose, classic cheekbones and chiseled planes. *Damn, even asleep you are sexy as ever!*

She closed her eyes, allowing her thoughts to run through the busy week that encapsulated her life. Everything was happening so fast that she barely had time to process or think things through.

All of a sudden, she remember her best friend, Clara, who she hadn't talked to in a few days. Moving quietly out of bed, she headed for her purse and dug her cell phone out. There were twenty missed calls, most of them from Clara, with eight text messages that she had missed. Wrapping a robe around her, she headed outside, grateful for the early morning light. She dialed Clara's number and waited patiently for the answer.

"Where the hell are you?" Clara demanded, answering in two rings. "I've been worried sick!"

"I'm with Tristan," She answered quickly. "I'm sorry…I know I've been a real lame-ass not calling you, but I'm just wrapped up around this man right now."

"Wow! I've never heard you say that. Is this serious?"

"I think so, Clara. I really like him. A lot. He means so much more than the other guys I've ever dated."

"Ok good. I'm glad that you're ok and you sound happy. What about the job? I haven't even had a chance to ask you what you think about it."

"I start tomorrow at the main office. I'm kind of nervous. How's it going for you?"

"OMG Harmony!" Clara's voice was excited and happy. "I totally love it! The clients are great! I have free time in between sessions, and I'm getting paid super fat!"

"That sounds amazing!"

"Yeah! And they even have this great tool that all the therapists, clients and staff get to use. It's such a high whenever I get done with it!"

"What tool?"

"Well it's more like a personal mind sauna. You get in and everything starts lighting up. At first you don't feel anything, but then you start to think about things bothering you in your life, and whoosh! It's better after that!"

"What do you mean by *whoosh*?" Harmony's voice was skeptical.

"I don't know how to explain it. They call it the E-2K."

"The E-what?"

"It's called the Ecstasy Two-Thousand. I sit in this machine and I see a series of disturbing, negative images. Then all these crazy thoughts come into my mind that bothers the hell out of me. The box lights up all around like a big video game and music starts to play. I start to relax and chill. I'm in there for a like ten minutes and I leave feeling totally happy and elevated."

"That sounds pretty cool."

"Yeah…but the only problem is that it only lasts for a few hours and then you want to use it again. It makes you feel so good that you want more."

Harmony was quiet, waiting for Clara to continue. "The worst part is that there are so many people who want to use it that there's always a line." Clara complained lightly.

"That popular, huh?"

"Oh yeah! The company is making another prototype just for their clients. I'm telling you…it's a total dream job!"

She heard a rustle of movement behind her and felt Tristan walking towards her. She quickly wrapped up her conversation with Clara, promising to call her later, and hung up. Setting her phone down, she turned to face him, the robe parting slightly to show her long, shapely legs. She could see Tristan eyeing her, his blue eyes twinkling.

"Good morning." He reached down to capture her lips, grazing them lightly.

"Good morning, lover."

"I woke up and you were gone," he pouted.

Tristan pouting? Super hot! "I'm sorry. I had to call Clara. She's been worried and blowing up my phone."

"And how is your temperamental friend?" he asked amused.

"She's good. Happy at NET Media. Apparently they've created a device that hooks you into feeling happy. She's all about using it right now."

Tristan pulled away from her, his eyes now cold and serious. *Whoa! What happened? Where'd you go?*

"What device is that?" His voice was flat and tense.

"I don't know. I haven't seen it yet. She called it the E-2K. It's supposed to replace your negative thoughts and make you feel better. She's been using it a lot, from the sound of our talk."

"Hmm….I wonder what this device is all about. We'll have to look into it. But right now, we've got to eat breakfast and start your training. I have a feeling today is going to fly by."

She wrapped her arms around him, pulling him back close. "You know, I liked waking up next to you."

He smiled, playfully squeezing her behind. "And I liked going to bed with you."

She smiled shyly, looking up at him with adoring eyes. "So what's our plan today?"

"First breakfast. Then you."

She laughed. "Oh Tristan! I swear you are such a man!"

He smirked and intertwined her fingers in his, pulling her back towards the house. They walked into the kitchen, surprised to find breakfast ready and waiting. There were eggs, bacon, toast, pancakes, fruit, and crepes.

It was lovely, opulent spread, making her acutely aware of the rumble in her stomach. Tristan handed her a plate and began to serve them. They walked towards the table, which was already set for their meal.

"Who prepares all this stuff?" she asked between mouthfuls of food.

"Glenda, the housekeeper. She always takes care of all the guests here at Sacre Tellus. Thank God, too! I wouldn't survive for long if I had to cook for myself. And I've found myself in some places in the world that were barely hospitable."

They sat comfortably together. Tristan answered Harmony's questions about his travel and work, filling her in on his lengthy service with The Tribe and some of his assignments, which had taken him to the far reaches of the world. She was fascinated by his stories, probing him for more information.

"Why did you join The Tribe of Light?"

"I didn't join The Tribe. I was born into it. My mother was an Air Trader, and my father was a Fire Starter. They met during their initiations, and I was born a year later."

"You've been with the Tribe since you were a child?"

"I have. I was trained in the arts of the Earth Keepers and became a tracker about eight years ago. It's the only life I know."

Harmony was quiet. She envied that he knew both parents and grew up in a community that was close-knit and tight. His concept of family seemed so foreign to her.

"What are you thinking?" he asked, his eyes studying her.

"I was wondering what that must have felt like – to have a family that wanted you."

His hand reached out to clasp hers. "This family could be yours too, Harmony. You just have to say yes."

"I have family, Tristan. It's Emily and Clara. They may not be blood relatives but they are all I have."

"You could have more. You could have me," he softly replied, twisting her heart with an ache.

But will I be enough? Her question rolled around in her mind.

They finished their breakfast in silence and Tristan got up and placed their plates in the sink. He returned back to the table and pulled Harmony up to him. " Listen, I need you to focus today. Don't let this stuff about The Tribe or The Corona mess with your head. You just need to trust me and know that this training will help you. Can you do that?"

She nodded, forcing herself to put their early morning conversation aside. This was all that mattered right now and she followed him up the stairs to his bedroom.

Tristan headed towards the bathroom, turning on the hot water and quickly stepping out of his boxer briefs. "Come on, baby," he called out. "Come join me."

Harmony slipped into the shower, enjoying the full force of Tristan, bathing in the steamy waters. He turned to face her, his blue eyes blazing and full of intent.

"I want to make love to you more than anything right now, but I've got to hold back and wait until we're done with the work this morning."

She felt herself stir inside. "Why wait?"

"Because I need you to concentrate. We'll have plenty of time for that later." His voice was firm, inviting her to concede.

He pulled her towards his hard, wet body and made quick time in washing her front and back. She relished the movement of his hands on her skin, watching him with hooded eyes. Against her will, her nipples contracted into tight buds and she felt herself swell with awareness, but Tristan avoided arousing her further. Still, he couldn't hide the fact that he was sexually attracted and attuned to her, his firm erection betraying his desire.

They moved with a fluid awareness of one another, sliding past each other's body to complete their shower. Tristan finished first, coming out to dry himself quickly. Harmony came out next, greeted by a thick warm towel that he held out for her.

She shyly allowed him to dry her, wiping off beads of water from her shoulders and back. He even carefully dried her hair, kissing her on the temple when he was done.

She quickly got dressed in her previous day's clothes, wondering who had washed and folded them for her. She made a mental note to thank Glenda.

Tristan led her to a room in the back of the house. It was locked, with a keypad in front of it. He entered a code and the door unlocked. He led her in, surprising her with a lone metallic box that stood in the middle. There was no other furniture or décor in the room. Just the metal box -which looked similar to a telephone booth.

"What is that?" She eyed it speculatively.

"It's another tool of The Tribe. It's called a Field Modulator."

"What does it do?"

"It sends your energy field different vibrations and frequencies and tests your ability to shield yourself."

"Oh," she was quiet, shifting uncomfortably. "I don't know how to control this shield that you placed."

"That's why we're here. You've got to train your willpower to tighten up the shield around you when you feel different forces of energy. The only way you'll know how to do that is if you experience what those forces are."

"But how do I use my willpower to affect my shield?"

"When you feel a change in the vibrations around you, you use your mind and intend your shield to go up, especially in places in your body where you feel it's weakest. You command it, and it follows your will."

"Oh…" *Surely it can't be that easy?*

"You're going to experience a range of frequencies, from sadness, anger, curiosity, rage all the way to love and joy. You need to feel what those frequency ranges feel like so that you can tighten your shield. This the first phase."

"What's the second?"

"We'll test your ability to shield off different levels of psychic attack."

Psychic attacks?! It had all seemed like fun and games in the beginning. But psychic attacks, energetic battles, force fields and mind control? *What the hell? I don't even know what I'm doing!*

"What's wrong?"

"I don't know if I'm ready for all this Jedi mind trick stuff."

Concern filled his eyes. "Look, Harmony, I know this isn't what you imagined your life might look like. But you're one of the exceptional people on this planet that has a very special gift. It makes you unique and valuable. You may not see it, but I do."

"I don't know what you see in me."

He tipped her chin up. His eyes were warm and caring. "I see a confident, beautiful, powerful woman who is strong, sexy and stubborn. I see you."

Her breath caught in her throat as her cheeks reddened with his compliment. "Ok, that's pretty smooth. You win. Let's get this over and done with."

Tristan grinned. "That's my girl."

He walked her over to the Field Modulator and opened a door. It really was like a telephone booth. He motioned for her to come inside and sit, placing a pair of headphones on her head.

"You're going to feel different sensations as you hear sounds over the headphones. Focus on bringing your attention to where you feel a dip in energy, and place the shield there. Ready?"

She nodded. Tristan disappeared behind her and an audible click of the door indicated that she was alone. *Thank God I am not claustrophobic. That would really suck big time!*

She looked around the metallic confines, noticing the patterns of sacred shapes that surrounded her. The sound of tinkling music, interlaced with beeps and waveforms, stimulated her senses. She brought her attention to her mind's eye, focusing on the external golden shield of armor that had been built the day before.

She could see the golden armor vibrating and radiating light all around her. Changes in frequencies and sound made her armor lighten and weaken in some spots. Bringing her attention to that area, she commanded her shields up, and the armor became whole again.

Bombarded with noise and sounds, she surrendered to the sensations. Certain frequencies caused a shiver, coldness, or darkening in her field. She watched closely, vigilant for cracks and ripples in her armor. Her fluidity and speed gradually increa sed.

The sounds slowed, and she was surrounded by silence. Looking up, she saw Tristan's smiling face greeting her as the door opened. She removed the headphones and stood up, teetering unsteadily as her circulation shifted. He reached out a hand to steady her and brought her out of the Modulator.

"How was it?" He asked curiously.

"It was strange at first, but that armor is amazing. It felt like a second skin - so connected to my thoughts and emotions. I don't have to give it back, do I?"

His laughter lifted her spirits immediately. "No. That's yours to keep for life. Consider it a gift from The Tribe."

She smiled, her eyes lighting with amusement. "So how'd I do?"

"Better than I expected. You're a quick learner. Only one emotional frequency got through and it doesn't surprise me that it did."

"What is it?"

"Abandonment."

"Great," her response was sarcastic. "My old friend."

"Don't worry. Most humans can't even filter out half of what you were able to do. I'm quite impressed. We'll see how that frequency will affect you when we get into phase two of the Modulator."

"I'm ready."

"You sure?"

"I have to know what I can and can't handle. The sooner I find out, the better I can deal with what comes up."

He caressed the side of her cheek. She sighed and leaned into his hand.

"You know, you continually amaze me?"

She smiled shyly at him. "Yeah?"

He bent down to place a chaste, sweet kiss on her lips. She felt herself glowing with euphoria.

"You make me want you," she whispered.

"As soon as we finish this, we can head back to The Chrysalis."

She pulled away from him and sat back inside the Modulator. "Let's not waste time then."

"Have I created a monster?" He teased her.

"A monster for you," she countered back.

He laughed, closing the door and separating them. She replaced the headphones. A sigh of longing escaped her lips.

"Focus." His words came through the headphones.

"How do you know that I'm not?" She shot back.

"When you daydream, your shield weakens. Just thought I'd tell you to stop thinking about sex."

"What makes you think I'm thinking about sex?"

"I can see your face from here and I know that look you get."

What look is that? She stuck her tongue out at him playfully.

"Focus baby."

"Yes sir!"

The whirring sound of music, noise, beeps and frequencies invaded her mind. This time it was different. Not only could she hear the sounds and witness the dips in her golden armor, she could see images forming in her mind. Being pressed in a cold, dark room. Being consumed by fire. Being covered in ants and bugs. She fought to keep her shield up. She tensed under the attack, and invoked her internal guides and Angels to help strengthen her shield. It worked. Her shield grew in luminosity and strength.

A suffocating feeling crushed her. Images wove in and out of her mind. She continued to battle each scenario, placing her shield up and projecting light into that image. It was successful until an image came that displaced her.

She saw Tristan looking at her with disgust on his face and turning around to walk out the door. She saw her arms raised up, pleading him to stay, and he shook his head *no*. He was leaving her. She gasped and screamed.

"No!"

Her armor instantly melted, and she felt searing pain run through her body. She ripped the headphones off, gasping for air.

The door of the Modulator swung open and Tristan hoisted her out. She cried uncontrollably as he held her close to his chest, rocking her while they sat on the floor. Images of his coldness and the disgust in his eyes flashed through her mind.

She thought her golden shield of armor was impenetrable, but that fear of abandonment, of him leaving, pierced a hole. She burned with fear and shame. *I can't believe I'm acting like such a cry baby!*

"It's ok," he soothed her with his gentle voice. "It's ok. I'm here."

"It was awful," she sniffed. "It was the most painful thing I've ever felt."

He caressed her back, kissing her hair while whispering assurances to her. "What made you so scared?"

Her eyes met him. "You left me."

He stiffened, his body taut and anxious. "What did you say?"

"You left me, Tristan. That's what pierced my armor."

He looked anguished. "Baby….I won't. I can't."

She shook her head. "You're my greatest weakness."

Chapter Thirteen

Harmony allowed Tristan to drive her to work that following morning. Her clothes were once again meticulously washed and prepared by Glenda, the housekeeper. She was quiet, nervous about going into NET Media, especially after the past two days of training.

Her thoughts drifted back to their conversation after the Modulator. Tristan had stopped her training and brought her back to The Chrysalis. He made sweet, tender love to her, trying to soothe away her fears with his warmth and need. It was as if he needed it as much as she did. It still haunted her. She didn't want to feel that again.

He held her throughout the night as they slept, occasionally whispering words of love in her ear. She meant something to him. She could feel that, and the possessive way he held her body assured her that she was his. Knowing that he wanted her now made the fear of his disappearance and rejection wane.

It was a sharp warning. Any projected attacks on her psyche had to be shielded immediately. Though he brought her to orgasmic release in The Chrysalis after the Modulator, she knew that it was to re-fortify her armor. He had even re-activated The Ring of Light while they made love.

It had done the trick, at least; she felt better. Harmony reached over to squeeze his hand. He reassuringly answered her with a kiss to the back of hers.

"I'll be thinking of you today," he whispered. "The past two days have been quite amazing!"

"I'll be thinking of you too."

"I'd rather you didn't. You need to put your shields up before you step into NET Media. Also, you need to shift the vibration of your shield so that you blend in with the other staff, other Coronas."

"Oh, I didn't realize that. I'm sorry."

"Don't apologize, Harmony," he replied stonily. "This is new for you, and you're walking into a battlefield."

"Gee when you say it like that...no pressure," her voice was tense.

"I don't take this lightly. With you in there, I feel like a storm is brewing all around me."

"Please, Tristan. Don't be upset. I need your support. This is intense for me."

"I know. I just feel a little helpless when you're around them. It's not good for my state of mind when I'm not in control."

"What will you do while I'm at work?" She attempted to divert the conversation.

"I'll be in meetings with different Tribe leaders. There's quite a few coming into town for this convention."

"This sounds bigger than just a regular trade show."

His voice and tone were serious. "It is. Anything The Corona does that impacts a large group of people and their consciousness is big. I don't think this is just any run-of-the-mill convention. Whatever it is....we're here to find out."

As Tristan drove her into the city, she absorbed the corporate suits entering high-rises, tourists in awe, and politicians en route to the Capitol. *I'm going to have to blend in with all of this?*

She didn't have much time to dwell on that as Tristan pulled up to the front door of The Frost Bank Building. She turned to look at him, struck by his sudden coolness. He didn't like her decision to go back to work. Hating the distance already forming, she quickly leaned forward and planted a kiss on his lips, willing him to respond. He finally did, deepening their kiss and leaving her breathless.

"Shield on," he commanded. Immediately she felt a glow around her. "Change your vibrations before you go in there. Blend in. I'll call you later."

She nodded, turning her focus to the feeling of the dark. A chill descended on her. She was ready.

She stepped out and faced the door. With her shield up, she couldn't risk turning back to look at Tristan. The turnstile opened and she dashed in, heading towards the elevator that would lead her to NET Media. She quickly flashed her badge and headed towards the Wellness Department to check her appointments.

She was surprised at how many people were using the gym, sauna, weight room and elliptical. Arriving at her office, she found Lydia staring at a series of spreadsheets. Lydia paused, sensing her presence, and gave her a welcoming smile. She gestured for Harmony to sit and passed her a list of names.

"These are the sessions that you have lined up today. You've got three clients that are new to NET Media. They're from a digital software company. Then you've got a lunch break, followed by two clients from a manufacturing facility that we work with, and then Eduardo Torres at the end of the day. Everyone is busy getting ready for the trade show."

Holy hell! Eduardo Torres is at the end of my day? She gulped. The first three were Japanese, and the last two sounded like they were Italian. *Followed by none other than Mr. Nervewracking.*

"Thanks," she murmured absently to Lydia. "I'll get my room ready."

"Good idea. Your first client is in fifteen minutes."

Harmony walked to her massage room. Taking in the relaxing smell of lavender, she prepared her table, turning on the warmer and placing fresh clean cotton sheets. Light, meditative music filtered through the speakers in the corner. She applied essential oils to her blankets and to herself, trying to ground and prepare.

A soft knock came at the door. It opened, and revealed a young Japanese man in his early thirties. She motioned for him to come with a smile.

"Welcome, Mr. Morito," she greeted him, bowing politely. He bowed back, with a large smile. His intelligent eyes assessed her.

"I will leave you to get ready, sir. When you're ready, please lay on the table face down and we can begin."

He nodded, silently appraising his environment before turning to her again.

"I…don't speak much English…" he responded. She relaxed.

"That's ok," she replied. "You don't need to talk, sir. Just relax." She slipped out the door, allowing him privacy to change.

When she stepped out, she found Eduardo Torres standing outside of her room. Leaning back against the wall with a hand in his pocket, he looked like a celebrity model posing for a magazine ad. Her breath constricted in her chest. *Damn! How does he do that to me?*

He smiled. "Hello, Harmony."

"Mr. Torres. Good morning."

"It is now that you're here." She blushed, choosing not to answer. "You've been given some interesting clients today. I'm surprised at Lydia's assignment. She must have a lot of faith in your abilities."

"Perhaps. I can handle it," she responded smoothly.

"Oh, I don't doubt you can," He shifted his stance, his blazer revealing a crisp white shirt and a red and gold silk tie. "I do want you to pay special attention to our clients today. See what you can pick up."

"I will do my best, sir."

He smiled and walked up close, looking down with his vibrant amber eyes. Those eyes could melt steel. She could feel that pull between them, drawing them into each other.

"I look forward to my session later, Harmony. I'm sure you will not disappoint." With that, he turned and walked away, leaving her bewildered as she watched his retreating back.

Taking a deep breath, she turned towards the door and opened it, allowing the lavender to take over any thoughts of Eduardo and his mercurial nature.

Mr. Morito was face down in the cradle. She approached him from the left side and took a grounding breath. Placing her right hand at his occiput and the left on the base of his spine, she assessed his energy field, watching with interest the different spheres and shapes that appeared. His body felt clear of any dark vibrations, and she continued to effleurage and massage tension out of his muscles.

They were nearing thirty minutes into the session when Mr. Morito finally sank into a deeper state of relaxation. That was when she spotted a bright green tubular light at the base of his occiput. As she holographically projected her mind to look into the green tube, she was astounded by the streams of code that appeared. It looked like a computer language. It made no sense to her, except that there was a string of code that appeared red, whereas everything else was a dark blue. She didn't know what to make of it, and continued to work on him until the timer signaled the end.

"We're finished, sir," she whispered. "I will leave and let you have some privacy to get dressed."

"Thank you, Harmony. I feel...good."

"It's my pleasure, sir." She bowed her head respectfully and walked out. Her next clients were already there – two more thirty-something Japanese men on their iPads and iPhone, barely cognizant of her presence.

Mr. Morito emerged from the room and immediately chatted with the other men. It was clear they knew each other. She turned around and headed back to her room, quickly stripping the bed and preparing it for her next client.

In ten minutes, she opened the door again, welcoming Mr. Takasaki into the room. His English was marginally better than Mr. Morito's, but he too was shy and taciturn.

She began her session once again, energetically connecting to his field with her hand at his occiput and the other at the base of his spine. She stroked firmly and moved stagnant energy around his body. Continuing to press deeper, she spied a similar green tubular column appearing on his body. This time it was not located at the occiput, but at the middle of his thoracic vertebrae, lodged inside of his spinal cord. The green tube was full of red lines of computer code, interspersed with a sprinkling of dark blue. *What is this stuff?*

Time flew by as Mr. Takasaki relaxed on her table. The timer dinged, indicating an end to their session. Outside of the massage room, she found her next client, Mr. Makai, waiting for her. They shared a few moments of chit chat as Mr. Takasaki dressed. When he appeared, he went straight to Mr. Makai and began speaking in rapid Japanese. She excused herself, making a beeline for the door and entered the room.

Closing her eyes, she breathed in the calming scent. She relished how her client's bodies responded to her touch. *This is why I do this. I love to help people.*

The door opened quietly and Mr. Makai walked in, shyly eyeing the table and nervously shifting in his feet.

"I…I never have massage before." Smiling gently, she gazed at him. His wiry, thin physique was a contrast to the large, sharp black glasses that framed his face, making his small eyes appear larger, more childish.

"It's ok, Mr. Makai. Just please tell me if there is something that feels uncomfortable, and I will honor your request."

"Thank you, Harmony," he murmured.

Outside of the room, she found Clara waiting patiently for her. When she closed the door, her best friend enveloped Harmony in a large hug.

"It's so damn good to see you!" she gushed. "It feels like forever!"

Harmony smiled, returning Clara's hug with a tight squeeze. She missed her friend and wanted to share in her good fortune and love. "You look great! I didn't realize how this corporate gig totally suits you."

"Let's have lunch after this client's done. I can't wait to fill you in!"

"Ok! Where to?"

"We don't even have to leave! There's a cafeteria that's on the first floor! Free to NET Media employees!"

"That's a perk!"

"Oh and there's more! I'll come back and pick you up when you're done!"

Harmony nodded and gave her hand a squeeze.

She returned to Mr. Makai and began her session again, energetically connecting to him as she placed her hand on his occiput and back. What she saw totally astounded her.

While she saw the green columns in Mr. Morito and Mr. Takasaki, she saw something completely different in Mr. Makai. As she pressed down into his shoulders, a bright yellow sphere encased his heart, stomach and pelvis. The boundary of the sphere was thick and impenetrable. Inside, she could see a light covering of cryptic computer code, but it was barely perceptible. As she moved down to the base of his spine, she felt him stiffen and saw the sphere move.

"That's...enough," his voice was stiff and direct. Her hands paused. *What didn't he want her to see?*

"We've barely started, sir."

"I'm...done."

"Of course." She respectfully moved aside and dried her hands. "I will let you get dressed, sir, and wait for you outside."

Stepping out of the room, her mind was conflicted with questions. Why did Mr. Makai ask her to stop? What she saw was so different from the other two gentlemen. It was obvious they all worked together, but she couldn't understand why he wouldn't allow himself to indulge in a massage.

When Mr. Makai stepped out of the room, he stopped and gazed deeply into her eyes.

"Harmony," his English was stiff and broken. "You can see. I know that. Please..."

"Yes sir?"

"Please hide...what you see....inside of me."

"Of course, sir." Remembering Tristan's words about creating a compartment just for The Corona to access, she quickly removed his face and her vision. "Your secret is safe with me."

He nodded and quickly left her side, joining his other two partners. She watched him walk to the elevator, briefly turning to look at her with an imploring gaze, and disappeared into the car. *What are you hiding in there that you don't want anyone else to see?*

She returned back to the massage room, stripping the sheets and preparing it for her next clients. Curiosity ran through her, but she refused to allow herself the opportunity to reflect, realizing that her errant thoughts could betray her. She focused instead on fortifying her armor and solidifying the boundary on the compartment she reserved just for Eduardo.

Clara knocked on the door, drawing her out of her reverie. They headed towards the elevator and joined the other employees going on their lunch break. Clara began sharing her weekend stories with her boyfriend, Mike, and their adventures at the pond. Apparently, Mike wasn't as experienced on the jet skis as he had promised, and managed to flip himself over a whole bunch of times. By the time they arrived to the cafeteria, Harmony had laughed herself to tears.

Clara filled her in on office gossip. Apparently Todd was dating another massage therapist. "He must have a soft-spot for body workers," Harmony mused.

"Yeah, or he's just looking for a happy ending," Clara giggled.

They entered the busy, enormous cafeteria – struck by the multiple choices of food. From burgers, pasta, Asian and Mexican cuisine to organic, raw, vegan fare – the dining room boasted an eclectic mix to please any palate.

Harmony saw the corporate execs eating in separate dining halls while different levels of staff mixed freely. With nearly a hundred people in that vast room, the sound bordered on cacophony. She followed Clara down the buffet line, choosing a caesar salad and sushi.

They found a table that faced the street, affording them the opportunity to people watch inside and outside the dining hall. Clara commented on the different clients that she had taken care of and the working conditions of the Wellness Department.

"This is honestly the dreamiest massage job I could ask for," she said, between bites of her chicken alfredo. "I mean...I don't have to set up clients, do any follow-up calls, or drive all over town. And did I mention how fat my paycheck has been? I've totally been splurging on myself this past weekend."

Harmony smiled. It was good to see Clara so happy, especially when she knew the struggle of keeping a full time practice going. It wasn't easy in a town that spit out more therapists than rain. The competition was stiff, and therapists held on to their clients like gold.

"Well, this is my first day, and so far so good."

"I'm glad to hear that. I think you'll really like it."

And then she felt him. Harmony could feel the hairs on the back of her neck and her forearms rise with Eduardo's presence in the cafeteria. He walked in with a group of smartly dressed men. As if feeling her stare, he turned his piercing gaze on hers, freezing the moment in place. His amber eyes were like liquid fire.

"Would you look at that dreamboat of man?" Clara murmured. Harmony knew that she was talking about Eduardo. She tore her gaze off him and focused on her food. "It has to be a crime to look that good in a suit. He's like sex on legs. Damn!"

Harmony focused on her salad, willing herself to chew. She wanted to place an invisibility shield around herself, but she knew it was useless. She could feel his presence growing, increasing in magnetism, until he stopped right in front of their table.

"Harmony." His voice was like spun silk. "Mr. Makai and his partners just shared their very positive experience with you."

She looked up, shielding her thoughts from him as their gaze met. "Thank you, sir. It was my pleasure."

"As I'm sure it will be mine later." He nodded towards her and turned around, walking back to the group of suits that waited patiently for him. Her eyes followed him as they entered a private dining area.

"What the hell was that?" Clara yelped. She turned around to face her friend's surprised and shocked face.

"I don't know what you're talking about."

"Eduardo Torres *never* speaks to anyone, let alone any therapists from the department. He barely even said 'thank you' when I worked on him, and he came over here to talk to you?!"

"I don't know. Maybe we just click."

Clara leaned back, folding her arms and studying Harmony with a shrewd look. "You like him."

"What?" she sputtered. "No...I don't...what? I don't even know him."

Clara smiled knowingly. "You do like him! What about that other guy, Tristan?"

Harmony shrugged, trying to look casual and unaffected. "He's cool and we have a great time together. But honestly! Nothing's going on. Eduardo is my boss. And he's got a girlfriend."

"Oh you mean that ice bitch that comes around?"

"I guess you've met her too."

"That woman just drips mean. She comes into the Wellness Department demanding massages and all kinds of body work. Just hope she never asks for you to work on her. It's not that much fun."

"I hope I never see her again."

"Well speak of the devil..." Clara whispered. They watched Mariska Hebrenovitch stride into the building with an air of arrogance and ownership. She spoke to no one, walking with determined focus towards the room that Eduardo and his fellow suits occupied. They could see Mariska bending low to whisper into Eduardo's ear. He stood up and followed her out the door. This time, he bypassed Harmony, ignoring her as he followed Mariska out of the building, disappearing from their view.

"What's her story?" Harmony asked curiously. "Why is she so cold?"

"She's threatened. She used to work here at NET Media as a therapist and Eduardo found her. Next thing you knew, she was his girlfriend and off the schedule. She routinely comes in and receives treatments, and acts as if she owns the place."

"Nice. Remind me to not get on her bad side."

"Yeah. Good idea."

Clara and Harmony finished their lunch and headed back towards the Wellness Department.

"There's this great machine you've got to try. The E-2K is positively amazing."

"What is it?"

"I don't know how to describe it. You pick a scenario that you want to experience – usually something stressful, negative or painful and then you step into the E-2K, and it runs all these lights around you. Your body starts to feel tense and all these different emotions run through you. If you can make it through, the last ten minutes are totally worth it."

"Oh yeah? Why?"

"Well in the end, the lights change and you start to feel better – like immediately. You start to see images that are positive and you feel high, happy and totally open."

"Interesting. How long does that last?"

"That stellar feeling only lasts for like four to five hours. Then afterwards you feel like you've dropped a few notches in the happy spectrum, and you just want to go back."

"That does sound like a drug."

"Well it's the kind of drug that I like. I've done it twice in one day and I feel like a new woman. Literally…it's like I have all this energy, happy feeling and this weird willingness to do something. Most of the time…I work out, because otherwise, I wouldn't."

Harmony gazed at her friend. "I want to see this machine. Can you take me there later?"

"Sure, you bet!" They had arrived at the wellness department. "I've got to go. My next session is in fifteen minutes. Catch ya later!"

She gave Harmony a quick hug and disappeared. Harmony headed towards customer services. Her next client was already there waiting for her.

She was grateful for having made her table ready. All she needed to do was fortify her shield and spray lavender and orange essence in the room. Taking a deep breath, she opened her door and motioned for Mr. Toceni to come in.

A portly, slightly balding man, his rich Italian accent mesmerized her as he introduced himself. She quickly excused herself and explained the process of getting ready again. When she stepped out of the room, Lydia was waiting.

"Why did Mr. Makai leave so suddenly?" Lydia was dripping curiosity.

Harmony felt a bump against her field and pushed her armor out to equalize the dip. "I'm not sure why he left. I think he was uncomfortable with me touching him."

"That's strange. He's had other massage therapists work on him. Are you sure you didn't say anything to set him off?"

Harmony flinched at the accusation, careful to hide her interaction with Mr. Makai under her shield. "I barely touched him and he said he was done."

"Ok," Lydia sounded relieved, stepping away from Harmony. "I guess some people just have off days. Mr. Torres really wanted you to work on our Japanese partners and take good care of them. I'm sure he'll back. Mr. Makai has been a close partner in the creation of our greatest tool, the E-2K."

"Of course," Harmony murmured. "Listen, I should get back. I have Mr. Toceni waiting."

"Yes. Thank you again for being so accommodating to our special guests."

Harmony gave her a small smile and turned back towards the door, opening it to find Mr. Toceni face down on the massage table. What was lacking above his head made a surplus everywhere on his body. *Great. My favorite. Hairy men.*

She immediately began by energetically connecting to his field before placing her hand on his occiput and the small of his back. Looking down, she felt a shiver of apprehension. A series of dark grey, worm-like apparitions appeared at the base of his spine, moving up and down his spinal cord. They slithered like a lazy slinky, bobbing up and down. *Ewww...I hate this part of the job.*

Taking a deep breath, she focused on making her shield impenetrable while working on his thick muscles. She didn't want any of those creepers clinging onto her field. She imagine that she was as slick and slippery as a gold metallic ball. It worked. The apparitions stayed within the confines of his body.

Solid and stocky, massaging Mr. Toceni was like effleuraging a brick wall. Hearing him sigh, she continued to work on him. She noted with dispassion the movement of the wormlike creatures as they formed shapes and undulated. As the grey worms separated, they created an image in between them of a factory that built machines and silver boxes. She noticed that the silver boxes had dark streaks of black lines along their sides.

She continued to work on him, forcing herself to stay away from his spine. The ding of the timer was heaven sent as she quickly dried her wet hands. Stepping out of the room, she took a deep breath to steady herself. He felt grungy, layered with soot and a grey worm sandwich.

Outside of her room, she found a handsome, dark haired man in his forties sitting patiently on the couch. Feeling her gaze, he looked up and smiled, dazzling her with his perfect white teeth, elegantly chiseled nose and high cheekbones. She smiled back, feeling the energy of Mr. Toceni draining away.

"Are you Harmony?" his Italian accent was deep and sexy. *Oh my....*

"Yes, sir."

"I'm Vincenzio Gambini. I see you have met my partner already."

The door opened and Mr. Toceni stepped out, greeting Vincenzio with a handshake. He quickly leered at Harmony before walking away towards the elevator.

"Sir, if you wouldn't mind giving me a moment to prepare the room, I will be with you in a few minutes."

"Of course. I'm more than willing to wait for a beautiful woman to deliver me pleasure."

A crimson blush enveloped her as she turned around towards the door. She disappeared in the safe haven of the massage room, hearing him chuckle as she closed the door. *What is it with these men? Surely they must realize the effect they have on women! Ugh!*

She quickly stripped the sheets, wanting to spray the table with bleach after her session with Mr. Toceni. She refrained, knowing that Clorox and lavender didn't mix well together.

Harmony quickly dressed her table, sprayed her essential oils in the air, and grounded herself. She could feel Vincenzio's presence on the other side of the wall.

Opening the door, she invited him in, keeping her eyes low to the ground. When she raised them again, he was sitting at the table, studying her. She quickly explained the process of getting ready and turned to head out the door before he stopped her.

"Do I get a happy ending after my massage?"

Her back stiffened as she slowly turned to face him. His handsome face was marred by a smirk that assumed too much.

"Mr. Gambini. I can assure you that is *not* the type of massage I offer."

"Well Ms. Carey assured me that I could receive whatever treatment I needed to feel relaxed and comfortable."

"I'm sure we have a list of services that can be to your liking, sir," she responded coolly. "But last time I checked, happy endings weren't on it."

His laughter bounced around the room like a pinball, striking off her field with a push. She gritted her teeth and fortified her shield even more. *How dare you? Happy endings. Please....*

"I'm simply joking with you, Harmony," his voice was teasing. "A beautiful woman with a feisty spirit is sure to be a challenge to any man."

"I'll take that as a compliment." She turned the door handle and began walking out.

"It is meant as one, *belissima*."

She closed the door. Leaning against the handle, she shook her head. *Great! What a day! First weird geek languages, then grey worms, and now Mr. Smooth-ass Gelato. Can this day get any better?*

She stilled her sarcastic thoughts, turning around to open the door. This time, Vincenzio was face down, his breathing deep and relaxed.

"I'm ready, *belissima*."

Damn it! I wish he would stop calling me that! She stepped over to his left side and energetically connected to his body. A dark blue column appeared on his spinal cord. Feeling a chill growing in her body, she realized that he was part of The Corona.

Taking a deep breath, she began to massage his body, using deep pressure towards his latissimus dorsi and moving down his spine. She could feel the blue column exerting pressure against her armor, and she projected her willpower to strengthen it. As she felt her shield flex, she noticed the blue column opening to reveal a grey building with metallic doors. Curious, she holographically allowed herself to enter the building and take stock of what was inside. She saw a production line with ten metal boxes, all uniform in appearance, with a glass roof and electronic gadgets inside. The glass roof looked dingy. *What a strange thing to see.*

Her massage continued until the timer went off. Vincenzio made no further comments until she bent low to inform him of the completion of his session. Turning around lazily, he looked up into her eyes.

"That was lovely."

"Thank you, sir."

"You are quite talented," his Italian accent was smooth and enticing. "I like your touch."

"Thank you. "

"Harmony, *belissima*, I know this is quite sudden, but I do hope you'll do me the honor of accompanying me to the NET Media party on Friday."

What party? "I'm sorry, Mr. Gambini," she responded quickly. "I have an unbreakable rule that I don't date clients."

His laugh was rich, vibrating around the room like a baritone saxophone. "I'm not your client. I'm simply passing through. We may never see each other again."

That would be a relief. "Still, sir, it does not feel like a good idea for me to take you up on your generous offer."

He sat up quickly, the top sheet barely covering his fine physique. It was distracting, his naked self sitting so close to her. "I'm not a man that takes no easily."

Oh great! The no theme. Is this universal amongst these men? "Well then, sir. Perhaps the more you practice, the easier it becomes." She bowed her head stiffly and turned towards the door, ignoring his laughter as she stepped out. Her brow furrowed in anger at his condescending treatment. *You got yourself into this. Get yourself out!*

After a few minutes, the door opened as Vincenzio stepped out, resplendent in his blue pin-striped suit. He looked more relaxed and self-indulgent than before he started. He smiled widely when he spotted Harmony standing by the water cooler.

"Thank you, Harmony. I will see you on Friday, yes?" his Italian accent was persuasive and honey-smooth.

"I doubt it, Mr. Gambini. I was not aware of the company event on Friday, and as such, I've already got plans."

"A date?"

"Yes."

"With me?"

"No."

"Well you can't blame a man for trying to seduce a beautiful woman." He smiled wickedly, walking past her towards the elevator. As the door opened, he turned around to face her, flashing a devastating smile. She shook her head in disbelief. *What is it with men who think you're going to just drop everything just because they're crazy rich and have a killer body?*

"So does that mean you're busy on Friday?" She jumped at the sound of Eduardo's voice. He had been there the whole time, leaning against a wall that was away from her view.

"Eduardo...Mr. Torres, I'm sorry," she stammered nervously. "I didn't see you." Her heart was pounding loudly in her chest, so much so that she thought he could hear it too.

He stepped gracefully towards her, his eyes blazing amber. He reached out to touch her elbow, momentarily closing his eyes, absorbing her information into his mainframe.

"I see. Mr. Gambini has been less than well-behaved."

"I'm sorry that you had to see that."

"Don't be. I expect that kind of behavior from him. Usually the therapists give in to what he wants. Your reaction is rather refreshing, if not brave."

"He's not my type."

"And what is your type, Harmony?"

"Someone who's not my client or my coworker."

"Are you suggesting we fire you?"

She froze. He was baiting her. "Are you unsatisfied with my work, sir?"

"Hardly," his smirk was disarming. "I find your work rather...addicting."

"Then why do you throw that kind of threat over me?"

"Because it pleases me that you would say no to these sleazeballs who happen to be our clients and partners."

"I wasn't lying when I said I had a date Friday."

"Well then you can bring him to our party."

"But sir, I'm not sure it's such a good idea. I don't..."

"No excuses. Consider yourself invited." Eduardo's voice was firm and decisive. Clearly he was not going to be swayed about this decision.

How could she argue with her boss? Especially when he was standing so close, and she could breathe in his strong scent. *Damn it! These men....*

He smiled, as if reading her thoughts. His hand was still on her elbow, caressing her skin softly and radiating heat throughout her body. She could feel him surreptitiously invading her senses, making her squirm.

As if his touch was connected to the center of her pleasure, she felt the stirrings of warmth begin to awaken deep in her belly. A part of her felt mortified that he could elicit such a carnal response. The other felt drawn to him like a drug. She looked up and saw his blazing amber eyes searching hers. She could see red streaks of fire energy seeping through his body, emanating from the blue column in the center of his spine. The spark between them grew like a fire on gasoline.

"What are you doing to me?" His voice was barely a whisper.

She shook her head. It was near impossible. With sheer willpower, she forced herself to move away from him, pulling her elbow free from his grasp. She could feel her armor bending and bowing.

"I should get the massage room ready for you, sir."

"Of course." He followed her into the massage room, sitting on a chair while watching her strip the table.

Harmony could feel Eduardo's gaze following her every move. Her armor felt weak, and she focused her willpower on stabilizing it. She judiciously fought to keep her thoughts blank, grounding her energy. She felt a cold chill descend on her as she masked The Corona energy around her. Finally, she turned to look at him, feeling ready to start her session.

"Your ability to hide your thoughts from me is fascinating." He stood up and moved close to her, trapping her between himself and the table. "Tell me...where did you learn that from?"

She smiled demurely. "Surely you must understand, sir. A woman never reveals her secrets."

"Ah...it's like that, is it?" his eyes darkened with amusement. "And pray tell...what other secrets are you hiding in that beautiful head of yours."

She closed her eyes, feeling him psychically probing into her mind. Firmly sequestering him to the compartment that she assigned to him, she doubled her force field with her intentions.

"Sir, some secrets just aren't meant to be shared with others."

He smirked, appraising her from head to foot. "Perhaps I have underestimated you after all, Harmony."

"You cannot gauge what you don't know."

Eduardo smiled, allowing their close contact to become intense, heated and intimate. "Well I'd like to get to know you better ."

Harmony felt herself swirling in the amber eyes that held her gaze. With supreme effort, she pulled herself away and began to busy herself around the room. She wanted to do anything to avoid having to look into his hypnotic gaze.

"Harmony..."

"Yes Mr. Torres?"

"You really are quite a beguiling woman. Whatever it is you're doing, I seem to find myself being drawn to you. Do you have anything to say for yourself?"

She bravely lifted her head to face him, her thoughts blank and her shield steady. "Sir, I'm not doing anything. I'm simply doing my job as a therapist. If you like my work, I consider that a compliment."

He smiled, reaching out to trace her jawline with a skilled finger, leaving a trail of burning fire behind in its wake. "I think you're more than just a therapist, Harmony. Your ability to cover your thoughts takes skill and training. How did you learn that?"

"Practice, sir. I don't like the feeling of having my personal space invaded by uninvited guests."

"And what would I have to do to be invited in?"

"Sir, you apparently don't care if you get an invitation. You just come in anyway."

He smiled, causing his amber eyes to glow like hot coals. "I'd rather you be more upfront in sharing with me."

"I don't know you enough to trust you."

"And yet you're still here, Harmony. I find that to be an interesting dilemma."

She tore her gaze away from him and moved over to the other side, freeing herself.

"Sir, if you'd like to get ready, I'll give you privacy. I'll be back in a few minutes and we can get started."

"I do like this cat and mouse game we've got going on."

"Well sir...I should just let you know now...I don't have any intentions of getting caught."

His laughter surprised her. "I do so like your spirit, woman. You make this challenge even more appealing."

She shook her head, dumbfounded at his obstinacy, walked out the door, separating them for a brief interlude. *This has got to stop. I can't keep trying to pretend I don't feel anything around him.*

With a resigned sigh, she turned the handle and stepped back in. She found Eduardo face down on the table, naked and waiting for her. She willed her armor back to full force and reached for the massage lotion. Placing her hands on his occiput and lower back, she energetically connected to him. She worked in silence as she focused on easing the tension in his back, shoulders and neck.

Looking into his body, she could see that blue column of light tinged with red streaks of attraction, residue from his earlier conversation with her. She followed the streaks into his body and saw that it emanated from a dark black seed at the base of the column. Unsure of what that black seed was, she holographically entered it to view its contents. What she saw filled her with sadness and compassion.

She witnessed a young boy pushed to the background of activity, fighting to get attention and be seen by others around him. The younger brother of a powerful entertainment family, he was overshadowed by his older brother, Nicholas, and his father, a powerful Corona leader.

Harmony also observed him as a solitary figure, holding everyone at bay—Mariska, his family, and his coworkers. He was an island, floating desolate and alone in life.

"So now you really see me." His voice was soft, catching her off guard.

"Mr. Torres, I'm sorry. I didn't mean to pry."

"You didn't. I offered it for you to see."

Her hands stopped mid-stroke. "Why?"

"Because it's lonely where I am. No one ever reaches me there." He turned around suddenly to face her. His muscular physique was distracting, and she carefully readjusted the flat sheet to cover his frame.

Her silence encouraged him to continue. "I thought I was more than ok being in this place of control and isolation. I didn't want anything. That was until I met you."

"Sir, I…"

"Let me finish." His voice was deep and husky. "Harmony, when I look inside your mind, I see a place of beauty and purity. I see someone who is capable of great love. Someone who could save a man drowning in his soul."

Her emerald eyes gazed deep into his. *Where's he going with this?*

"Every time I'm around you, I feel like there's a lift inside of my spirit – like I'm taking a breath of fresh air. That's why I've come around so much. I don't know what you're doing, but I like it."

"I'm not doing anything, sir."

"You're being yourself, and that's more than these copycats around here can claim."

"What do you want from me?"

"Give me one night, Harmony. That's all I ask."

"What? You're kidding, right?" Shock overwhelmed her system. *He cannot be serious! This is some kind of a set-up, a joke.*

"No," his tone was clipped. "I've never been more serious about anything in my life. I want one night with you – just to see whether what we have is real or not."

"Have you forgotten something? You have a girlfriend. I'm in a relationship. This is not a good idea."

"Mariska and I are not in a committed relationship. We never have been. She has other lovers, and well….I don't."

"Can't you see how wrong this is? I work for you! It goes against my personal code of honor to be involved with a coworker, client and someone else's boyfriend. You're all three!"

His smile was rueful. "I do see your point. It means nothing to me though. I see us as two consenting, mature adults coming together to celebrate union for one night."

"I'm sorry, Mr. Torres. I can't do it."

His eyes changed, taking a more detached and cooler glint. "I thought as much, Harmony. You're a woman of strong conviction. It's something I admire in you. I respect your decision, but I will not deny this attraction between us."

"Sir, I feel that too, but I will not act on it out of respect for you, our partners and myself. If my presence here at NET Media is too much for you, I will most certainly understand if you decide to let me go."

"Let you go?" he laughed harshly at her words. "That's preposterous. You're not going anywhere. If this is the only way right now that I can see you, then I want you here."

She remained silent, unsure of what to say.

Eduardo gazed at her, sensing her internal conflict. He could see her fighting against him – both in her body and her mind. It caused him to change and pull away immediately. A mask fell on his face, leaving him cold.

"Now, I believe I need a debriefing of the clients that you've seen today." His voice was all business. Gone was the gentle profession of a lonely man. She was now facing the detached VP, whose smoldering look could burn the clothes off her body.

"What would you like me to do, sir?"

"Give me your hands," he commanded, placing his in front of hers. Intimidated, she placed hers in his, feeling the jet-fuel of heated, restrained desire course through her on contact. She closed her eyes and focused her attention on opening the cell reserved for him.

Eduardo was silent as he absorbed the contents of the encapsulated vestibule of her mind. White heat coursed between their arms, wrapping themselves around each other like a circuit. She could feel her armor bending in some areas. Pressure crushed on her, and she and felt a headache coming on. After a few minutes, he finally spoke.

"Amazing. You did a great job, Harmony. I could see the programming code that Mr. Morito and Mr. Takasaki had erroneously created. Now we can fix that on the E-2K – make it better, less prone to glitches and viruses. As for Mr. Toceni and Mr. Gambini, they have not been forthright about the sources of their crystal glasses. I'm disappointed that these men have already produced ten E-2K's with faulty wiring and contaminated crystals. That's deplorable."

Harmony pulled away, sinking gratefully into a chair. She felt drained and siphoned. Having Eduardo in her mind and shielding at the same time took great concentration and force. Her eyes closed and she felt nothing.

When she opened her eyes, she found herself lying on the massage table. Eduardo was standing above her, fully clothed and looking concerned.

"Hey...are you ok?" his voice was gentle.

"What happened?" Her voice shook as she tried to sit up. Another wave of dizziness ran through her. She laid back down, her hands on her temple to ease the pounding pressure.

"You passed out after you sat down. I brought you up on the table so that you weren't lying on the floor."

"I don't know what came over me."

"I think you've taken on all the energy you can handle today, Harmony. Perhaps you should go home. Rest up so you can return here tomorrow."

Feeling herself more grounded and steady, she sat up, gratefully accepting the water bottle he handed to her. The cool liquid eased the tension and pain in her head.

"Thank you," she murmured. Looking up at him, she found him staring at her intently. She immediately checked her shield and felt relief as it radiated around her. "Did you get the information you needed?"

"Yes, I did. Thank you. We'll be addressing these issues tomorrow. Can I offer you a ride home? I don't feel like it's a good idea for you to be driving."

"No thank you, sir. I can manage. I feel better. Thank you."

He stood up, assessing her before turning towards the door. He paused after opening it to look back at her. "Harmony, I hope you believe what I've shown you. It's who I am, and it's what I can offer at this time."

Their gaze held one another in a state of suspended longing and attraction. She could feel his energy wash over her shield, trying to penetrate it to see into her mind. She couldn't allow him that.

"I'll see you tomorrow." He nodded coolly and walked out.

She turned towards the massage room, feeling the thick energy left behind by the powerhouse known as Eduardo Torres. It was hard to concentrate on cleaning up.

Taking one final look around, she stepped out of the room and headed for Lydia's office to clock out. She noticed the list of therapists and their schedule for the following day. Checking hers, she noticed that she had six clients again, with three Asians clients in the morning and two Australians in the afternoon, followed by Eduardo Torres. *Great. Another day like today. I don't know how I'm going to handle all this fun!*

She checked her phone and noticed a missed call from Tristan. Searching around for Clara, she found her on the floor below, in the middle of a massage. She decided to leave a note. Turning around to head towards the elevator, found herself face to face with Mariska Hebrenovich. *Awesome! I was totally wrong. This day is only going to get juicier after all.*

"I don't know who you are," Mariska hissed icily. "But I suggest you stay away from Eduardo Torres. Do you understand?"

Harmony assessed her, seeing green streaks discoloring the blue column in her body. She could tell that Mariska harbored some intense emotions of jealousy. But towards her?

"I don't know what you're talking about."

"Don't play that game with me. I see how Eduardo acts after he's been around you. I've never seen him like that before, and I don't like it."

"Well you can be assured I don't have any interests in him. I have a boyfriend." *More than that...*

"That's never stopped the Torres brothers. Those men don't care if you're married, in a convent, or say no until you're blue in the face. If they want you, they'll have you, no matter what."

"So why are you telling me this?"

"You touch what's mine, and I will find you and make your life a living hell."

"Oh really? Kind of like yours?" Sarcasm dripped out of Harmony's voice as stepped into the elevator . She wanted to get away from the ice witch that was throwing accusations her way.

"This isn't over."

Her emerald eyes flashed defiantly into Marisa's icy blue. "You start something with me, it'll be the worst decision you'll ever make."

The door closed, separating her from Mariska's shocked, open-mouthed look. She leaned back, sagging with relief as the elevator began its descent. Heading outside, she took a deep, cleansing breath.

She was so glad to be out of there. She was grateful that Tristan had the foresight to leave her car in the parking garage. Walking towards it, she felt a buzzing in her purse. It was a text message from Tristan.

**Call me when you get home. Don't call me til you're there.
They're tracking you.**

Chapter Fourteen

Harmony was exhausted when she got home. Her emotions felt raw and ragged, and her head felt like it was about to explode from all the concentrated efforts to keep her shield up. Heading straight for the bathroom, she began to run a bath, placing essential oils of lavender and eucalyptus in the running water. She headed for her altar and grabbed some crystals – quartz, black tourmaline and malachite – all intended to pull the negative vibrations and energy off her and transmute it into calming, life-enhancing forces. Grabbing her phone, she quickly texted her address to Tristan, letting him know that her door would be unlocked for him.

Slipping into the hot bath, she released a sigh of relief. Her thoughts slipped briefly to her clients, pausing in her interaction with Eduardo. *I don't know. I'm so confused. Why is this happening to me?*

She heard the front door open and movement in her living room. Closing her eyes, she knew it would just be a matter of time before Tristan came in. Pulling a long quartz crystal from the floor of the tub, she ran it up and down her body, willing it to pull any stagnation away so that she could return to her center.

"Hey," Tristan's soft voice greeted her as he opened her bathroom. She welcomed him with a tired smile.

"Hi, baby," she murmured gently. "Wanna join me?"

"Absolutely." He stripped off his clothes and gingerly stepped behind her, filling the tub to overflowing with his large frame. His long legs eased on either side of her, and she was grateful for her extra-large tub.

"Tough day?" he asked, running his hands up and down her arms.

"I don't know if tough is the word I would use. Demanding. Pressure filled. Tense."

"You know you don't have to do this."

"I know. I'm not sure how long I'll be able to last in this job."

"What happened?"

She held nothing back, except for what she had seen inside Eduardo. His desire to share that vulnerable part of himself made her feel responsible for protecting it. She did share Eduardo's request for one night alone with her. Tristan froze. She turned around to face him. His eyes were cold and dark and his mouth was set in a grim line.

"One night, Harmony? He wants one night with you?" Fury radiated through his words.

She nodded, speechless.

"What did you say?"

"Of course I said no. I also reminded him that he was in a relationship and so was I."

She was hesitant in speaking the last words, knowing that she and Tristan had not formally declared anything solid between them. A few imprints, mind-boggling sex and admissions of love didn't label what they had.

She wasn't even sure what exactly she was to him. She knew he loved her. Wanted her. Wanted her to join the Tribe of Light. But was that it? Was that his true motivations for seducing and training her?

Tristan sighed heavily, running a hand through his hair. He was silent, causing Harmony to feel a rivulet of anxiety run through her. She could sense his anger under his brooding stare.

"What's wrong?"

"I'm totally against this one night stand. This is how The Corona gets hold of you."

"I knew you would be. That's why I said no."

"But are you against it?"

She was quiet, allowing his question to play around in her mind, carefully choosing her answer. "I am, Tristan. But there's something between me and Eduardo that I can't put my finger on. It's like our connection feels older than just this meeting. The pull that we have towards each other is almost as strong as what I feel for you."

"Well, perhaps this will answer some of your questions." Tristan placed his hand on her arms, allowing her mind to fill with visuals and images.

A beautiful woman, dressed in white, stood at the altar, her tear-stained face in agony as she waited and waited for her groom. Everyone in the church looked uncomfortable as their eyes were filled with sympathy at her pain and her loss. Her sobs filled the quiet hall, interrupted only as she fainted, overcome with the grief that her beloved had not shown up...

Harmony gasped, pained as the image dissipated only to be replaced by another.

A village stood in burning disarray as a ragged and dirty young girl held her arms out towards a young boy who was being dragged away. He was screaming her name and crying as soldiers pulled him onto a horse, sprinting away from her and his home. His shrieks of fear and anger filled the air...

Harmony's heart ached for that young child as the vision disappeared, allowing another to come into place.

A dark cell, cold and grimy, shrouded the figure crouched in the corner. A young woman, dressed in a resplendent velvet red gown, held her hands to her face in fervent prayer, sobbing quietly, distraught and sad. The door of the jail cell opened, and a handsome man with bright amber eyes solemnly came in. He held a hand out to her. Standing with grace and dignity, she wiped her eyes dry and reached for him, knowing that he was leading her to the guillotine ....

"Ok," her voice was a strained whisper. "That's enough."
"As much as I hate it, I understand the connection that you and Eduardo have. I don't like it, but in the end, the choice is still up to you."

Her green eyes searched his, looking for confirmation that it didn't matter to him of their past connection. *Or did it?*

"Don't," she whispered softly. "Don't question my loyalty to you. He's not what I want."

"It's not what you want that I'm worried about."

"You worry too much," she responded lightly, wanting to shift the conversation before it got too heavy. Her day was already weighing her down. She didn't want any more pressure.

"You're worth worrying about," he growled softly against the smooth column of her neck. It elicited goose bumps on her arms as he trailed soft kisses from the base of her neck to her earlobe. Catching the soft lobe in his teeth, he licked the sensitive skin, extracting a moan from her lips.

She reached up and pulled his head close, whispering as their lips met. "Well I have an idea on how to erase all those worries from your mind."

"Do you now?" his voice was husky against her lips. "Care to show me?"

She smiled wickedly. "Oh, I fully intend to."

She delicately licked the outline of his lips, lightly tracing the curvature and dipping in to taste him. "I might even let you watch."

With an aroused groan, Tristan crushed her to his chest, deepening their kiss and claiming her lips savagely. She responded to his touch, melting towards him. His hands ran up her side, caressing her breasts, pulling at her nipples until she gasped and moaned in pleasure. Her hand trailed down towards his abdomen, raking her nails down to grasp his firm erection. He groaned as she began to move up and down, firmly encircling him in her hands. She relished his panting as his lips moved down her throat.

She gasped as his fingers found the opening of her center. They dipped into her slick wetness and rubbed over her swollen clitoris. A moan reverberated through her body as she arched towards him, desire rising deep in her body as a vortex of light began to form. Her hand continued to stroke him, increasing the pressure and pace. He moved and thrust against her, splashing water over the tub.

"Yes baby...that feels good!" he murmured against her breast, relentlessly coaxing her with his fingers. He rubbed a spot inside her pussy that made her shudder, working away at her clitoris. A moan of pleasure erupted from her lips as she shook with abandon, releasing all that pent up energy. He pushed relentlessly through every ecstatic wave.

She pulled away looking at him with hooded eyes. Her body was reverberating with awakened sexuality. "I want you..."

"You've got me."

"In my mouth..."

Understanding that carnal look in her eyes, Tristan stood up, running his hand up her body. She leaned into his touch, moaning softly as he drew circles on her skin, licking her lips at the sight of his stiff, engorged erection. She reached up to stroke him, kissing the tip of his crown before opening her mouth to fully take him in. Sheathing her teeth, she began to suck and lick him, eliciting groans of pleasure as he pushed deeper into her. She moaned and continued to suck him, massaging his base and moving in rhythm to his body.

Tristan began to thrust deeper into her mouth; her tongue lapping, circling and sucking him harder. His movements became more rhythmic as she stroked him from the base to the tip. A shudder ran through him as his orgasm began to wash over his body. She could taste his hot creaminess in her mouth as he emptied himself, his body shaking and an animalistic groan escaping his lips. She swallowed, allowing his essence to fill her body. Looking up, she could see blazing fire and lust hooding his eyes. He leaned down to kiss her, his tongue dipping into her mouth. His invasion inflamed her. She reached up to hold his head down, deepening their kiss, until she felt herself wanting him again.

He broke away, breathing heavily, as he reached down to unplug the tub, draining the water all around them. Pulling her up to stand in front of him, he reached for her towel and gently began to dry her. She tried to help, but he quickly shooed her hand away.

Surrendering to his loving ministrations, she closed her eyes and threw her head back.

Tristan quickly dried himself next. Swooping down to pick her up, he carried her to her bed and eased her down. He laid beside her, his hand caressing her face. His eyes searched hers, as if looking for answers.

"What's on your mind?" she asked softly, tracing his full lips with her finger. He quickly caught her hand, bringing it up to his lips for a chaste kiss,

"The leaders of the Tribe have been brought up to date with what's happening at NET Media. They're very appreciative of the work you're doing right now."

Her eyebrows rose up, not expecting their conversation to take this turn. "I'm not sure what I've done. I just hope that they can get what they need in the time that I'm there. Otherwise…"

"Stop." He admonished her. "Don't second guess or doubt yourself. You're doing exceptionally well – much better than the Tribe or I would have thought."

"How much longer do I have to do this?"

"The Tribe says that they'll know more after the trade show. They want you to try to hang on until the end of the show which could be the end of this weekend. Can you handle that?"

"Yes. Can you?"

"I'm trying. It's not easy."

She heard the frustration in his voice. "What's troubling you?"

"This one night thing that Eduardo's asking. It pisses me of royally that these bastards are still in my life after all these years."

"It won't come to that. I promise."

"We'll see. The Corona is cunning. I never put anything past them."

"Shh…let's not talk about The Corona, the Torres brothers or anything else related to this job anymore. I just want it to be you and me. Can we do that?"

His smile answered her question. She could see his eyes lighting with love and adoration for her. It melted her. She lifted herself up to kiss him, relishing in the softness of his lips and responding to the movement of his hands on her body.

Somewhere between her question and his response, they lost themselves in the invitation to touch, to remember and to return to the center of pleasure. All concerns faded in the background as they were obliterated by sensations that consumed them. They passionately carried their bodies to the edge of release and pushed through the veil of control. Tristan and Harmony made love until they were shaking, breathless, and awash in orgasmic waves.

~~~~~~

Harmony drove into the parking garage of the Frost Bank building, reminding herself to activate and fortify her shield. As she headed towards the elevator that would take her to the NET Media offices, she thought gratefully about her previous night with Tristan.

Something deep inside made her feel like she was bait, waiting for a bigger fish to bite than just the Torres brothers. She shook her head, resolving to feel differently when she left the building today.

She arrived at the NET Media office to find it bustling once again. There was a film crew moving through the different offices, asking random employees questions while shooting and blinding them with their bright lights. She prayed for anonymity as she wove her way towards the Wellness Department.

Like the previous day, the department was filled with people exercising, lifting weights and running on treadmills. The vibration of healthy radiance filtered throughout the gym and she smiled as she saw Todd Wenzley waving to her from one of the treadmills. He looked happy, and she was secretly relieved that he had stopped texting her.

When she arrived at the spa, she ran into Clara, who was busily perusing the appointments of the day. Clara's face immediately brightened when she saw her.

"What happened to you yesterday? I was looking for you and you blazed!"

"You didn't get my note? I left you one."

Clara frowned. "No, that's weird. I got nothing. Next time text me."

Harmony nodded and looked at her scheduled appointments. She had three more Asian computer techs in the morning, two Australian financiers in the afternoon, and capped off with Eduardo Torres.

"You're working on Eduardo Torres?" Clara was thunderstruck, looking at her schedule. "Is there something going on between you two?"

Harmony laughed. "No. Nothing. Zip. Nada. He must just like my massages. Besides, you know what would happen if anything ever went there."

"What?"

"Mariska."

"Oh yeah….that one." They both laughed.

"How are things with your new guy?" Clara turned a curious eye towards her. She was fishing for more juicy details. Harmony had been elusive and evasive about sharing her time with Tristan, wanting to protect his identity and their relationship from prying minds at NET Media. It pained her that she had to keep parts of her life from one of her oldest, dearest friends.

"He's really amazing! I try not to overthink it too much. I just want to enjoy him as much as I can for however long it lasts."

"Gee, how romantic."

Harmony laughed. "Don't be like that. You know how I am when it comes to guys. I get totally excited and fall too fast, and then it's done before I know it."

"But did any of those guys in the past make you feel like this guy does?"

"No," she smiled sweetly. "They didn't. They couldn't even measure up. I'm telling ya – this guy has really raised the bar up. Big time."

Clara clapped her hands in excitement. "I'm thrilled for you, honey! You, of all people, deserve to be happy. See, I told you. You just had to wait for the right one to come along."

Harmony smiled, her green eyes flashing happily. "I sure do hope he's the right one. It feels that way."

"Then that's all that matters. Listen...I have to go. My first client starts in half an hour and I've got to prep my room. Lunch?"

Harmony nodded happily. She walked towards her massage room and opened the door.

"Good morning." Eduardo's voice made her jump. *Holy hell!*

"Mr. Torres...what...what are you doing here?" she stammered. She wasn't prepared to get hit with his intense presence so early in the morning. She felt her shield bow around her and immediately willed it to strengthen and grow. A sigh of relief escaped her as she felt it swell.

"I thought I would speak to you about your clients before they arrived."

"Of course, sir." She began to prepare her room, refusing to meet his eyes.

"There are two financiers that are coming this afternoon. I would like for you to take extra special care of them."

She stiffened, hearing the implications in his words. She thought of Vincenzio Gambini and his request for a happy ending. *Is that what he wants from me?* She shuddered in revulsion. She heard Eduardo laugh softly.

"No, Harmony," his voice was raspy and soft, sending shivers up her spine. "No happy endings for you. At least not with these clients. That would be an utter waste of your gifts and abilities."

She turned around and faced him, bracing herself for the impact of his beautiful face and charming smile.

"What are you asking from me sir?"

"I believe you have the ability to draw out a negative block and place in a positive outcome. Do you get my drift?"

"Sort of. Can you be more clear?"

"These two financiers are important backers of our E-2K program. There is some resistance in fully funding this initiative. I want you to find where that resistance lies and remove it."

She was silent, studying him, pondering his request.

"Harmony," his tone was persuasive. "These men are already a yes. They simply need reinforcement. That's where you come in."

"How so?"

"You simply remove that energy block that resists a full yes and place the vibration of acceptance in. I know you can do it."

"How do you know that?"

"I've seen it." She was silent. "Will you do it? Please?"

She gazed up into his honey eyes. He leaned closer, his face inches from her.

"You're a very talented and gifted energy worker. I'm very lucky that you work for our company. You have a bright future here."

She smiled, the warmth not reaching into her eyes. She knew what he was doing, bringing his charmingly persuasive self closer into her field. But would she? Could she?

"What you're asking me to do is to interfere with how someone feels and thinks. I don't know if I can do that."

She could feel his breath on her face. She tried to pull away. He was too close, too strong.

"I'm not asking you to go against their will. All I'm asking is that you see where that resistance lies and give it a little nudge. Surely you can do that, right?" His voice was smooth and hypnotic.

He was distracting, and as much as Harmony didn't want her body to, it responded to him in an unconscious way. *Dammit! Why do you do this to me?*

He leaned back and smiled. "Because I want you, and I want to see how far you're willing to keep pushing me away."

"Eduardo...Mr. Torres. I will do what I can. No guarantees or promises. Don't get your hopes up."

His charming smile lit up his eyes. "Harmony, you truly are a gem. You will definitely be rewarded for all your hard work."

He began to move towards the door, pausing before turning the handle. Looking back, he quickly assessed the whole room. "I will speak to Lydia about moving you to a larger office, one that will better fit our executive clients. I will be back later for debriefing."

He walked out of the massage room, leaving her shaken and perturbed. *Is this how it's always going to be? Him charging in and me fighting him off?*

She sighed and began to prepare her room. She could still feel Eduardo's presence around her. Closing her eyes, she strengthened her shield, feeling it push away the lingering vibrations of his energy field. A vortex of light descended from the top of her shield, moving through her spine and radiating a golden light around her. She called in her guides and asked for their support, feeling serenity envelope her.

A knock at the door brought her out of her meditation. It was time to go to work. She opened the door with a smile, greeting Mr. Tokosaki, her first client.

As she began her session, she could once again see the column of blue light emanating from his spine. He was part of The Corona. There was a visible movement of energy and salamander - like beings moved up and down his column. As she examined the movement, she noticed a small red sphere float like a bubble amongst the ocean of blue. Holographically peeking into the sphere, she could see an array of numbers and letters, moving in a rapid sequence. Everything was in neon green, except for a sequence that appeared a bright red. She didn't know what that sequence represented and was grateful for her ignorance.

Her session with Mr.Tokosaki was followed by work with Mr. Akita and Mr. Makito. Both of the gentlemen were also Corona members with a blue column of light in their spines. Each held spheres of information and had the sequential arrays of neon green code patterning. Mr. Akita held a sequence of golden yellow, whereas Mr. Makito had another shade of red. Harmony was not sure how these different men were related to the E-2K. She wasn't sure she wanted to know.

Lunch came sooner than she expected, and she was grateful for the break. She cleaned and prepared her room for her afternoon clients and went in search of Clara. She found her friend finishing up her last client. With extra time on her hands, she wandered through the Wellness Department, exploring the other classes, equipment and offerings of the company.

A familiar voice filtered out of Lydia's office, freezing her in her tracks. She quickly moved against the wall to listen.

"Lydia, I don't like her working on Eduardo." A whiny, petulant tone rang clearly.

"Mariska, Eduardo is the one signing up for her sessions."

"Find another therapist to work on him."

"I just can't assign *any* therapist to work on him. He's specifically wants her."

"But why her?" Mariska grated as anger dripped from her voice.

"Probably the same reason why he chose to have you work on him in the beginning. You had certain skills that he needed to access. Harmony is no different."

"I want her moved."

"You'll have to talk to Eduardo about that. He assigned her here for a reason."

"Well find a reason to get rid of her or place her in a satellite office. *Away* from him." Mariska demanded hotly. Harmony smiled, finding some twisted pleasure in how much she was affecting the cold, domineering woman.

Lydia sighed patiently as if talking to a small child. "Look, I make the schedules. I don't say where these therapists get assigned to work. Right now, is not a good time. We're fine-tuning all the pieces that are contributing to the creation and launch of the E-2K. We need her. She's getting the information about what's blocking production. You just have to be patient."

"Patient?" Mariska's voice was close to hysterical. "Every time that woman touches him, I feel the imprint of her body on him. It makes me want to gag."

"Are you jealous?" Lydia sounded amused.

"Please….don't be ridiculous," Mariska scoffed. "She couldn't possibly give him what I can. Besides, it's only a matter of time before it comes out that she's a Lightworker. There's no where she can run to where The Corona won't hunt her down. We'll eventually own her, too. And then I'll really make her pay for putting her hands on my man."

"He's not your man, Mariska. There's no ring on your finger," Lydia reminded her gently. "We all know that Eduardo is the most elusive bachelor in town. You can try and land him, but there's no guarantee with that one."

"We'll see about that!"

Harmony slid back in the darkness of the hallway, allowing it to shield her as Mariska and Lydia walked out of her office. As she watched them head towards the elevator, she released the breath that she'd been holding. So they knew. *Dammit! I don't have much time. I've got to get out of here quick.*

"Hey there!" Clara's voice interrupted her. She whirled around quickly, planting a smile on her face. Clara's brows furrowed at Harmony's flushed appearance.

"What's wrong? Why are you hiding there?"

"I just caught a conversation between Mariska and Lydia."

"Oh yeah? Was it juicy?"

"Mariska's super pissed off that I'm working on Eduardo. She's got something against me. Bad."

"Can you blame her? You didn't see how he looked at you at lunch yesterday. He's clearly interested. If I were her, I'd be worried too."

"I'm not interested in him."

"You sure about that? I can feel you too, don't forget. You get all nervous at the mention of his name. Why?"

Harmony blushed. "I don't know. I guess because I feel some kind of weird attraction, but I'm staying away, because I know he's not good for me."

"That's a smart decision. Ok…so are we going to lunch now?"

"Yes but first...I want you to take me to the E-2K. I want to see it."

Clara led Harmony to the entertainment wing of NET Media. Filled with video games and virtual reality machines, it was a techie's dream come true. For Harmony, it was a confusing array of beeps, dings and over-stimulation. .

They walked to the back of the large department. Alongside the wall stood three sleek, silver rectangular boxes that looked like telephone booths. Inside each silver machine was a small screen, with headphones attached to the monitor. The headphones had a network of patches attached to the top and a blood pressure cuff and finger probe connected to the base. It looked like a clinical experiment, and Harmony shivered, feeling a sense of foreboding as Clara explained the procedure of using the E-2K.

"First, you apply the headphones and make sure the patches rest above your head. Then you put on the blood pressure cuff and attach the probe to your finger. You dial in the experience you want to have and the emotions you want to feel."

"This sounds weird."

"I know, but trust me, it's totally worth it. The heavier and darker the experience you want to have, the better you feel afterwards."

"How does that work?"

"Well, say you want to experience war. You get flashes of all these images that are about war and hear these frequencies that feel really disturbing. It literally makes you want to jump out of your skin. But if you can hold on for even ten minutes, then everything changes, and you get to see all these beautiful and uplifting pictures and hear all these amazing sounds. When you get done, you feel like a million bucks. You're so happy and light."

Harmony looked at her dubiously and turned a narrowed gaze towards the E-2K. *What's so damn special about this thing?* Turning towards Clara, her stance was firm and determined. "Ok. I want to do it. Dial me in."

"You're sure about this?"

"I'm positive. I want to know what the big deal is about this machine."

"So what negative experience do you want to see?"

"I don't know. Surprise me."

"Ok, since this is your first time, let's try something easy. How about robbery and theft?"

Harmony shrugged her shoulders and nodded. As she stepped into the E-2K, a wave of familiarity washed through her. Déjà vu. It reminded her of the Field Modulator.

Taking a deep, steadying breath, she sat down on the bench and placed the headphones atop her head. She put the blood pressure cuff on and attached the probe to her index finger. She heard the door close, and soon she was immersed in darkness. Her breath caught in her throat. *I hope I'm not making a mistake by doing this. I just need to see why there's so many people working on this machine.*

The monitor flickered to life in front of her as an ominous and creepy sound filled her ears. She felt the hairs on her arms and neck stand up as pictures appeared on the screen. She watched in fascination as banks were robbed, homes ransacked, villages plundered, jewelry stores stripped, and people were mugged.

The eerie soundtrack was dark and discordant, enough to make her skin crawl. She sweated, feeling upset and nervous. A suffocating feeling began to rise, encircling her throat like a vice. She felt like she was about to lose control – wanting to rip the headphones off of her. *Hang on. Just hang on a bit longer.*

Minutes crawled by painfully slow and just when she felt like she couldn't bear another excruciating moment, everything changed. The images shifted from negative, painfully disturbing pictures to beautiful sunsets, high mountain vistas, people laughing and babies cooing. The sounds altered from heavy oppressive dark beats to light airy instrumentals. It was soft as a butterfly's wings in the breeze.

Harmony felt herself relax and breathe more regularly. She even found herself smiling as she was drawn deeper into the hypnotic trance of the E-2K. She felt a lightning bolt of pure joy enter her body through her crown, the connection point of her headphones. Tingling sensations of light rained down on her, elevating her mood.

When the program was finished, she removed the headphones and stepped out of the booth. She felt fantastic, even euphoric, and flashed Clara a brilliant smile.

Everything insider her felt so light that she could barely even recall the disturbing images that had started off her E-2K experience. She didn't care. All she knew was that she had never felt so elated and wonderful before.

"Now you know what I mean, right?"

Harmony nodded, overcome with a feeling of joy. "I feel so…happy."

"Yes, I know. That's why they call it the Ecstasy 2000. It's the best high ever! Totally clean without being illegal!"

"High?" Harmony was confused, her elatedness still vibrating inside.

"You feel good right now, but in four to five hours, you'll feel different. Just wait and see. Right now, just enjoy the ride."

They began walking out of the entertainment department and headed down to the first floor towards the cafeteria. Harmony felt radiant, smiling warmly and waving happily at everyone she passed. She turned to see Clara's look of amusement as they entered the crowded cafeteria. Harmony was in a world of her own.

She was mesmerized by the beautiful, shining faces of all the people she saw. *When did everyone look so amazing and happy? When did the world explode in color and brilliance? How did I never know that this level of euphoria existed?*

She smiled at the array of food, commenting on the colors and flavors. Everything felt so vibrant and bright. The decadent smell made her gasp with delight. Every cell hummed with joy. As she sat down at the table to eat, she felt her phone buzzing in her pocket. When she looked at the caller, her face lit up.

It was Tristan. She mentally gave herself a hug as she thought about him. *How can I be so lucky to have such a super-hot hunk of a man to love?*

Reading the text, she was surprised at the message: **WTF?!?! Meet me at 4th and Congress. NOW**

Harmony's mouth dropped. *What just happened?!*

She felt a brief flash of annoyance, but an overwhelming sense of buoyancy replaced it, washing any negative feelings away. She wondered what the rush was but didn't care. She would get to see him! She felt herself grow light with excitement. She looked at her watch. Only twenty five minutes remained of her lunch break, and she was famished.

Grabbing everything to go, she said a hurried good-bye to Clara and headed out the door. Eating on the run was no easy task, but Harmony managed to do it with a smile on her face. She still felt fantastic! Even the text message could barely scratch her euphoria. *Life rocks!*

She spotted Tristan sitting at a bench, brooding and guarded. She could feel his eyes assessing her as she walked towards him. Her desire for food was all of a sudden replaced by a growing hunger for something else. As if her body was synchronized to her thoughts, she felt a warmth in her pelvis begin to grow and a tingling heaviness in her breasts. *Dangit! Is it possible not to think about sex whenever I see this man? Really...*

"Hey you!" she greeted him, feeling flushed and radiant.

His eyes narrowed at her smiling face. Something was off. "Sit down," he snapped. She automatically complied, confused by his detachment.

He reached for her hand and closed his eyes, receiving a series of imprints of her morning that downloaded in a flash. When they opened, they were cold with anger and shock.

"You used the E-2K?" His voice was harsh and piercing.

"Yes. I did." *What's wrong with him? Can't he see how happy I am?*

"Why?"

"Because I wanted to know what the big deal was about this machine."

"And?"

"And...I feel super great! I'm happier than I've ever felt before!"

"It's an illusion, Harmony. It's a false sense of security."

She felt like he had slapped her in the face. Her voice sounded hurt when she replied. "Why are you being this way? Can't you just let me be happy?"

Tristan sighed angrily. "Listen to me. When you use the E-2K, it affects your shield. It weakens it."

"How do you know?"

"Because we originally created the prototype for the E-2K, and it fell into the hands of The Corona. We know what it's capable of, and it's dangerous."

"But Tristan," her lip trembled. "I feel so...joyful. How can you say that when I feel so good?"

"That is temporary. This feeling won't last very long. And you're not going to feel so stellar afterwards."

"But what about my shield?" She began to feel a slight sense of panic creeping in. "What do I do?"

Tristan produced the crystal star tetrahedron pendant from his pocket. "I want you to wear this. Don't take it off for any reason. This pendant is programmed to hold your shield up and fortify it even more."

As Tristan placed the necklace around her neck, she felt a veil of light descend around her. Though she still felt euphorically happy, it was contained and controlled. Her eyes rose up to his.

"There's something else I need to tell you," she nervously spoke.

"What?"

"Mariska and Lydia know I'm a Lightworker. And if they know, then..."

Tristan was quiet, processing her information. "Then you're not safe."

"But they keep sending me these high-level executives and their team of tech wizards. Why do it if they know I'm on the other side?"

"They're baiting you," Tristan responded softly. "More than likely, they're trying to find the Tribe workers in their midst."

"But Eduardo downloads mainly the information related to the E-2K. Why not get that on his own? He's obviously got people who are skilled."

"But they don't have your skill," Tristan looked her in the eyes.

"What do you mean?" Confusion furrowed her brows.

"You have an oddly strange ability to look into people's bodies and energy field and manipulate what you see. It's almost like being a puppet master."

"That sounds ridiculous."

"I know. The Corona and Eduardo are keeping you at NET Media for a reason. The fact that they know who you are just makes me even more suspicious of their motives."

They both sat on the bench, gazing at one another. Harmony could feel Tristan's searching her face for answers. His protectiveness thrilled her, and she knew that her safety was of paramount importance to him.

"Why did you come?" she asked softly.

"Because I couldn't stay away and leave you unprotected around all those people."

"That's the only reason why?"

"No. I had to see you – make sure you were ok. When you used the E-2K, I knew something had changed drastically within your field. I could just feel it. It freaked me out a bit." He drew her close and kissed her gently.

Sighing, she allowed herself to soften and open to his advances. His kisses became more insistent and demanding, and she could feel her body responding quickly, getting hotter as she kissed him back with abandon. He clutched her back possessively while his hand cradled her neck.

She felt herself melting towards him, wanting him like she had never before. She didn't care that she only had a few minutes left of her break. If he tore her clothes off, she wouldn't fight it.

She just wanted to be filled with the ecstatic bliss that was reverberating through her now.

Tristan broke away first. "Do you want to leave? You know you don't have to go back to work?" he asked, his voice thick with desire.

"Dammit! I forgot...I just got caught up in the kiss."

"Well, you can leave right now."

"No! I'm going to see this through. I have to at least finish today."

"Ok, fine, I'll walk you back." Disappointment tinged his voice. He rearranged himself so that his excited state was less apparent. She smiled and winked. In his tight jeans, his bulge was like a neon-sign of his desire.

"You know I don't like this decision," he spoke tersely.

"I'll make it up to you later. I promise," she whispered in his ear suggestively.

"I'm taking you up on that."

They walked hand-in-hand towards the Frost Bank building. Harmony could still feel the effects of the E-2K on her system. She was deliriously happy, basking in the rays of Tristan's affection. When they reached the revolving doors, he brought her back to his arms, planting an urgent and deeply passionate kiss on her lips, making her breathless and heady.

"See you tonight?"

She nodded happily, blowing him an air kiss before turning toward the turnstiles. As she stepped through it, she stopped in her tracks, facing Eduardo Torres head on. His amber eyes had darkened into a furious burnt orange at the sight of her. Without a word, he whirled away, leaving her open-mouthed in shock.

Chapter Fifteen

Tristan watched Harmony disappear into the cold, interior of the Frost Bank building. His eyes glinted with anger as he stared at Eduardo Torres. Every part of him had to reign in self-control, forcing himself to turn around and walk away. *What I really want to do is go in there and beat the living shit out of you.*

His anger was palpable, radiating around him like a force field, causing people on the sidewalk to give him space. He turned the corner quickly, only to find himself face to face with Nico Torres, the other brother and president of NET Media. Nico was walking back to the Frost Bank Building, accompanied by a few men dressed in black suits.

"Well, well," Nico drawled, sizing Tristan up and down. "Look what the cat dragged in."

Tristan drew himself in and blasted his shield up like a fortress. He was instantly glad they were outside in the public eye or else he would have gone straight for Nico's jugular and taken him down.

They were a formidable match. Both men were over six feet tall, muscular and well built. Where Tristan was golden and light colored in nature, Nico was the opposite with jet-black hair, olive toned skin, hazel eyes and classic Spanish features. He was handsome and magnetic, but Tristan saw none of that. He only saw his enemy.

"I would say it's nice to see you," Tristan responded coldly. "But we know it'd be an outright lie."

"What are you doing here?" Nico's cut-to-the chase approach was cold and demanding. He attempted to psychically peer into Tristan's field, finding it impossible to get through. A grimace ran quickly through his face. He hated being thwarted.

"That's none of your business."

"Visiting your little friend?"

Tristan glared at Nico. "Leave her alone."

"You're in no position to bargain with me," Nico snapped. "She is *my* employee, and I take care of what is *mine*. Or did you forget that?"

Tristan sneered. "Right! You take care of what's yours. Like you did with Serena? You sure have a messed up way of showing how much you care."

"Back off, Tristan," he responded icily. "You should have stayed out of my business then. Hopefully you've learned your lesson and stay out of our business now."

"You can't have her."

Contempt filled Nico's eyes as he spoke. "It's too late. We already own her. She just doesn't know it yet."

"The hell she doesn't."

"This little love affair that you *think* you have – enjoy it for now. By the time we're done with her, she's going to hate you."

"You really are a twisted fuck, you know that?" Tristan spat. "I should have killed you when I had the chance."

"Like you could," Nico taunted.

"Oh I could alright, and the pleasure would be *all* mine," Tristan responded hotly. "But if you touch one hair on Harmony's head, I will hunt you and your brother down. This time – there will be no one to stop me."

Nico scoffed, shaking his head with disdain as he began to walk away. He paused, turning his head to call out. "You and your ragamuffin bunch of energy workers are really pathetic. Go back to your fairy homes and leave us to run the world."

"Go to hell," Tristan replied and began to walk the opposite direction. He fumed with violent rage at the close contact with Nico. Never before had he felt such hatred towards another person. And to know that they had Harmony in their midst made him bridle with fury.

He pulled his cell phone out of his pocket and began dialing a number. Two rings later, he was connected.

"Emily," he spoke tensely. "We've got a problem."

Harmony felt like she had been with cold water as she headed towards the elevator. Eduardo's hardened look pierced her bubble of happiness. She saw something close off in his eyes as he turned away from her. *Why should I care?* After all, Tristan was the only man she had eyes for. *Right?* What did it matter that Eduardo saw that kiss? He was publicly claimed by Mariska, regardless of whether he believed it or not.

She arrived to the Wellness Department to find two well-dressed men, immaculately groomed in their late fifties waiting outside her room. Greeting them warmly, she flashed a charismatic smile. *These must be the financiers.* Her eyes narrowed as she studied them quickly. *I wonder what they're holding on to inside.*

She extended her hand and introduced herself to the first gentlemen, Peter Skarsgaard. Inviting him into the room, she assessed his demeanor. A brilliantly blue-eyed Swede, he radiated privacy and detachment. She felt a shiver run through her, recognizing him as the billionaire playboy who lived a lavishly public life. *Why is he here? He could be getting a private massage anywhere!*

Peter barely acknowledged her presence, turning his back to her as he began to change. She turned away to give him privacy, slipping out the door. She spotted Eduardo in Lydia's office. It was clear they were in the middle of a serious conversation. She felt her heart sink. *Are they talking about me? Great....I'm totally going to lose this job. Dammit!*

With a sigh, she turned the handle to the massage room and stepped in, finding Peter face down on the massage cradle. She quickly explained her procedure for massaging clients and received his consent for treatment. Placing her hands on his body, a tingling sensation crept up her arm as she made contact with his skin. With closed eyes, she holographically peered into Peter's body, noting the dark indigo blue column in the center of his spine.

She remembered what Eduardo had asked her earlier – to find the resistance in these men, remove it and transplant a different program instead. *How the hell do I do that?*

Her fingers firmly slid up and down his back, pressing with precise measured strokes that opened his muscles and kneaded out any tension and resistance. As she got to the area of his heart, her fingers began to shake. It felt like she was pushing against rubber, the edges defined and blunt. *What is that?* She demanded. *Show me!*

As if following her command, she visualized a large red sphere around his heart, covered in blue light and interwoven with green vines. Jealousy. Green splotches, colors and shapes usually represented that dark emotion. *What are you jealous of?*

She coaxed that area of his heart to open, unearthing an image that flashed in her mind, catching her by surprise. It was Eduardo, Mariska and Peter. Green sinuous lines covered Eduardo, leaving only Mariska's face and body unmarred and clean. She could see Peter embracing Mariska and kissing her passionately. Harmony got it. Peter Skarsgaard was jealous of Eduardo and was involved with Mariska.

How am I supposed to change this?

Taking a deep breath, she concentrated her focus as she conjured up an image in her mind of Peter and Eduardo coming to terms about his feelings for Mariska and amicably shaking hands, as if sealing a business deal. She directed that clear image straight into the red sphere inside of his heart area, replacing the previous image of separation and jealousy. Using her hands, she wove an intricate set of geometric symbols to seal the new program in place.

Initially, she felt Peter stiffen as she introduced the image into his subconscious and his mind. After ten minutes of him resisting, she finally felt him relax under the ministrations of her hands. His body loosened and opened as he integrated the new program into his being. When she felt his body finish, she began to close and complete their session. The timer dinged the end.

She moved away, allowing Peter time to collect himself. He sat up and regarded her with shrewd eyes.

"Eduardo was right about you." His voice was smooth and accented.

"How so, sir?"

"He said you were exceptionally talented – a real asset to our organization."

"I'm just a massage therapist, Mr. Skarsgaard."

"Clearly, Ms. Mendelson, you underestimate your talents. We would be more than delighted to help you develop your skills."

"I don't know what you're talking about."

"Really?" Peter's voice was amused, playing with her. "You mean you had nothing to do with implanting those thoughts in my mind?"

She felt her shield bow wildly around her. She closed her eyes, willing her armor to grow and strengthen. She could feel Peter trying to pierce into her. Her head pulsated with pressure. Clenching her hands, she increased her willpower – intending her shield to shine with golden force. She could feel his penetrating pressure beginning to ebb.

"Mr. Skarsgaard," she responded calmly. "I do body work. That's all I do."

She headed towards the door, turning back to face him momentarily. "I will let you get dressed, sir."

"Harmony," he interrupted her exit. "I would appreciate it if you could keep this conversation between us private. There are many wandering eyes and ears in this place."

"Of course."

She stepped out of the room, her breathing shallow. *That was a close call. Too close. These people are really insistent.*

The door opened and Peter stepped out gracefully. He gave her a secretive smile and shook her hand, squeezing it conspiratorially. Nodding curtly towards the other man waiting, he began to walk towards the elevator. Harmony watched his retreating back, wondering what his other motives were. Feeling the gaze of her next client, she turned towards the elderly gentleman and smiled.

"I will have this room ready in a few minutes, sir."

His gentle smile lit up his green eyes, making him seem younger. "Please, take your time. I can wait."

She turned back towards the room and began to prepare. She could feel the effects of the E-2K ebbing from her body. Her level of ecstatic joy was diminishing, leaving her slightly fatigued and nervous. *Is this what Clara and Tristan meant? I don't feel so high anymore.*

Opening the door, she welcomed her next client in. With graceful dignity, the older gentleman walked into her room. He turned to gaze at her, his green eyes flashing as he smiled.

"I've waited for quite some time to meet you, Harmony." He extended his hand to shake hers. Slipping her hand into his, she marveled at the warmth and firmness of his touch. His silver hair was cut short and framed his handsome face. He was debonair and charming. Butis voice sounded like something she had heard before but was unable to place it. *Where have I heard that voice before?*

"It's a pleasure to meet you, Mr..."

"Mendelson. Felix Mendelson."

She froze, her hand dropping from his grasp. *NO! It can't be!* Her mouth opened in shock.

"Mr. Mendelson," she nervously uttered his name. "I'm...glad to meet you."

Felix Mendelson sat down on the massage table and gestured for her to take a seat in front of him. He assessed her from head to foot, nodding in appreciation. "I didn't realize you would have grown into such a beautiful woman."

Her insides quaked, and her shield shook violently around her, ebbing and flowing with barely any control. She closed her eyes and willed herself to calm down.

All her life, she wanted nothing more than to meet her mother and father. And now...here he was in her massage room. She felt sick and nervous inside. *What kind of messed up game is this?*

"Harmony," Felix said gently. "Do you know who I am?"

She nodded, unable to meet his gaze. She could feel tears welling up in her closed eyes. Dashing her hand against her lids, she forced the waters back. "What are you doing here?" she whispered.

"I came to meet you."

She finally opened her eyes. "Why? After all these years?"

"I didn't know where to find you. Your mother left after she told me that she was pregnant with you. I was never given the invitation to be a part of your life."

Her green eyes met his. "Why now? Why here?"

He smiled. "Harmony, I came when Eduardo told me that you were hired at NET Media. I came as soon as I could."

She remained quiet, reeling at his admission.

"I wanted to see you – meet you," he continued. "I know it may not seem like much, but I'd like to be a part of your life. I'd like at least to get to know you. To know my daughter."

She stepped back. Taking in his sleek, confident presence, she narrowed her eyes. *Is this a trick?* "Mr. Mendelson, with all due respect, I don't know who you are. I grew up without a father or a mother. You have to understand if I'm a little suspicious."

"I do understand. That's why I'd like to open that door for a relationship to happen." He shifted to look deep into her eyes. Green on green. Lightning flashed in her eyes.

"Is that all you want?"

"No…there's more. I'd like to invite you to join The Corona."

Her world stopped spinning. Cold dread washed over her. *So that's it. They want me in. And they sent you to get me.* "I don't know anything about you or The Corona."

He smiled, making her shiver at the coldness that touched his eyes. "Well I'm here to rectify that."

"I don't know if I want to know you or The Corona, sir."

His smile slipped. "That's a terrible dilemma to be in - not knowing your opponent or your ally. I'd like to help you. We could be partners. After all, we know more about you than you realize."

Her body stiffened with open vulnerability. *What do you know about me?*

"We've been watching you for quite some time. Your involvement with Tristan Alexander puts you in a precarious and difficult situation. You're not a Lightworker or a member of the Tribe yet. What I'm offering you is something you haven't had before."

"What is that?"

"Family. I'm offering you an opportunity to be part of my family – your family. This is your bloodline, your lineage, your calling. That's why I'm here."

His voice was hypnotic and convincing. She couldn't shake that feeling though that she had heard it before. His eyes studied her face, sensing her conflict. She radiated a maroon red vibration of stubbornness and self-control.

"Your gifts and abilities can become more powerful if you have the proper training. I would see to your education myself. And...I would have my daughter at my side."

Tears sprung forth from her eyes, unable to hold back the pain any longer. She felt the overwhelming pressure overtake her. She felt fragile and tired.

"Mr. Mendelson," her voice was shaky. "I appreciate your offer. You don't know how much it means to me to see you, know you or even be around your presence. I've longed to meet you for so many years. But..."

"But what?"

"You're a stranger to me. You want me to join The Corona, but I don't know you. I don't even know if I can trust you. I've spent my whole life dealing with not having any family around. And then you show up out of the blue and expect me to follow you?"

Felix softened, watching her cry. "I understand your resistance. Your mother felt the same way when she initially met me. After all, we were on opposite sides. But we were drawn to each other – it was more than we could fight against."

"And yet you left her," Harmony accused him, sniffing back the tears that threatened to flood her body.

"I didn't want to leave her," Felix's voice was filled with anguish. "When she found out that she was pregnant, she struggled with staying or leaving. I pleaded with her to stay, but she was such a strong-headed woman. When she left, I suffered greatly. Even though I love her still, I cannot forgive her for taking you away."

"You're asking me to trust without knowing you."

"I am."

"I need time."

"Of course, I understand. I will be more than happy to give you that time."

"And space."

"I can do that, too."

"And privacy."

"I can't guarantee that," he responded stiffly.

"And somehow you want me to trust you?" her sarcastic response was cold and biting.

"Harmony, we have a vested interest in you. Your safety is our priority."

"Then you'll understand if my sanity is mine."

"What you're asking is something I'm not willing to do. The Tribe of Light has already sent their tracker to find you. Why do they want you?"

"I don't know."

"Don't know or won't tell me?"

She stood up and walked towards him.

"Mr. Mendelson, I've had a lot happen in a couple of weeks. I feel vulnerable and pulled in a lot of different directions. I can't give you the answer that you want right now."

Felix eyed her speculatively. "I'm not asking you to give me your answer right now, Harmony. All I want is for you to weigh your options." He stood up quickly and extended his hand towards her.

She hesitated before she slipped her hand into his. It felt comforting and secure. "Ok. I'll think about it."

He nodded, gazing at her with serious green eyes. "You don't know how long I've waited to look into your eyes. To see you after all these years of wondering. You remind me so much of your mother."

She stepped away, pulling her hand back. "I wouldn't know. I don't know my mother."

He began to walk towards the door, opening it as if to leave. He paused to look back at her. "I know that I'm a complete stranger to you. But if you give me the chance, I can be something more. A father. Even a mentor. The Corona could take care of you, and you'll never have to worry about anything ever again."

She nodded, their gaze boring deep into one another. "I'll let you know what I decide."

Nodding, he closed the door behind him, leaving her alone. This time, the tears flowed freely. She had finally met him. Her father. Her link to the past.

Hugging herself, she rocked back and forth as her cellular memory unleashed waves of abandonment and fear. *What is wrong with you? You should be happy! You finally got what you wanted! So why do I feel so awful?*

She wasn't sure who to trust anymore. Her hands were shaking as she pulled her cell phone out. There was only one person that she knew wholeheartedly that she could trust: *Emily Morgan.*

Emily answered her call on the first ring. "What's going on, Harmony?"

She took a deep breath, her voice shaking with tears as she responded. "Emily. I need to see you. I can't wait 'til Saturday. I feel like my world is going crazy."

"Of course, honey. Come tonight. I can sense what's happened to you. It's best if you come straight after work. Don't let Tristan or Eduardo know that you're coming. Amplify your shield and when you're on your way, take off the crystal pendant."

Harmony was stunned. "How did you know about the pendant?"

She could sense Emily smiling on the other side of the phone. "You should know by now, my dear, I have my ways."

"Ok. I'll be there at 6 pm."

"Yes. See you soon, dear." Emily's voice was warm and comforting. Harmony knew that she would be able to talk to her plainly and truthfully about what was going on.

Their conversation ended just as a knock on her door interrupted her. Eduardo entered the room, cutting her with his gaze. He closed the door behind him and sat down on the chair opposite her. They stared each other down. He eyed her red, puffy eyes and flushed skin. Looking around, he handed her a box of tissue. As she reached for it, their fingers touched.

Harmony could feel the electrical magnetism between them. Despite his attempt to remain aloof and detached, she could see the slow burn in his eyes as he drank her in. Her green eyes flashed with fury.

"You set me up."

"No. That wasn't a set up. Felix requested to see you."

"He wasn't on the schedule this morning. I would have recognized that name. Why did Lydia change it?"

"Because he asked, and as an executive board member, he has right of way. I'm sorry that it caught you off guard."

She stood up and turned away. "Are you, Eduardo? Are you really sorry that you keep flipping my world upside down?"

She could feel him moving towards her and she braced herself. The touch of his hands on her shoulder made her flinch as he turned her around. Tipping her face up, he forced her to meet his gaze.

"I'm not sorry at all for being attracted to you. Or wanting you. And I'm definitely not sorry that I hired you. You want to talk about flipping worlds upside down? You've definitely caused havoc in mine."

How dare you! I have done no such thing!

"Yes, Harmony," he answered, reading her thoughts. "You have." She glared at him, refusing to back down. "From the moment I saw you, I wanted you. You plague me with your beauty, your scent, your touch."

"A plague is not a compliment," she responded sourly.

"That's how I feel. I can't get you out of my mind. I find all kinds of excuses to be around you, to see you, to have contact. It's driving me crazy. And it's driving Mariska insane with jealousy. So much so that I asked her to stay away from NET Media."

"You did what?"

"Yesterday. I barred her from coming back to NET Media and inciting drama. Apparently, she doesn't listen and bombarded Lydia Carey today."

Harmony pulled away from him, his touch intoxicating her senses. Her shield bowed wildly once again. She closed her eyes and willed it to return to its center, but it continued to dip around her. When she opened them, she found Eduardo staring at her, his amber eyes glowing brightly.

"Your relationship with Mariska doesn't involve me. Please try to control her. She's a scary thing when she's pissed off."

"It's too late. Consider yourself involved." His hand reached out to touch her arm. Closing his eyes, Eduardo downloaded the information of her day. When he opened them, she could see that his amber eyes had turned dark orange.

"Just as I had suspected. I knew Peter Skarsgaard had his eye on Mariska. I just didn't realized how deeply he felt. Thank you for showing me that."

"I didn't really have a choice, did I? You just kind of took it from me."

"You always have a choice. Don't forget that. Why else do you keep putting your shield up around me?"

She was quiet. *Damnit! He knows about my shield.*

"You can't hide from me," his voice was seductive and sexy. "I know you."

"Does my privacy mean nothing to you people?" she asked scathingly. "You make this job impossibly difficult when you come here and raid my thoughts. And then you send my father in to meet me? Is this some kind of sick joke to you?"

He was silent. She pushed him away and began to gather her belongings.

"Harmony, none of this is a joke to me. You arriving at NET Media has caused a huge ripple in my life. There is something between us that I can't deny."

She ran her hands through her hair, closing her eyes in disbelief. *This man is impossible!*

"Don't turn away from me, Harmony," his voice was low. "I saw you this afternoon with Tristan Alexander. Is he your boyfriend?"

"That's none of your business."

"It is when you're working for my company. Are you a spy for The Tribe? Have you been planted here to find out information?"

She gazed at him defiantly. "I have never met The Tribe. And up until recently, my life was what you would call boring. Now, I have to juggle my feelings, watch my words and filter my mind. I'm beginning to wonder whether taking this job is worth it."

He leaned in closer, trapping her between himself and the wall. She could feel his masculine vibration emanating force and power. He pressed against her, causing her breath to catch in her chest. His hands gripped her arms.

"Let go of me."

"What are you afraid of?"

Her eyes flashed angrily as she stared into his. "You have to ask?" She felt his magnetic energy wrapping around her like a vortex. The alluring primal coat awakened a dark sense of desire deep within her. "I feel like some kind of game to you."

"Life *is* a game."

"Don't start being philosophical with me."

"What would you rather I do?" He leaned down and she could feel his warm breath caressing her face. Turning her head, she closed her eyes, willing her body to fight against him. Despite her willpower, a growing warmth in her belly ignited fire inside her.

"I'd rather you let me go. This is totally inappropriate."

"I'm finding it difficult to move away from you. Not when your body fits so well with mine. Tell me, Harmony. Why do you fight your attraction to me?"

That's it. I've had it with these ego-maniacs. She pushed against him, breaking their contact. "Just because I feel a physical response towards you, Eduardo, doesn't mean I have to act on it."

"Maybe not now, Harmony," he replied, easing up and letting her have some space. "But one day, you will be mine. And this," He picked up the crystal star tetrahedron pendant casually. "will not be enough to protect you."

She grabbed her purse and headed for the door. Before opening it, she turned towards him. "You assume a lot. Don't forget...I still have a choice." She walked out, fuming in anger, disgusted at her own weakness and lack of control.

Eduardo followed her out of the Wellness Department and inside the elevator. There was no one else.

"How can you deny this attraction?" he murmured. Placing a hand behind her back, she felt a jolt of white hot electricity run through her spine.

"I'm saying no because you're not good for me."

"You've never experienced a man like me."

She turned a cold look towards him. "And that's supposed to win me over?"

Smiling, he looked down at her. "I don't need to win you over. I just need you to see."

"See what?"

"See that we're made for each other."

"You've got to be kidding me. You really are delusional."

He laughed. "Perhaps. But at least I know what I want."

"You're mad."

He continued to smile. "Yes...I have been called that."

The elevator dinged indicating the ground level floor of the parking garage. The door opened and Harmony made a bee-line towards her car. She felt Eduardo following her to her Toyota Forerunner. She glared at him, feeling annoyed that he was still so close. As she neared her car, she heard a squeal of tires and turned her head.

A black Mercedes Benz was rounding the corner at breakneck speed, heading straight for them. Eduardo yelled her name and pushed them out of the way in time to barely miss being hit by the speeding car. They fell over the hood of a nearby white Toyota Camry, scrambling quickly as the car headed towards them. The Mercedes skidded and bumped violently against the white Toyota before the driver hit the brakes and accelerated away, leaving them both shaken and breathing heavily.

Harmony lifted her head from her crouched position, shaking in fear and surprise. Eduardo was still holding her close as he watched the black Mercedes speeding away.

"Are you ok? Are you hurt?" His mouth was so very close to her lips, fanning her with his breath.

"No." Her body felt cold with shock. It was a contrast to the intense heat that he radiated as he laid over her. His sinewy muscles pressed against her sensitive flesh. Her breathing grew erratic as he bent closer.

"You're sure?" He searched her face worriedly.

Unable to answer, she simply stared at him. Time froze in place as he bent down, his lips lightly brushing hers, sending tingling sensations down her spine. The touch of his mouth was soft and gentle, pressing lightly against her lip. Surprise mixed with confusion as she felt his tongue trace her lips tenderly. Heat blossomed in her core, lighting her body with radiant energy and fire.

An uncontrollable urge to taste him overwhelmed her as her mouth opened a fraction more, allowing him to boldly press closer, invading her mouth and caressing her tongue with his. As she softened, his kiss turned more insistent and demanding, drawing from her a response that she could not fight back.

He evoked a strong carnal desire from her, a savage lust from deep inside, as she felt him claim her mouth with passionate ferocity. A tornado of emotions ran wildly through her body, causing her to break away and gasp for air. He bent down, resting his forehead against hers.

"God, woman!" he whispered harshly. "The way you make me feel…"

Oh no. I can't do this! She pushed against him frantically, causing him to lift up off her. "Stop…I can't do this."

She eased herself to a sitting position, running her hands through her hair in an attempt to settle the wildness that coursed through her. She couldn't meet his eyes. Her breathing was still heavy and erratic as she tried to still the havoc of sensations that swirled madly inside. Having Eduardo touch her so intimately was too much stimulation and sensory overload for her.

"Why did you do that?" She asked shakily.

"Because I wanted to. I've wanted to the moment I saw you."

"Eduardo, I can't do this. I'm not available. Neither are you. I'm not crossing any lines. Understand?"

He nodded, his eyes dark with desire. "It seems to me those lines just got blurred."

She shook her head in frustration. He continued to watch her, taking in her breathless, weakened presence.

"That was a mistake. I don't know what came over me."

Eduardo slipped off the car and came to stand close to her, lifting her face so that they were eye to eye. "There is no mistake, Harmony, only experiences."

She felt his touch sear her skin, causing her to jerk her head away, not wanting to get lost in his amber eyes. "I have to go."

Eduardo sighed, stepping away from her. "You sure you're ok?"

Harmony nodded, refusing to look him in the eyes. Shifting the topic to ease the tension, she gestured towards the direction the Mercedes Benz had gone.

"What the hell was that? That car was totally out of line. It could have nearly killed us."

His eyes narrowed at her words. "Harmony, I'd take more precautions if I were you. It's a good idea to watch your back."

"What do you mean?"

"Your father is a Corona member, your boy toy is a Tribe of Light Tracker, and you work for me. You're right in the middle of a hairy situation."

"My boy toy?" she asked incredulously.

"You heard me," he reached out, whirling her around to face him. "So what is he? Is he more than that or are you teasing us both?"

"You're mad!" she shook her head in disbelief. "And like I said - it's none of your business."

She quickly stepped out of his grasp and began walking to her car. She could feel his gaze penetrating her back. As she opened her door, she turned to face him.

"For what it's worth...thank you. For saving me."

He smiled, his amber eyes glowing. "The pleasures all mine. And thank you for kissing me back."

She shook her head in frustration and disappeared in her car. As she placed her key in the ignition, she heard her phone ringing. Looking at the caller, she saw that it was Tristan. She placed her phone on silent.

Hearing Emily's words, she quickly took the crystal pendant off and placed it on her rearview mirror. With another glance at Eduardo, she began to pull away, heading out of the parking garage into the bright sunshine.

She turned the corner and headed towards the freeway. Her phone continued to ring and she ignored it. How could she talk to him after she had just kissed Eduardo? Confusion and guilt filled her. She only had one place to get to: Emily Morgan.

Chapter Sixteen

It took less than thirty minutes for Harmony to pull into Emily's long-winding driveway. She arrived at Emily's house in West Austin to find her rocking calmly on a porch swing. The sight of her guardian immediately eased her worried and stressed mind.

"You've been busy," Emily's directness poked right through Harmony's shield. She relaxed. She knew she wouldn't have to protect herself from Emily.

"Yes, more than I'd like to be," she responded glumly, sitting next to Emily on the swing. They swung in silence for a moment, gazing at the fading sunset in the distance.

She turned to look at her guardian, amazed at her ageless beauty. Even though Emily was in her seventies, her smooth, unwrinkled face was calm and masked her emotions. Emily had been her guardian since she was twelve years old, taking her away from her self-absorbed and controlling grandmother. She was grateful to have left the woman who had raised her since birth. Her grandmother clearly despised her, feeling imposed by her daughter's reckless behavior. She was only too glad to pass her on to Emily.

Once a leader for the Tribe of Light and Head of the Air Traders, Emily carried great wisdom and the regal bearing of a matriarch. She had never told Harmony the real reason why she had left the Tribe or had severed contact with them. Harmony had her suspicions but never found the opportune time to ask.

"I see the dilemma you're in. Tristan and Eduardo." Emily chuckled.

"I don't think it's funny," Harmony fumed. "These men are putting a lot of pressure on me right now. And it seems like my world is colliding with theirs."

She went on to explain to Emily about her afternoon with Tristan, Eduardo and Felix Mendelson. Emily's face remained impassive and clear, but her grey eyes flashed with worry.

"I see." Emily finally spoke after hearing her lengthy story. "The question you have to ask yourself is which one would be the best person for you. Who has the best agenda? That answer does not have to come right now. There are many things that will be revealed to you very soon."

"What do you mean?"

"The appearance of Felix Mendelson and other Corona elite is disturbing. Even more, the arrival of the Tribe of Light leaders is more perplexing. Tribal leaders don't leave Quattro Terra. This convergence has something to do with the E-2K. What was your experience with it?"

Harmony tuned in to her body. Gone was the elated feeling of joy that ran through her after the E-2K. What was left was a feeling of fatigue, memory loss, and discomfort. She shared her experience with Emily, explaining the before and after effects.

"It's just as I suspected."

"What do you mean?"

"Forty years ago, the Tribe began conducting research on changing brain chemistry and patterns of emotions based on reactions to specific experiences. We were working with Lightworkers who had been under the control of The Corona."

"What happened?"

"We used our prototype to rearrange the patterns that The Corona had implanted into these people. It was beginning to shift their consciousness, and we had an explosive growth in awakening. Maybe it got to our heads – our success – and we became sloppy in how we protected our information."

"Sloppy? How so?"

Emily's looked out at the distance. "Instead of holding the research findings in a centralized data bank, we embedded the information – the program – in some Lightworker's cellular memory. That is where we made our mistake."

"Oh?"

"There were three Lightworkers who held the data bank of information: myself, Serena Morgan, and your mother. Your mother fell in love with Felix Mendelson. They were young and idealistic. When she discovered that she was pregnant, she and

Felix decided to encode you with their genetic library, in hopes that would bring peace to both sides."

Harmony was stunned at the news. *Genetic library? What does that even mean?*

Emily continued. "The Corona had a different idea, however. Their primary initiative was to extract information from your mother. Felix was simply bait. He had brought her to The Corona in hopes that they would release him. They didn't, and she became their prisoner. She felt like he betrayed her, and it broke her heart."

Emily gazed at the darkening sky, speaking softly. "The Tribe of Light sent a team to find her, and she was able to escape, severing her ties to Felix and The Corona. She felt that he was only using her to get the research information, and she could not double cross The Tribe like that."

"But I don't understand why she had to leave me, too."

Emily turned to look at her, taking in her large green eyes, wide with confusion and sadness. She reached a comforting arm around to bring her closer. "Your mother had a plan. She transferred her cellular memory bank of The Tribe, The Corona and the research project into your DNA, your blueprint. Together we then created a complex matrix of codes and symbols to close and seal the portals, blocking The Corona from accessing it and finding you."

Tears coursed down Harmony's face. *Doesn't my life, my mind, or my body belong to me?*

"Your mother made the hardest decision of her life by leaving you Harmony. She knew that if she stayed, they would find you and take you away from her. That's why I was entrusted to be your guardian. I've shielded you from The Corona all these years. The only time I failed was when you were a teenager and they kidnapped you. Thank God we found you in time before they could do any damage."

"How do you know?"

"I scanned and thoroughly checked you myself. The seals were still intact. However, you were not in the frame of mind to learn about this kind of information."

Harmony laughed bitterly. "And to think I told Eduardo my life was boring."

Emily smiled. "Far from it, my dear. Your life has been far from ordinary."

"Are the seals still closed?"

"Yes, they are. But the choices you've made are placing them in precarious danger."

"My choices? What do you mean? What have I done?"

Emily appraised her. "I don't think you realize the impact of your decision to work at NET Media. You put yourself right in the heart of The Corona Empire. All the research and creation of the E-2K has been done through NET Media. And when you use the E-2K, it weakens the force field around the seals."

Harmony placed her head in her hands. *Oh my God! What have I done? I have made a mess of things!*

"The Tribe has been feeling the pressure of your presence for many years. They felt like you were too much of a liability, holding the holographic library of The Tribe in your genetics. That is why they sent Tristan to retrieve you. They wanted to intercede before you got too heavily involved with NET Media or The Corona. I can see now it's too late. You've developed feelings for Eduardo, too."

"That's not true," Harmony denied hotly. "It's just a physical reaction. My allegiance is with The Tribe. It's with Tristan."

Emily's eyes narrowed as she filtered through Harmony's words. "Don't be too hard on yourself for having feelings for Eduardo. He's an attractive, charismatic and highly energetic man. His feelings for you have been hardly contained."

Harmony said nothing, knowing Emily was right. Her feelings for Eduardo were there inside of her, and she couldn't ignore its existence.

"I'm sure Tristan is having a difficult time with all of this. I see what he feels for you. He's never exhibited that with anyone – not even Serena."

Harmony remembered what Emily had said earlier about Serena. "Emily, you said that Serena was one of the three people who had the E-2K plans implanted in her DNA. Is that what caused her death?"

Emily was silent, pained by the memory and loss of her only child. "There were many factors that contributed to Serena's death. Nico's jealousy. My overprotectiveness. Tristan's involvement. At the heart of it, though, The Corona wanted that information and they sent Nico to get it. No matter what the cost." Her voice was filled with regret.

She turned and gazed deeply in Harmony's eyes. "Remember something very important Harmony. Your affiliation to The Tribe or The Corona will supersede even your blood ties. Once you join either one, they own you. That is why you must choose wisely. The Dark or The Light."

Harmony thought about Felix Mendelson and his offer. "Felix said that he wanted to be my father. He wanted me to join The Corona and train me himself. Is that just a lie? Is he just following The Corona's orders or does he really care about me?"

Emily looked away, squeezing Harmony's hand. "I can't answer that, dear. You will have to figure that out on your own."

"I'm so torn. I'm not sure what's happening anymore. I just want to belong - to feel safe. I'm so tired of trying to fit in and always being the outsider."

"I know this is hard for you. Don't be too hasty in making your decision. Your mother sacrificed a lot to protect you. One day you will understand."

"But where is she? Why hasn't she tried to contact me?"

"Harmony, everything gets revealed in due time. You have to be patient."

"Emily, what is so damn important about the E-2K that these two organizations want it so bad? Why would you have to protect and hide me?"

"The E-2K's original intention was to help recalibrate the brain and open it up to its full psychic potential. When The Corona discovered our research and got hold of part of the program, they manipulated the coding sequences so that it could be used as a form of subliminal mind control. They want to control the masses, and have been slowly creating the technology to make that happen. The E-2K is the first in line of that series."

"It's very alluring to use the E-2K. Clara was right when she called it a legal drug."

"That makes sense." Emily's voice was solemn. "When you use the E-2K, it depletes the Dopamine and DMT centers of your brain. These two neurotransmitters are responsible for making you feel happy and connected to Source. The lower the levels of these two substances in your brain chemistry, the worse you feel. That ensures that they control you. You will want to go back to the E-2K to feel better."

"I know. I felt it. I had never been so happy before in my life. Everything felt so right."

"It's an illusion."

"That's what Tristan said, too."

"The Corona's plan is really brilliant, if not disturbing and morbid. They control the pharmaceutical industry, and they created an antidote for people who suffer the effects of the E-2K."

"What antidote?"

"They created a synthetic substance that mimics an anti-depressant and is a mood stabilizer. It makes you feel happy and elated when you realize the effects of the E-2K have worn off. The nanotechnology inside the antidote allows The Corona to go into your brain and begin creating its own micro-circuitry. They start reprogramming your polypeptide chains. Essentially, you become enslaved to them."

"Holy hell...that's pure evil!" Harmony gasped in horror.

"That's why we're trying to stop them. This isn't just about you anymore, Harmony. The fight is so much bigger. This is a spiritual revolution that The Tribe is fighting. We are fighting to save the conscious and free spirit of mankind."

Harmony shook her head wildly, fear running rampant through her body. "I've gotta get out of there. Now! I can't do it anymore Emily. It's too much. I feel like I'm losing my mind."

"Stop!" Emily commanded. "Get a grip on yourself! You started this! Now finish it!"

"But how?" she protested weakly. "I'm just one person, and I don't know what I'm doing!"

"Stop belittling yourself," Emily scolded. "Have you not paid attention? Tristan has been training you, teaching you to shield yourself and creating complex energetic grids to protect you. And have you not been using your force field?"

"Yes, but all these Corona men and women keep trying to break it down."

"And what about compartmentalizing your thoughts so that only Eduardo could see what you wanted him to see. Give yourself credit for that. That's very high level work."

"But Emily," Harmony's voice dropped to a whisper. "I'm afraid. What if The Corona gets hold of me and forces me to unlock the programs?"

"Well, dear, that's why you're here, isn't it? You want to know what's happening and how to protect yourself even further."

"I suppose so." Harmony mulled over Emily's words. "What else can I do?"

"The first thing I want you to realize is that you're an electrical being and that your psychic powers are under your control. Understand?"

"Yes. I do."

"The second thing I want to impart is how to affect the electrical systems of others – humans and the material plane."

Harmony's eyes widened. "I can do that?"

"Absolutely. You've got to control your thoughts and emotions for that. Focus on the electrical program you want to affect and send a pulsation of thought and energy to change that."

"You make it sound so simple."

"It doesn't have to be difficult, Harmony. Just effective. Now listen…when the time comes to either shield yourself or send an attacking electrical energy, you must apply the Law of Three."

"Law of Three?"

"First, you must activate your force field – your merkaba, your Light body – to match the energy of what you want to affect. You do this by command and intent. Don't question yourself because doubt will lead to weakness and insecurity. You don't have time to second-guess your actions. That could be your life hanging in a balance."

"Ok," Harmony responded nervously.

"The second law involves another level of sacred geometry. You must ask for the symbol of what you're trying to affect appear to you. This will show up physically, psychically, mentally or emotionally. When that sign appears, you must take a programming crystal – either the crystal that Tristan gave you or another power tool of your own – and let it be the bridge that carries your intention."

Harmony nodded, affirming her understanding.

"Third, you must direct that electrical pulsation of thought energy and direct it to the coding sequence you want to change."

"How will I know that?"

"You have the coding sequences imbedded in your DNA."

Harmony nodded. "Alright, but how am I supposed to access it?"

"You do it with your intention. Wait to receive the coding sequence and then initiate the third law, which involves you putting the electrical pulsation in place. Seal it with the sacred geometrical symbols of a star tetrahedron spinning in a clockwise and counterclockwise direction. You know this. You've already done it."

Harmony thought about Peter Skarsgaard and how she manipulated his energetic field. Emily was right. She did know what to do. "I get it now. Perhaps that's why I'm at NET Media. Perhaps the time is now to end this tribal war for the E-2K."

Emily nodded, smiling at Harmony. "You're wise beyond your years, my dear. And your abilities are stronger than you realize. There's just one more thing you need to do."

"What's that?"

"You need Tristan to help you strengthen and fortify your root chakra."

A furious blush covered Harmony's face. "How?"

"In order to be in the seat of your power, you must have a strong sense of yourself, your center and your ability. You're safe and in control. If you go to The Corona weakened and afraid, they will be able to take over much easier. If they do, I cannot guarantee that I or The Tribe will be able to help you."

Harmony nodded. She knew she was treading dangerous waters. *Maybe I'm just wired for crazy!*

"You must go to The Chrysalis and activate the Ring of Light again. This time, open to the coding sequences of both The Tribe and The Corona within you. It's important to elevate the magnetite levels in your brain."

"Magnetite?" Harmony was confused. She had never heard of this substance.

"Magnetite is a crystalline substance that is iron based and located in the pyramidal cells of your brain. It helps you reach a transcendental meditation state – a higher vibration of being. Create a compartment for the magnetite in a part of your brain for safe keeping, and when you need it – access that level of consciousness and use the magnetite to help increase the power of your electrical pulsations. This will allow you to charge people and objects with energy. This is vitally important."

"How so?"

"Give me your hand." Emily placed her hand an inch away from Harmony's. She watched in fascination as a golden wave of energy began to grow around Emily's hand. The golden wave undulated in a synchronous pattern and touched Harmony's hand. She immediately felt a warmth spread through her as thoughts of a bright sunny day appeared in her mind. Her body relaxed and she felt ease wash through her.

"If you want to affect the vibration or emotions of someone, you apply this electrical pulse with that command. You control what you want that person to see and how they feel. It's temporary, but it could buy you the time you need."

Harmony mulled over Emily's cryptic words. "Need for what? What do you see, Emily?"

"Harmony, be careful. Don't give in when the pressure feels overwhelming. Have faith that Spirit will pull you through any difficult situations."

Harmony nodded, feeling uneasy. She took a deep grounding breath, gathering her thoughts and Emily's instructions. Her body felt weary and tired, her mind full, and her emotions raw. Images of Tristan and Eduardo's faces floated intermittently in her mind.

"What are you thinking about, dear?" Emily asked her gently.

"I guess I'm a little scared. I don't want to hurt Tristan or Eduardo."

"It's understandable. Opening your heart, your sacred space, to another takes great courage."

"I've never felt this way before. And to feel so much attraction to both men is overwhelming. It's triggering some strong reactions inside."

"Such as?"

"Fear. Fear of abandonment. Fear of not being loved. Fear that I'm not good enough. I don't know. I wonder if Tristan will leave once I decide to join The Tribe or if he'll be forever gone if I join The Corona. The same goes with Eduardo."

"Your fear is understandable, but you have to let go of playing the victim role. You're a strong, confident and intelligent woman who is in control of her mind, her life and her emotions. I didn't raise you to be a weakling."

Harmony smiled. "No, you most certainly didn't."

"What else is bothering you?" Emily prodded.

"All this stuff sounds so complicated. I just don't want to mess up."

"You won't. You're wired for this kind of work. It's who you are."

Harmony nodded solemnly. That would have to do. There was no sense in beating herself up further. Emily apparently had more faith in her than she did. She would have to trust her guardian implicitly.

She looked at her watch and realized the lateness of the evening.

"Wow...I should go." She began to gather her purse and belongings. "There's a NET Media party tomorrow to unveil the E-2K."

"And you're going?"

"I don't see how I can escape it. Eduardo personally invited me to come. My father will be there, too."

"Then you must take Tristan. He will help reinforce your shield."

"I don't know that he'll come, with so much of The Corona there."

"You don't know Tristan."

She smiled ruefully and blushed. A buzzing vibration brought her attention to her purse. When she reached for her phone, she saw it was him calling.

"Time to go." Emily smiled. She enveloped Harmony in a warm and loving hug. "I'm always here for you, dear. Don't forget that. No matter what side you choose, I will always be with you."

Harmony closed her eyes and hugged Emily fiercely. "I'll call you soon," she whispered in Emily's ear. She grabbed her belongings and headed towards her car.

Getting in, her eyes were drawn to the crystal pendant hanging on her mirror. Without any hesitation, she put it on, feeling the sensation of serenity and focus in her energy field. She turned the key, and the car started to life. It was already midnight, but she dialed Tristan's number anyway.

"Harmony," His voice was tinged with concern. "I'm glad you called. Are you ok?"

"Yes." Anticipation coursed through her. She wanted to see him. Be near him. Taste and touch him. "I've been with Emily Morgan this evening. I'm just leaving her house, and I'd like to see you."

"Ok, I'm here. Where are you?"

"I'm not far. I'm in West Austin, maybe ten minutes from Sacre Tellus. Is it too late?"

"It's never too late for you."

She smiled at his response. "I'll be there soon."

She began to drive away, a feeling of renewal washing away her fatigue. Somehow, receiving the encouragement from Emily to have Tristan help her fortify her root chakra gave her the desire and courage to go to him now. She felt another buzz coming from her cell phone. It was a text message from Eduardo: **Thinking of you**

Her eyes involuntarily looked up at her rearview mirror to find a car following her closely. She froze. It was a black Mercedes Benz.

Chapter Seventeen

The eight miles it took to get to Sacre Tellus from Emily's house seemed to take forever. Harmony nervously glanced at her rearview mirror, watching the Mercedes. She was unable to see through the darkly tinted windows and cold dread filled her inside. *Who is that? Is it Eduardo?*

She continued to drive towards Sacre Tellus. She had a feeling that whoever it was wasn't worth meeting at midnight. Breathing a sigh of relief, she saw the winding entrance towards Sacre Telllus. She felt the energetic force field bow in to let her pass. The Mercedes stopped at the entrance as if bumping against a wall. It disappeared from her view as the gates opened and welcomed her in.

She saw Tristan standing by the fountain, waiting for her. The moment she turned her car off, he was at her door. She opened it and launched herself into his arms. He bent down to nuzzle her temple, soothing her frazzled nerves.

"I'm glad you're here." He spoke softly.

"I am, too. Someone followed me here."

"I know. I saw the car on the security camera and ran the plates."

A cold shiver ran down her spine. "Who was it?"

"Mariska Hebrenovitch."

An icy gust of wind whipped her face. *Holy shit!* "That woman is insane."

"I'd say. She has some balls to follow you all the way to Sacre Tellus."

She heard the change in Tristan's tone. "Why do you say it like that?"

She felt him stiffen in her arms, causing her to pull away and stare at his impassive face.

"Mariska is no stranger to Sacre Tellus. I found her five years ago and began to train her in the ways of The Tribe. The Corona found her shortly after and convinced her to join their side. There was no dissuading her."

Harmony thought of The Chrysalis and all the tools that Tristan had shown her. A wave of jealousy washed over her. *OMG! Were they lovers?*

"No, Harmony," Tristan answered her unspoken thoughts. "I never found Mariska attractive. She was too greedy and egocentric for my taste. And...she's not you."

She relaxed in his arms, knowing he was speaking the truth. She forced all thoughts of Mariska out of her mind. At least for the time being. She was safe here in Sacre Tellus.

"I want to know how your day has been." She nodded, opening her field to him. He downloaded the information, gasping in anger as the images of Felix Mendelson and Eduardo filled in the gaps of her time away. She hid nothing, even the parking garage and the kiss. She relayed the information Emily had shared.

"I see." His words were clipped. "We've got some work to do before you attend this party tomorrow night. I suggest we go to The Chrysalis tonight and stay there tomorrow. After your day today, I think you'll be safer here. Glenda will see to your needs for the party tomorrow."

"You're not angry?" she gazed into his eyes.

"About what?"

"Eduardo. The kiss. Everything."

Tristan sighed heavily. "I know what I'm up against. I also know what I feel for you. You're asking if the kiss bothered me?"

She nodded uncertainly.

"Yes, it did. But what can I do about it now? I see your conflict. I feel the attraction between you two. Can I force my will and make you choose?"

"I don't know. Can you?" she asked him softly.

"I can, but I won't. I would rather you came to me of your own free will and volition."

She wrapped her arms around his waist. "I'm here now, Tristan. Does that answer your question?"

He cupped her face in his large hands and brought his lips down to taste hers. She sighed, feeling a lift in her spirits.

"I'm glad you came. I wanted to see you."

She nodded in agreement, feeling her body sag with relief. Her confession about the kiss felt like a huge weight off her shoulders. Yet she could see how her words affected Tristan.

"Hey," she softly whispered, reaching out for his hand. "Are we ok?"

Tristan gazed into her eyes, not saying anything for a while. "We will be. This is all too new right now. I'm not prepared to handle these feelings of possessiveness and jealousy. It's mine – I understand that. Still…I don't want to share you."

"You don't have to, Tristan. I choose you."

His eyes closed and she could feel his pain underneath. Guilt washed over her as she realized that she was partly to blame for that. *Dammit! Why did I have to kiss Eduardo back?*

"Come." He stated simply, taking her hand and leading her down to the crystalline laden man-made pond. The almost full moon was bright, lighting their path and making it easy for them to see. The Chrysalis was lit with candles and glowed invitingly.

She turned to gaze at Tristan, feeling his gaze on her. For the first time that evening, he smiled, making her catch her breath at his handsomeness. He drew his hand to caress her cheek, inviting her to lean into his touch.

"We're going to be alright," he whispered, drawing her close. "We've just got to get through these rough spots first."

She sighed. He understood and was willing to give her another chance.

"Let's go." He began to undress, throwing his clothes in a pile on top of a nearby lawn chair. Without waiting for her, he dove into the orgonite rich waters.

She quickly removed her clothes and dove in, following him. Feeling her body lighten up, she allowed the orgonite laden water molecules to pull out the angst of her day. Images of her father, Eduardo and Mariska began to run through her mind quickly, left behind with each passing stroke. She could feel Tristan swimming beside her and she flashed a smile of pleasure as they swam in silence. She flipped over onto her back, allowing the water to buoy her as the radiant light of the moon bathed her naked body.

When they arrived at The Chrysalis, she felt relaxed and calm.   Finding a large luxurious towel waiting for her, she wrapped herself and began to dry off. Tristan came behind her to wipe off the drops lingering on her shoulder. Tilting her head, she leaned back towards him. His lips trailed hot smoldering kisses down her neck, eliciting a trail of fire, awakening her.

"I've wanted to do that all day," he murmured against her skin. She could feel the surge of energy rising between them. She wanted nothing more than to feel his naked skin against hers. Dropping the towel, she moved in closer. Their lips met passionately as his hands ran up and down her side, squeezing her breasts with sure fingers. A sigh erupted from her as she licked and sucked his bottom lip.

He grasped her hand and brought it down to cup his firm erection. She began to move her fingers with deliberate intent, stroking him gently and with firm pressure. His hips swayed in synchronicity with her movements. His fingers trailed down to the center of her pleasure, finding her pussy wet with longing. He skillfully touched her clitoris, rubbing the tender nub back and forth. His touches and kisses were inviting, urging her to dive into the growing vortex of sensations. She leaned back and gazed deeply into his eyes.

"I want you," she whispered seductively.

"Show me," he commanded, releasing her from his arms.

Bending gracefully, she grasped his hard erection in her hands and placed a kiss at the tip of his crown. Opening her mouth, she began to suck and pull him in, licking his firmness and applying pressure with her tongue and fingers. Tristan groaned, holding her head and thrusting deep into her inviting mouth. She grasped his buttocks to bring him in closer.

She could see a bolt of electrical fire coursing up his spine. It moved from his base all the way to the top of his head, igniting his crown chakra. She wanted him - wanted to taste him, wanted to feel his desire for her spill into her tongue. With renewed force, she increased her suction, feeling him touch the back of her throat. His movements became wilder as he ground himself into her waiting lips.

"Stop," he gasped, pulling out of her mouth quickly. "Not yet. Come here."

He grabbed her hand, pulling her up against his muscular body. Bending down, he savagely kissed her, drawing the fire bolt of desire up her spine to explode in her head. He could taste himself on her lips, further fanning the flames of lust. He grabbed her hair and pulled her back so she could see him.

"Inside. Now. I want you." His voice was rough and raspy.

She shivered with delight. Taking her hand, he led her inside The Chrysalis. Small tea light candles flickered around them, casting a sensual and soft light. The scent of rose and amber filled the room and the gentle breeze blew in through the open windows.

Without a word, he brought her to the edge of the bed, pulling her down so she could sit. He bent down in front of her and gazed deeply into her eyes.

"I want you so much, Harmony, it hurts."

Her eyes widened at the rawness of his admission. Parting her legs wide open, he bent lower to blow on her open lips. A sigh of pleasure escaped her. She was so wet, swollen with need for him.

A pulsation of red hot fire brewed in her loins. As his lips came into contact with her juicy center, her back arched to receive his tongue. He lapped up her womanly flavor, inhaling her musky feminine scent. She smelled like the Earth and tasted like the most decadent meal.

Lying back, she surrendered herself to his sensual attention. His fingers found their way into her opening, pushing deep into her corridor of pleasure. A ripple of fire ran through her.

He pulled away to look at her, wide open and wanton with hunger. "I want you to do something for me."

She pushed herself up on her elbows to look into his eyes. At this point, she would do anything for him. "Yes."

"I want you to see a vortex of light coming down through your body. See this light coming from The Creator above and wrapping all around you."

She nodded and closed her eyes, visualizing a column of white light energy coming from above her head and surrounding her body. She felt the light seeping into her spine, evoking a connection from Spirit and coming down to awaken her power centers. She felt grounded and connected.

As she watched the energy moving up and down her body, she felt his fingers rubbing her clitoris and entering into her sacred temple of sex. She undulated her hips. Electrical pulsations of desire ran through her in waves.

"Now, I want you to move that vortex of light from the Earth up your body. Connect to The Divine Mother and feel her activating your body's energy centers."

Harmony nodded as she continued to feel his fingers thrusting into her, driving her body higher into a state of ecstatic bliss. She focused her mind and intention on drawing the Earth's energy up through her. As she felt the dark maroon wave enter her body, she began to moan.

Her first power center exploded in a dark red blast of energy, moving the vortex in a clockwise direction. She groaned as it filled her body with a wave of pure pleasure. She saw the dark maroon wave move towards her second power center in her pelvis, eliciting a similar response, blasting that chakra open. Bright orange waves of intense ecstasy swept through her as she watched it spin in a clockwise direction.

"Do more. Bring it closer home," his voice coaxed her body to respond, licking her juicy opening.

She envisioned the maroon wave encircling around her third power center, filling her abdomen with golden yellow light as it spun in a clockwise pattern. Shifting her hips, she could feel him growing more insistent as he removed his fingers and inserted himself deep into her.

She gasped at how he filled her inside, touching the raw, sensitive nerves. Her body began to drive against his as the maroon wave washed into her fourth power center, expanding her chest with pink and red light. Her heart pounded furiously as Tristan thrust into her. The fourth power center burst into a clockwise spiral before the maroon energy moved up to her throat.

A moan escaped her lips as she saw her throat chakra catch on fire with blue light. Heated desire washed over her as the clockwise tornado of energy moved in synchronicity to their bodies. Tristan was moving faster and faster, and she seized his buttocks, drawing him closer.

She watched the maroon Earth energy rise up to her forehead, igniting a purple fire in her Third Eye. She could feel her pineal gland opening as the violet flame surrounded her mind. She could barely think, her body responding to his touch and his movement automatically.

"Hang on, baby," he groaned. "You're almost there. Keep going."

She watched the maroon wave reach the top of her head. It activated her portal of connection to Source, winding like a helix in a clockwise direction. She felt wide and open as pure energy washed through her body, shaking her to the core.

"Now call in the Goddess and ask her to join us. I'll call in the Creator." He gasped, his body a pounding machine of pleasure and power.

She opened her eyes, hooded in deep mystery to gaze at her lover. His body was covered in a fine sheen of sweat as he sank deeper into her. She sent an energetic call to The Goddess, asking her to join them in union.

Her body rose higher and higher to the sacred call. Her heart connected downward as his shot upward – creating a spiraling vibration of Divine Love.

Tristan continued to thrust into her, his breathing ragged as he pushed her into the abyss of pleasure. A pure white light descended into their bodies, activating them in love and unity. She moved her hips in response to his, lost in pure sensation. His hand reached between them to rub on her highly charged clitoris, pushing her to the edge.

She felt herself weaken and melt, until the explosive energy of their orgasm crested over her. Crying his name with abandon, she surrendered to the full force of radiant sexual release, allowing it to shake her to her core and unleash its potent power. Tristan met her orgasm with his own, stiffening as he jetted his seed into her sacred garden. He groaned and collapsed on top of her.

The only sound in The Chrysalis was their ragged breathing. Tristan gathered Harmony in his arms, feeling her body relax and return to its center. He kissed her hair, occasionally rubbing his hand on her back. She felt safe, loved and whole.

Time stood still. The room vibrated with highness and light.

"Wow! That was phenomenal!" her words were slurred. She felt drunk with the energy that moved through her.

"Yes," Tristan smiled. "It's always that way with you."

She raised her head to look into his eyes. "Tristan..."

"Yes?"

"Can you know in a short time that you love someone?"

"You can."

"Well, I think I love you."

He turned to look at her and smiled. "Is that the sex talking?"

She laughed lightly. "No, I mean it. I've never felt this way about anyone before."

His eyes crinkled with happiness. "Oh baby, I know what you mean. I love you too. More than you can imagine. I'm glad you finally remembered."

"Yeah...Why?"

"Because this time...we didn't have to wait so long to discover each other again."

He sent her an imprint.

An old couple sat on the porch swing, holding hands while looking at the sunset. He was a bald elderly farmer, whose rough and work-calloused hands, held the tender, wrinkled fingers of his high-school sweetheart. She had returned after fifty years of being gone. Their eyes were bright, happy and awash with love. It had been a long road to find their way back to each other. Who ever said it was too late to begin something new?

~~~~~~

Harmony awoke to the soft light of the early morning filtering through the curtains of The Chrysalis. She turned her head to find Tristan sleeping soundly next to her. His blond hair was strewn carelessly framing his face, making him look relaxed and unguarded. She relished seeing him in this state, knowing that the load he carried for The Tribe was heavy. She wondered how much his involvement with her had caused old wounds to open.

She thought unwillingly about Felix Mendelson and The Corona. Her heart felt a deep ache at the man who introduced himself as her father, a stranger. He offered her a future, a family, a home. She felt the bitter pain of realizing that it came with a price. There was so much pain in their shared history, and she felt utterly torn. She could not let herself be another victim to someone else's agenda. She had to be free.

That was it. Harmony bolted up. She didn't have to join either side. Emily Morgan had proven it to her. Even more…she contained the genetic library of both organizations. She could learn to fly under their radar. *Right?*

But what about Tristan? How could she be an independent party – a guerilla in the midst of power – and still have a lover who belonged to one side? *Could I really do this on my own? Would I ever be safe?*

She felt Tristan stirring beside her. Bringing her attention to the present, she looked down to find him studying her.

"You ok?" his voice was soft, his brilliant blue eyes probing.

"I am now." She leaned down to plant a soft kiss on his lips.

"I keep telling you that you don't have to do this. You can walk away from The Corona and come join us. We're your family, too."

She smiled. "Yes, I know. Call me crazy, but something in me feels like I have to do this."

"You're crazy then."

"Thanks...." Her words were sarcastic.

"You're also hard-headed."

"Great! Any other labels you want to place on me?"

"No." His teasing smile mollified her. "I'm simply helping you prepare for your day."

"This is great motivation."

"This morning is going to require some intense work."

"Well... if last night was any indication of that kind of work, sign me up."

He smiled at her suggestive comments. "Today, you must manage your energy field well."

"That's an understatement."

His head shook ruefully. "I feel like a real ass for sending you off to this party."

"You're not sending me off anywhere. I'm choosing to attend."

His eyes shot to her face. "See what I mean? Hard-headed."

She poked him playfully and stuck her tongue out.

"I'm coming with you," he spoke suddenly, causing her to stiffen.

"You're going to put yourself in the middle of The Corona? That doesn't feel safe."

"Neither is letting you go in there by yourself."

"Nothing will happen. It's a party. Downtown. With lots of people."

"You don't know these people, Harmony," his voice was rough. "They don't care about law and order. They manipulate the environment at their disposal. You cannot trust them."

"That's why you shouldn't come. It'll make me worried and nervous."

He laughed harshly. "I'm coming. No point arguing about it. Emily even saw it herself. So why are you fighting this alone?

You don't have to take on the whole organization by yourself. It's not wise."

She sighed. Arguing with him was not going to budge his stubbornness. "Ok. So then how do we prepare for tonight?"

"We have to do some tantric energy work to get our shields up tight. It's paramount that we hold on to this built up energy and not release it."

"How do we do that?"

"I'll explain in a little bit. First, we should eat. You'll need your strength today."

Tristan climbed out of bed and headed for a small eating area. He opened cabinets and doors and revealed a little refrigerator, stocked with snacks and ready to eat food. Harmony watched with amusement as he began brewing coffee. The aromatic smell of Ethiopian Yergecheff filled the air, waking her senses up.

She moved out of bed, letting the comforter slide off her nude body. She approached Tristan with catlike grace, pressing herself behind his naked body and wrapping her arms around him. He leaned his head back onto hers.

"I like watching you," she murmured, planting a soft kiss between his shoulder blades.

"Have a seat." He motioned towards the small white table. "I'll make you breakfast."

She smiled, walking towards the waiting chairs. She watched him move easily around the small kitchenette, completely unabashed about his nudity. The early morning light cast a golden glow on his tanned skin, shadowing the muscles on his back and stomach.

Harmony gratefully accepted the coffee. She sipped the concoction of coffee, milk and agave nectar. It was heavenly.

Tristan put a bagel piled with smoked salmon, capers, sliced tomatoes, and cream cheese on a plate in front of her. He sat down beside her and began to eat. Harmony ate quickly, delighted by the simplicity of their meal and the intimacy of their morning.

"This morning is important," he said between bites. "You've got to apply the Laws of Three and change matter."

She coughed suddenly. "That sounds like a tall order."

"You can do it. You've got to learn how to manipulate the electrical pulsations that you naturally emit from your body."

"How can I do that?"

"You've got to focus your thoughts with clear vision. Don't doubt what you're doing. You've got to open your channels and receive the instructions to do what you want to do."

"You make it sound easy."

"It doesn't have to be difficult. Let go of your limitations about your abilities. You're more powerful than you realize."

"You keep saying that, and I feel like just keeping my shield up is a lot of work."

"You've already proven that you can sequester your mind. Now you've got to create a vault of useable energy that you can direct."

"Ok," she leaned back to sip her coffee. Her bagel was gone and she felt stuffed. "At least that's a language I can understand. Have a place for everything. Check."

"And you also have to learn how to open the meridian channels in your hands so that your second chakra can be activated to travel energy through it."

Her eyebrow rose as she looked at him. "That sounds challenging."

"Stop," He gently admonished her. "You're a massage therapist. You already run energy through your hands. You've got to download the meridian channels today and access it at will."

"You mean I have this morning to learn about the meridian channels? Please tell me there's not going to be a quiz."

"No quiz," he replied teasingly. "But if you're really good, I may reward you later."

"Oh please, teacher?" she shot back.

"Enough. Let's get started." He grabbed her hand and led her to the bed. Pulling the covers back, he gently eased her down.

"Remember what I said - no release today. You've got to hold on this energy in and send it to your storage vault. Got it?"

She smiled, as if challenging his initiative. "No release. Got it."

Tristan sat in front of Harmony, their eyes locked firmly on one another. With a deep breath, Tristan closed his eyes and psychically linked into Harmony's genetic codes. He was surprised when he met resistance and found her internal programming safeguarded with a vault.

"Wow," he replied. "You must really contain some special programming."

"Why do you say that?"

"Your cellular DNA codes are locked up like a bank vault. That's a good thing." Harmony looked relieved.

"Let's get started," Tristan began. "In order to use the Law of Three that Emily taught you, you have to be able to amplify your force field and generate a key that will unlock your opponent's coding sequences. Without that key, your work will not hold up."

She nodded, thinking of Peter Skarsgaard. Eduardo had asked her to change his coding sequence and replace his programming with something more acceptable for The Corona and their needs with the E-2K. She wondered how effective her work really was.

"So how do I generate this magic key?"

"Well that's where it gets tricky. You'll have to access their Book of Life, their Akashic Records, to retrieve that key."

"How do I access their Akashic Records if they don't know what I'm doing?"

"I'm not sure how you'll open the Records if that person doesn't say yes. I guess, you'll have to access either their higher selves or the higher programming that's in charge."

"That sounds easier said than done."

"I know, but you have to be wily about retrieving that key. It could save your life in a moment of crisis. I hope you won't ever need to, but I still have to prepare you anyway."

She nodded. "And what do I do once I have the key?"

"You'll have to apply the Law of Three to get to the program's genetic matrix. Once you place the key into the coding sequence, you'll have to activate the DNA coding sequence ATG to change the program and make it stick. If you don't activate the ATG codon, then it won't happen. Once you do this, a series of geometrical symbols will come to you."

"Wait a minute," Harmony interrupted. "ATG sequence? This is getting complicated. I don't know anything about genetics!"

"Don't let that stop you. I'm telling you this so you can place this information in a vault in your mind. You will remember when you need to. I have faith in you."

"Ok, go on…"

"The ATG codon is a start/stop series of amino acids that signals a change in the DNA sequence. When you intentionally command it to activate, it responds to you. That is why you have to place that key before the ATG sequence. When you holographically see the DNA matrix, the ATG sequence will appear as a red dot. From there, you initiate your activation protocol."

"I don't know, Tristan," her voice was uncertain. "This sounds way above my head."

He stared into her eyes, his voice was firm and decisive. "You can't doubt yourself, Harmony. This all takes place in a matter of seconds. If you allow yourself to question what you're doing or get distracted, you may get hurt. You can't take that chance."

She remained quiet. *Activation sequences. DNA. What the hell am I doing? This is not me!*

"Don't! This is you. You've been preparing for this all this time. The Corona can't touch you. The E-2K can't touch you. Only you can prevent yourself from reaching your max capacity. And don't forget," he continued, "you can affect not only people with this activation, but also crystals, machines and programs. The possibilities are endless."

"Wait a minute, you said I could affect machines? Does that mean the E-2K?"

"Exactly. Don't limit yourself or your abilities." He smiled gently at her.

"Ok, I'll try it."

"Let's move on. It's time to re-initiate the Ring of Life. We've got to fortify your shield and make it more complex. Your time in the E-2K weakened it a bit, but we'll change the matrix so that you can vibrationally run higher than the E-2K's programming."

Tristan stood up and walked over to the control pad against the wall. He punched in a code and The Ring of Life glowed and whirred with activity. Harmony watched in fascination as The Ring spun in a clockwise direction.

Tristan returned to sit in front of Harmony, taking her hands in his. She watched his comfort and grace, taking in his masculinity and confidence. Tristan caught her gaze and smiled mischievously.

"If you keep looking at me like that and blushing, I'm not sure I can behave myself to train you properly." He had already glimpsed the string of naughty images that flashed quickly through her mind.

"Get it out of your system," he teased. "You'll need to free up your mind as much as possible."

"You don't know how hard it is to focus when you're sitting in front of me looking so damn hot and naked."

He smiled suggestively, leaning forward to place a chaste kiss on her lips. "Believe me, the effort on my part to remain in control, instead of jumping you, is supreme. But I have to do what is necessary to get you ready. Let's get this flow of energy ramped up." He squeezed her hands encouragingly. "Start with the cyclical breathing of five seconds in and five seconds out."

"Why does it have to be five and five?"

"That's the time it takes for your cerebrospinal fluid to move from the base of your spine to your brain and then back down again. We have to build your energy from this central command point."

Harmony visualized her breath moving like a beam of white light up her body as she inhaled, then cascading over her with her exhale. Focusing on the flow of her breath and energy field, she felt more grounded and centered.

"Now expand that light from your spine throughout your body. Feel that light energy waken and connect your organs, cells and tissues. Move this energy through your field, touching the physical, emotional, mental and spiritual layers of your body. Let go and feel it."

Harmony felt an expansive wave of energy wash through her. She gasped in surprise at how easy it felt. Peace and joy radiated through her as resistance faded.

"Great job," Tristan said. "Now move that light outward to the edge of your field. Feel it."

She focused her intent and thoughts to expand outwards, allowing the white light to move the different layers. She could feel pressure in her head. She glimpsed a series of geometrical shapes, mathematical formulas, and other patterns. Clarity descended on her.

With a deep breath, she pushed the white light energy further out, activating her spiritual layer. She could barely make the outlines and shapes of beings that surrounded this field. It existed approximately four to five feet outside of her physical body. *So that's how I connect to the Angels , Masters and Guides!*

Harmony could feel herself clearing and growing stronger. Coupled with the emanations from The Ring of Life, her cellular memory was opening and restructuring. A feeling of bliss and power vibrated through her as her golden shield became stronger.

Harmony was caught in an ecstatic trance, feeling the resonance of The Ring washing over her. She barely felt Tristan pull her close and insert himself gently into her sex. Her eyes flew wide open. She wasn't expecting this. She shifted her hips, allowing him greater access to her.

"Still. Be still," he gently admonished. "Remember, this is not for release. We need to amplify the energy between us. Now that your shield is activated and the coding sequences are coming down from The Ring, I need to help you increase your powerhouses. Focus on building your energy centers up with light."

Her green eyes met his brilliant blue orbs. She could sense the control that Tristan directed. They maintained contact as she felt a blue river of electrical current run from his manhood and deep into her sacred center, igniting her root chakra. The activated power center was surrounded by a halo of blue light. It ascended up to her second and third power centers, leaving them surrounded in a field of vibrant blue energy.

As the blue electrical current moved to her heart, Tristan placed his right hand on her chest, activating her fourth power center. Electrical pulsations emitted from his hand, coming into contact with her heart.

Harmony felt like she was being hit with a bolt of lightning. Her fourth chakra lit up with a halo of electricity. She watched the river of energy spark up to her throat charka, her fifth power center, setting it afire with a blazing light.

As the electrical energy moved higher, she saw Tristan place his left hand on her forehead, activating her sixth power center. A blue swirling band of light leaped out of his hand and entered into her mind. It unlocked her pineal gland and unraveled a string of numbers, letters and shapes. She gasped as the library of knowledge opened up and her Tree of Life was revealed.

A golden wave of understanding dawned on her. She didn't have to know what to do to enact her powers. She just had to surrender to the flow of energy, and her guides would direct her to the right course of action. She was simply the vehicle to transport the intent.

"Now you're getting it," Tristan said gently. The electrical flow of energy moved up to the top of her head, her crown chakra. She felt a flame of pure energy beaming out of her head, connecting her to The Ring of Life and the barrage of symbols.

The Ring of Life began to ease in its clockwise movement. As it came to a stop, it began to shift direction and moved in a counter-clockwise pattern. The Ring hung approximately a foot above their heads, and Harmony felt the column of energetic vibrations surrounding her. Tristan continued to hold her gaze, gently moving in and out of her so slowly that it was barely perceptible.

"Now take that energy that you've built up and place it in a compartment in your mind. If you need to access it, then unlock it with your command and retrieve it. You can intend what you want that energy to do. Thought follows intent. That's how responsive it is."

Harmony nodded, feeling dizzy. Her body felt alight with pleasure and elation. Tristan was still inside her, his hands still in contact with her heart and her head.

She mentally sequestered the large influx of energy into a container and placed it in a part of her brain, her frontal lobe. She generated a series of geometrical symbols and codes to seal and protect it. She willed a heavy lid to cover the container and closed that area of her brain. She felt confident that reservoir was there should she need it.

Tristan removed his hands from her forehead and chest. He gingerly eased out of her, still firmly erect, glistening with her juices. She winced as he pulled away, her body wanting to respond to his touch.

"Later," he smiled. "We'll finish this later. But first, you've got a party to attend."

She turned her head to look at the clock. It was nearly three o'clock and the party started at seven. It only seemed a matter of minutes had passed since they had started. Tristan pulled her up to a standing position. He bent his head to gently kiss her full, waiting lips. A bolt of fire ran through her body as she pushed herself against his firm, muscular frame. She could feel his erection against her thighs. She felt herself growing weak with desire.

"Hold on to that, love. You're going to need all that energy for later when you see The Corona."

"Don't remind me," she whispered. His words brought her back to reality.

"You've got to do your best to blend in."

"How do I blend in with The Corona when they already know what I am?"

"You'll have to try and fly under their radar. Unfortunately, I won't be able to do any such thing. I'll stick out like a light bulb in that party."

"Then don't come," she pleaded.

"Over my dead body. I am not going to let you go in there alone."

She sighed. He took her hand and led her out of The Chrysalis, towards the warm, inviting waters of the pond. They dove in, allowing the water to envelope them with a calming and restorative energy. They swam in silence. Harmony stole a glance at him. He was quiet and his eyes were pensive.

They arrived at the edge of the pond, stepping out to find dry towels waiting for them. *Holy hell, I hope nothing happens tonight. Please God, let it just be a company party. No drama. No bullshit. Just fun and drinks.*

Chapter Eighteen

Harmony gazed at herself in the mirror. She barely recognized the extravagantly dressed woman facing her. Glenda had gone all out. She was dressed in a black Versace gown, adorned with small quartz crystals that accentuated her plunging neckline. Her crystal pendant hung delicately between her breasts and contrasted with her tanned, golden skin.

Twirling around, she assessed her svelte figure. She hoped she wasn't too overdressed for the company party, but Clara and Eduardo had both told her it was a formal affair. Grabbing her clutch purse, she took one last look at herself before applying maroon lipstick to her full lips. She was finally ready.

She headed to the main room of the house, hearing voices. When she arrived, she found Tristan deep in conversation with three other men. Their hushed tones made her pause in mid-step, hesitant to interrupt their conversation. As if feeling her presence, Tristan turned around to face her. He looked dashing in a black tuxedo, with a maroon cummerbund.

Tristan walked up to her, placing a kiss on her cheek. "You look beautiful," he murmured, sending shivers of delight down her spine. "Come. There's some people I'd like you to meet."

Harmony turned to face the three gentlemen, who eyed her with curious interest. They were in their mid-forties and dressed casually. A man with dark curly hair reached out to introduce himself.

"I'm Karl Renquist, a personal friend of Tristan's. These are Brian Sonata and Michael Burks. We're just passing through town on business and thought we'd visit our old friend here." Karl patted Tristan on the back and smiled at him warmly. *Perhaps they're members of the Tribe, also.*

"You're right, Harmony," Tristan responded smoothly, reading her thoughts. "They're members of The Tribe of Light. They're travelling here with the Elders."

Harmony gazed at each of the men independently, assessing their faces while masking her thoughts. "Any particular reason why?"

Karl smiled, sensing her guardedness. "We're here to assist you and Tristan in whatever way we can. It's a great pleasure to meet you. We've heard a lot about you from the Tribal Elders. It's not every day that the Elders leave their homes. You must be a very special person to draw them out."

She blushed, feeling their eyes studying her. Her energy field felt pressed all around. She turned towards Tristan. "We should go. I feel like the hour is getting late."

Tristan nodded and bid his farewells to his friends, leading her away. As they passed through the long, dark hallway, Tristan abruptly stopped her and brought her close.

Tipping her head back, he bent down to capture her lips, fiercely kissing her with passion and urgency. As if on command, she melted into him. Encircling her arms around his neck, she drew him closer and deeper into her lush kiss. His hands held her hair in place as his tongue mercilessly plunged into her mouth. Her loins burned.

"Have I told you how you beautiful you look? This dress looks amazing on you." he growled softly in her ear, his finger tracing the plunging neckline of her gown. She gasped as his fingers lit a trail of heat on her bare skin.

"Let's make this party short," she pleaded.

Tristan smiled. "I'm ready to blaze whenever you say the word."

"Ok. You know…I have needs. Needs that I believe can only be taken care of by you."

"Only me," he firmly replied.

"Only you."

Tristan bent down and placed a chaste kiss on her waiting lips. He continued to lead her down the hall and out of the house, towards the courtyard where a red Jaguar convertible waited for them.

Harmony gasped. *Where is his Tacoma? Or my Forerunner?*

Tristan smiled mischievously. "Relax, baby. This is a loaner from The Tribe. It's used for special occasions."

"Like fast getaways?"

"Exactly," he smirked, opening the passenger door for her. She gracefully eased into the seat, smiling at him in anticipation and appreciation.

Tristan got into the driver's seat and started the car, which purred to life easily. He smoothly pulled out of the fountained courtyard and headed out past the wrought iron gated fence.

As they left Sacre Tellus, Harmony felt the stirrings of anxiety and unease growing in her stomach. She could feel a wall growing around Tristan, shielding him from her energetically. It further increased her nervousness.

Tristan turned to look at her, smiling and keeping his eyes focused on the road. "It'll be ok. We'll be in and out in no time."

"I hope so," she bit her lip, trying to allay her doubt.

Tristan drove quickly, entering the busy Friday afternoon rush hour traffic with ease. It was almost 7 o'clock, and the city was alive with nighttime activity. He drove down to the Convention Center, finding a parking space in the garage.

As he turned the car off, Harmony was seized by a ripple of panic. "Tristan, we don't have to do this. Let's go."

Tristan smiled at her unease. "Harmony, if I let you walk away from this, you won't know just how powerful you really are. Don't shy away from your destiny."

She shook her head, refusing to believe him. "How can you say that? You're the one telling me I can leave any time. Why is now different?"

He reached over and gently squeezed her hand. "You're not thinking of yourself. You're thinking about me and what could happen. But I'm telling you right now...don't worry. I'll be alright. Trust me."

Her green eyes looked deeply into his blue finding only support and love. She felt herself relax a bit. "Ok, I trust you. Let's get this over with."

He led her out of the garage and towards the entrance of the Convention Center. They entered the lavish ballroom, strewn with streamers, balloons and expensive floral arrangements. NET Media had spared no cost in entertaining their staff, board of directors and guests. Harmony felt tension radiating through her as she observed the elegantly dressed women and men. She was grateful for her black Versace gown, knowing that she fit right in.

"Harmony! You made it!"

She whirled around, instinctively knowing that voice and instantly relieved that Clara was there.

"You look fantastic!" Clara gushed, taking in Harmony's beautiful attire. She appreciatively eyed Tristan, who stood on guard next to her. He smiled warmly at her, extending his hand.

"Hi, I'm Tristan."

"Clara." Turning, she gave Harmony a big hug and whispered in her ear, "OMG! He's such a super babe! Lucky girl!"

Harmony turned to smile affectionately at her best friend who began to fill her in on the party. She felt herself beginning to relax. *Maybe this won't be so bad after all.*

Tristan's eyes left Harmony and Clara and began to scan the room. They rested on Eduardo Torres, who was talking with a group of darkly dressed men. One of them was Felix Mendelson. As if sensing his gaze, Eduardo turned to face him, staring at him impassively with cold eyes.

Harmony followed Tristan's gaze and froze. She could feel Eduardo's eyes burning her skin. She looked away and turned to face Tristan.

"Ok, we're here. Can we go now?"

"But you just got here!" Clara protested. "You can't leave me now. The fun is just starting!"

"Yes, indeed," a masculine voice interrupted their conversation. "The fun *is* just starting."

Harmony's back stiffened as she heard Eduardo's voice. A shiver of apprehension ran through her as she turned to face him. She was surprised to see Mariska standing beside him, her eyes a glacial blue. She felt Tristan clasp her hand firmly and squeeze it. She exerted her willpower and felt her force field exert around her. Around him.

"I see you decided to bring a guest." The two men eyed each other with barely disguised contempt.

"This is quite a successful event," Harmony responded quickly. "Congratulations. We, unfortunately, have another engagement to attend to this evening. We just wanted to stop by and show some support."

Eduardo laughed. "Perhaps we can persuade you and your guest to try the E-2K before you depart, Harmony."

She shook her head. "That's very kind of you, Mr. Torres, but we really must be leaving."

"You're not going anywhere," Felix Mendelson said, walking their way. Harmony looked around, feeling pressure mounting. She and Tristan were surrounded by a group of tuxedoed men, all dressed in black. Clara was nowhere to be found, having slipped silently away. Harmony felt a cold dread growing in her stomach.

"Mr. Mendelson," she said quietly. "I assure you that we want no trouble here. Perhaps it was a mistake to come." She began to turn around, and stopped as the men dressed in black blocked her escape.

"There is never any mistake, Harmony," Felix said, his voice harsh. "You must simply stay a bit and allow your guest to try out our invention."

"Yes," Tristan bitingly responded. "Your invention, which you stole from us."

Felix smiled, his eyes narrowing with dislike as he assessed Tristan. "You cannot take what is freely given."

"That's a load of bullshit."

Felix leaned in menacingly. "It's over Tristan. You're over. You and your pathetic band have nothing on us. And you can thank your sweet little date here for helping us perfect the E-2K."

Tristan looked at Harmony, whose bewildered eyes met his.

"Oh you don't know how much information we gleaned from Harmony when she worked on your Lightworker programmers," Felix continued with a smirk. "I bet she doesn't even realize just how much we were able to extract."

Harmony glared at Eduardo, whose penetrating gaze revealed nothing.

"Now, let's go visit the E-2K, and you can see for yourself just how useless your psychic powers really are." One of the men in black approached Tristan and opened his jacket, revealing a revolver with a long silencer.

Harmony gasped. "Please. Just let us go. We don't want any problems."

"You should have thought of that before you brought this vermin into our midst. But I should thank you. You have far exceeded my expectations. Now we can finally get rid of this problem for good."

"No!" Harmony yelled. Eduardo grabbed her arm and led her to the back of the room, towards the five E-2K machines that stood like a stainless silver Stonehenge. She tried to pull her arm free, but he tightened his grip firmly around her. She willed her shield stronger as she felt his energy seep into her body. *Dammit Eduardo! You are really pissing me off!*

"Like you bringing him here didn't completely insult me?" His voice was menacingly cold. She turned to look at him, feeling his burning amber gaze heat up.

They stopped in front of the first machine. She could see a line of people waiting to try it out. People came out smiling in bliss and ecstasy. Eduardo whirled her around to face Felix and Tristan.

"Go in, Harmony. It's time for you to let go of this foolish nonsense. Stop playing the hero and join your clan." Felix's voice was cold and serious. "This man is nothing to you. We are your future."

"No!" She responded hotly. Anger radiated through her. *How dare he!*

The man dressed in black holding the gun at Tristan's side pushed the weapon closer into his ribs.

"You say *no* to me one more time, I will not hesitate to shoot him. Don't test me."

"Please," she begged. "Don't hurt him. It's me you want. Let him go."

"Get in." Felix's voice was harsh and demanding.

She turned to look at Tristan. "Tristan…"

"Erase everything. Wipe her memory clean." Felix commanded.

Harmony froze. She knew that voice. *Erase everything. Wipe her memory clean.* It was him. He was the one.

She whirled around furiously. "It was you! You bastard! You're the one that kidnapped me!"

He sneered. "Kidnapping is such a harsh accusation, Harmony. I'd like to think it was more like borrowing."

"Borrowing?" she shrieked. "You put me through hell so you could take something that wasn't yours in the first place. Then you come masquerading and pretending to be my father? What are you? Some kind of sick maniac?"

He glowered at her. "Don't be so judgmental. Remember, I'm a part of you."

"Never! You're not a part of me. Ever!" She spat vehemently.

"We'll see about that! Get her in the E-2K. NOW! After you're done with this, I own you. You will be under my command."

"We'll see about that!" she snarled, twisting her arm free from Eduardo's grip. She took one last look at Tristan before stepping into the booth. Eduardo's hands strapped her to the seat, placing the headphone with the neural attachments to her skull and wrapping her arm inside the blood pressure cuff. His eyes never left her face as he prepared her for the E-2K.

"I didn't know he kidnapped you when you were a child."

"What do you care? You're one of them anyway," she snapped angrily.

"I was kidnapped as a child, too," he responded softly. "Only I never got away."

"If you succeed and wipe my memory clean, then you better remember this." Her eyes glinted with determination. "A part of me – a deep part of me – will always long for freedom, and I will do anything to fight for it."

"Then perhaps you're braver than I am," he answered sadly. "Goodbye, Harmony."

She closed her eyes as darkness covered her inside the E-2K.

A whirring sound appeared in her headphones as images began to flash in front of the screen. They were horrifying: witch hunts, bombings, war and terror, massacres. Pain from all angles. She could feel her heart rate rising. She needed to control the wave of panic that was beginning to grow. She could not give in to their mind control.

She willed her eyes to close and her shield to strengthen. She could feel it bowing and warping around her, testing her resistance. She only had a few seconds. Her mind quickly ran to her father. Rage catalyzed her courage, and she focused on bringing her attention to her heart. They might try to destroy her mind, but she would not let them get to her sacred heart space.

She brought her attention to her inner sanctum. She created a simple white pagoda, open on all sides. It was a faint barrier against the onslaught of stimulation, but she believed in it and tried to feel its serenity. With a desperate cry for help, she called on the Most High, her Masters, Teachers, Loved Ones and Guides.

She felt her pleas were answered when a white light descended into the pagoda and blanketed her in a column of energy. She activated her coding sequence and invoked the angels of the energy field to bring her guidance and direction.

Her inner third eye opened and she found herself standing before a great door. She knew it was her library of knowledge, her book of life. With a quick command, the doors opened and she entered. She could feel the pressure around her and knew she would have to be quick.

Guardians of Light, please show me the key to unlock the E-2K's programming codes.

A golden sphere descended from above her. It suspended in front of her gaze and began to turn. She could see the Flower of Life lightly emblazoned on its matrix. A string of numbers and letters gradually solidified, creating what looked like a golden key.

When it was completed, the sphere stopped spinning and began to fade, dissolving in front of her. She reached for the key and placed it in her mind. The key dissolved from view, psychically tucked in her reservoir vault of stored energy.

She could feel her blood pressure and heart rate rising. Her eyes opened for a moment, as streams of vicious images and piercing sounds attacked her. Shutting them tightly, she energetically connected to the E-2K, sending a beam of light to its central mainframe. She imagined seeing the E-2K as a human organism and requested her third eye sight to find its cellular memory bank.

Instantly, she was taken to a blue column of light that was spinning rapidly in a vortex of energy. She watched in fascination as the E-2K's programs ran freely, moving in a series of codes, running up and down the column of a double helix. She wasn't sure where to insert her program. But first, she had to match the vibration of the E-2K.

All around her, she could hear the barrage of sounds coming through her headphones. She needed to absorb and magnify the energy of this mind-control to match it. Her body was filled with the cacophonous buzz of sounds as coldness washed over her. The E-2K's program felt like a warbled mass of numbers and letters being switched off and on. Time was running out.

She took a deep breath and brought her awareness inward, focusing on energetically connecting to the E-2K's vibration. An internal click resonated through her and confirmed her match. She then commanded for the sacred shape to appear. A golden star tetrahedron began to form in front of her, spinning clockwise and counterclockwise.

She quickly opened her partitioned mind to retrieve the key. Placing the key into the Star of David, which absorbed it quickly, she mentally sealed it into place. She drew a series of geometrical shapes to activate the key and then gently grasped the glowing tetrahedron in her hands. She could feel the warm heat radiating through her arms.

She watched in concentration at the series of codes, seeing a bright red dot floating from the bottom and slowly making its way to the top. *That was it.* That was the start/stop signal.

Opening her mind further, she retrieved the reservoir of energy, running it with focused intention down her arms and into the star tetrahedron. Pulsations of light ran through her arms and out her hands as she followed the red dot.

She was surrounded by blasts of violent sounds and menacing images. Her body shuddered as her force field shook with the effort of trying to keep her protected. It bowed wildly and out of control. Furrowing her brows, she forced herself to concentrate and watch the stream of code, following the red dot.

When it appeared right in front of her, she inserted the star tetrahedron into the coding sequence, activating the ATG start/stop codon with her mind, and blasted the program with an intense stream of light. She focused her whole body, mind and spirit to act like an arrow, directing all the energy straight into the matrix. A brilliant flash of light erupted after the dot as the matrix began to unravel. The code began disintegrating in front of her eyes.

She yanked every element of her being from the program. The E-2K began to shake violently as she felt herself being tossed around. A loud boom and an explosion erupted outside of the E-2K. Fear gripped her heart as screams of terror filled the room. Darkness folded all around her and an eerie silence filled the headphones.

Chapter Nineteen

Harmony opened her eyes as she sat inside the dark box. Opening the door, she found the ballroom pitched in black. Everything was dark and she could sense people talking frantically.

She had energetically overcharged the E-2K's mainframe, and it had totally blown the circuit. She quickly tore off all the attachments around her and crawled out of the booth. She could hear feet moving quickly around her. *Where is Tristan?*

She stood up and began to touch her surroundings. The rough, graininess of the upholstered walls stopped her searching hands, and she leaned against them. Everyone was running around wildly, heading for the door, the only source of light in the whole room. She could vaguely see the shapes of people rushing past her. A hand grabbed her arm roughly.

"Going somewhere?" Mariska's cold voice stopped her.

"Get your hands off me."

"No. You're coming with me."

"The hell I am. I'm not going anywhere with you."

"You will if you want to see your boyfriend alive."

Harmony froze. *Damn it! They still had him!*

She allowed Mariska to lead her away from the door and to another exit in the back of the room. This one was not lit, and most of the crowd was pushing in the opposite direction. Mariska opened the door and pushed Harmony roughly through it.

She found Tristan was surrounded by Eduardo, Felix, Peter Skarsgaard, and five other gentlemen. They eyed her angrily.

"What did you do?" Felix shouted with rage.

"Nothing." Harmony's eyes widened innocently. "I used your machine liked you asked. Happy now?"

"No! You ruined our system." Felix snarled. "Whatever you did messed up the program. This is going to take months to fix."

She smiled sweetly. "We had a deal, Felix. I use the E-2K. You let us go."

Felix laughed, his voice dripping acid and contempt. "You're in no position to barter with me. You destroyed something of mine. Now I will destroy something of yours."

"No!" she screamed.

A sudden explosion blasted the door open. Harmony ducked as grey smoke filled the room. Everyone started coughing and she crouched low, moving away from Mariska. A group of people appeared, cloaked in black. Leading them was Emily Morgan and Karl Renquist, Tristan's friend. They quickly surrounded The Corona.

"What the hell?" Felix screamed.

"This ends here, Felix." Emily's voice was piercing and direct. "Let go of them."

"Over my dead body! Shoot them both. NOW!"

The Corona henchmen removed their guns, taking aim. Before they could pull the trigger, Karl released a bolt of lightning from his hands and wrapped it around the gunmen's hands. Whipping their wrists with ease, Karl knocked the guns away.

Mariska screamed in terror. Emily shot her a look, whipping her hand out to release a golden orb that immediately fastened around her throat. She gasped, clutching at her throat in agony.

Eduardo took a step towards the group, unleashing a hail of psychic arrows at them. But Emily deflected the attack by shielding them in a sphere of golden light.

Felix, Peter Skarsgaard and Nico Torres rushed in, joining forces with Eduardo to override the force field of the Tribe of Light. Harmony could see it beginning to weaken. She looked over at Tristan, who had managed to separate himself from The Corona men. He placed his finger in front of his mouth to relay silence to her.

As The Corona men focused on weakening the shield and directing all their attention towards The Tribe of Light members, Harmony crept up behind them, oblivious to their gaze. She and Tristan met halfway. He placed his hand on her shoulder, imprinting her with his plan of attack.

She quickly nodded and began to form a field of energy in front of her. She created a golden ball of light that was filled with the program to incapacitate and render her opponents weak and useless. Tristan ran the energetic blasts through her arm, and shot it out towards The Corona men.

She felt a penetrating spear of liquid fire radiate through her as it attacked. The influx of energy surrounded the men, running through their bodies like a sound wave and disrupting their internal electrical system. She watched them fall as if being hit with a club. Their bodies convulsed uncontrollably as she and Tristan continued to direct the golden wave of energy through them.

Felix's eyes rolled up in their sockets, the burst of light shaking him senseless. He frothed at the mouth, shuddering and seizing uncontrollably.

"Stop, Harmony!" Emily commanded. "You'll kill him."

She was hit with a sudden thought that maybe she wanted him to die.

"Harmony, stop!" Tristan firmly shook her, interrupting her concentration and bringing her back to reality. She immediately let go, allowing the energetic emission from her hands to cease.

Felix stopped convulsing. His eyes were closed and his body was still. The other Corona men were unconscious on the floor, their bodies a tangled mass of twitching nerves. She sagged against Tristan, who caught her and held her up.

"Hey," his voice was gentle and concerned. "You're ok?"

She nodded weakly. She gazed up into his eyes, taking in his concern.

"You did it! You beat them!"

She shook her head with disbelief. She couldn't believe it was over. Emily came over to her and enveloped her in a protective hug. She held her close as Harmony's eyes welled up with tears and overflowed. They said nothing, just rocking in silence and relief that their battle was done.

"Well done, my dear," Emily congratulated her with a smile. "You did a remarkable job. Better than any one of us could have expected."

"What will happen to them?" Harmony eyed the group of unconscious men.

"They'll be arrested and taken to jail. Kidnapping and assault are serious crimes in the Council."

"But will that be enough, Emily to keep them there? These men are powerful and connected."

Emily smiled at her concern. "Don't worry, Harmony. We brought a big blow to The Corona organization today. We could not have done it without your help."

"But how do I know that what I did made a difference?"

"You effectively destroyed their E-2K program for good. They will not be able to unravel the virus that Mr. Makai placed just as you dismantled the energetic program into the code."

Harmony looked at her in awe. "How did you know what I was doing?"

Emily picked up the crystal pendant that hung on Harmony's chest. "Do you see this? This powerful crystal is a transmitter of energy and information. We watched you travel into the matrix of the E-2K and insert the key into the start/stop sequence. Like I said, we're very proud of you."

A sudden movement amongst the pile of men caught their attention. They were beginning to stir.

"Karl," Emily commanded. "Call the police. Have your men handcuff these guys and wait for the cops. We need to go before they wake up."

Karl nodded, quickly moving with the other Tribal members to handcuff and restrain the men. They were still groggy and barely conscious as they were moved against the wall.

"Put a blindfold on them," Emily continued. "If they look at you, they can shoot psychic arrows and debilitate you. We can't take that risk."

"What about the police?" Harmony asked worriedly. "How will they protect themselves from these Corona men?"

Emily smiled knowingly. "We're not just calling any regular cops, Harmony. We're calling in Special Forces. They're trained to deal with psychic attacks from these kinds of people. They'll be arriving soon."

"And what about Mariska?" Their eyes travelled to the disheveled blond beauty that had passed out in the corner of the room.

"She'll go with them. Don't worry about her. We've got this under control. You and Tristan should leave now though so you don't attract any attention."

Emily turned to Tristan and offered her hand. He silently regarded her before accepting her handshake in his. "Thank you for taking care of my girl," she said, looking him in the eyes. "Let's hope this chapter is closed for good."

Tristan nodded. He was ready for the pressure of fighting The Corona to cease in his life. He turned to look at Harmony who was expectantly looking at them.

"Let's go. I believe I owe you a date."

She smiled as she slipped her hand into his.

He smiled as he led her away from Emily and the Tribe of Light members.

"Harmony!" a voice called out. She turned to see Felix Mendelson glaring at her, his eyes narrowed with murderous rage. "This isn't over. We'll find you."

He looked older, unkempt and disorganized. His tuxedo was dirty and twisted. Gone was the powerful, controlled man.

"Go ahead, Felix. I'll be ready. And next time, there won't be anyone to stop me from finishing what I started tonight."

Felix tried to speak, but Karl gagged him. He struggled furiously against his restraints.

Harmony turned to Tristan's waiting hand. He led her past the group of handcuffed and blindfolded Corona men. She could feel Felix sending an energetic ray of darkness in an attempt to enter her field, but she detected its presence and exerted her shield, deflecting it away. She saw Felix slump over in defeat.

Her eyes passed over Eduardo, whose still body was slumped against his brother. Her heart felt a twinge of pity and sadness.

Tristan led her out of the room and towards the exit at the end of the hallway. As they were leaving, a heavily armed special ops team marched in. Harmony breathed a sigh of relief. Now she could relax. Her nightmare was finally over.

Chapter Twenty

The bustling nightlife greeted Harmony and Tristan as they headed out the door. There was still a flurry of activity coming out of the Convention Center. Well-dressed men and women waited to resume their party, chatting amongst themselves in confusion.

Tristan grabbed Harmony's hand and led her down a side street, hidden from the prying eyes of the party-goers. They walked quickly to the parking garage, saying nothing as their steps carried them farther and farther from their troublesome evening.

When they arrived at the Jaguar in the parking garage, Tristan finally stopped and pulled Harmony close to him, bending his head to brush the top of her head. Her body sagged in relief against him.

"Are you really ok?" he asked, his hands running up and down her arms to warm her.

"I'm better now that we're out of there. That was hell, Tristan. I thought they were going to hurt you!"

"I had a plan," he murmured.

"Well your crazy plan worked." She gently pushed away from him, looking up into his blue eyes. "It was scary, but I'm glad you're ok. How did you manage to get Emily to go along with it?"

Tristan opened the door and assisted Harmony in getting into the passenger side. He eased into the driver's seat and turned to look at her.

"This was Emily's idea. From the beginning, she believed that the elements needed to push you to access your powers would strategically appear, and you would be forced into it. Otherwise, you wouldn't have believed that you had the abilities."

Her eyes widened in shock. *Emily was behind my training all along. Had she known about Felix Mendelson, too?*

"No," Tristan responded, reading her thoughts. "Felix Mendelson was a wild card that The Corona pulled to try and sway your allegiance. They didn't hesitate to use their most powerful leader to retrieve you."

Her eyes turned dark and a bitter taste entered her mouth at the thought of Felix. She shuddered, relieved that the whole ordeal was over. She didn't want to see that man ever again.

A *ding* from Tristan's phone interrupted them as he pulled it out and read the text quickly. Putting the phone in his jacket pocket, he turned to gaze at her, his eyes assessing her beautiful flushed face. He had never seen her look more radiant.

"You know, I have to admit," his voice was warm. "You were a bad-ass in there. Your abilities and self-control in action were amazing. You really surprised me." She flushed at his compliment. "I knew you could do it."

"That was the scariest thing I've ever had to do. I thought we were going to die."

"No way...we had it under control."

"I just hope it's over."

"It is."

Calmness settled over them. Tristan turned and took Harmony's hand in his, bringing it up to his lips to kiss it gently. Her eyes watched him, amused at his tenderness.

"Have I told you that you look gorgeous tonight?" his voice was seductive and soft, causing her to flush.

"Not in those exact words..."

"Well...what do you say we celebrate our success with a real date?"

She smiled at him. "What do you have in mind?"

"I've got a special plan for you."

He turned on the car and led them out of the parking garage. He drove down the busy street, avoiding the Convention Center, and headed for the Driskill Hotel. Pulling into the valet lane, he stepped out and dropped the key into the waiting attendant's hand. The attendant grinned at the convertible, his eyes widening at the possibility of a joy ride.

Tristan opened her door, pulling her close to him once she was on the sidewalk.

"This dress makes me think of all kinds of things I would like to do to you later," he whispered. A rivulet of desire ran down her spine.

"Why wait for later?" Their lips met in a searing kiss.

"There's something I want to show you first." He led her through the opulent lobby, adorned with well-dressed men and women ready for a night on the town. They passed the ballrooms and headed for a room at the far end of the hallway.

Tristan turned to Harmony and smiled. When the door swung open, she was greeted by a room full of people who immediately burst into applause at their entrance.

Harmony was shocked. *Oh my God! Who are all these people? What's going on?!*

She looked wildly around at the smiling faces, surprised to see Clara, Emily Morgan, Karl Renquist and his friends, Mr. Makai and others who were strangers to her. They surged forward, pulling her into their waiting arms.

Clara was the first, squealing in glee as she enveloped Harmony. "Thank God you're ok! I didn't see you afterwards. Emily told me what happened."

She blushed hotly, her eyes drawn to Emily who was smiling affectionately at her. She separated from Clara and came into Emily's waiting arms.

"You did it, darling! You fought and won. I'm so proud of you!"

Her eyes misted with tears. "Have you known about this all along?" she asked Emily, pulling away to look into her eyes.

"I saw this unfold when you were a teenager, Harmony. I've trained and cultivated your abilities throughout these years, knowing one day, you would be called to defend yourself, your family, your Tribe."

She nodded, hearing the words that validated that she belonged - that she had family, that she was not alone. Turning around, she found Tristan standing in the distance, surrounded by Karl and his friends. Feeling her gaze, Tristan looked up closing the gap between them. She could feel the love and admiration emanating from his eyes as he stared at her.

The crowd of people separated, leaving Harmony to stand alone. She turned towards a group of strangers, dressed regally in robes of turquoise blue, winter white, royal red and pale grey. They were the Tribe of Light leaders, representing each of the Tribe that made up the council: the Water Bearers, Air Traders, Fire Starters and Earth Keepers.

Tristan walked up to her and grasped her hand, squeezing it firmly in his. He slowly led her towards the twelve Tribe of Light leaders. Bending down on one knee, he bowed his head, uttering, *"Pater, Mater, Deus. Lumen quod intra te honoro."*

Bjorn Cassidy, dressed in a red cloak, a symbol of the Fire Starters, said first. "Rise, my son. Please introduce us to your lovely guest."

Tristan stood up and nodded respectfully to the other Tribal Council leaders. "Great Council, I'd like to introduce Harmony Mendelson."

Harmony gave them a small smile, feeling suddenly nervous as the curious eyes lit on her. She bowed her head humbly and raised her eyes to meet Bjorn's scrutinizing gaze.

"We are pleased to meet you, Harmony," Bjorn said majestically. "We've been watching your progress and your participation in Tribal activities. You have truly surprised us in the face of such insurmountable obstacles. May I ask, what has your experience been with The Corona?"

She eyed him closely, guarding her thoughts. "I found most of the men and women in The Corona to be controlling and energetically aggressive. My interactions with Felix Mendelson and Eduardo Torres definitely proved that. Why do you ask?"

"We've had a long-standing battle with The Corona, but this is the first time that we've rallied together to help one person. You're that person."

"Why now? Why me?"

Bjorn smiled at her question. "You're both an asset and a liability, depending on which side you align to. That is why we chose to help you. We'd like to formally invite you to join The Tribe of Light."

He waved his hand to acknowledge the rest of the waiting Tribe. Harmony gazed over towards them, receiving their nods of approval and welcoming smiles. She looked towards Emily Morgan, who stood separate from them. Emily smiled at her and motioned for her to come forward.

"Excuse me, sir," she excused herself and walked towards her faithful guardian.

"What should I do?" she whispered at Emily when she arrived. She felt all eyes in the room watching her.

Emily gently caressed her face in both hands, tilting her up. "You've proven yourself to be a warrior of light. You've overcome your fear, doubt and insecurity about who you are and what you're capable of. Your decision to join The Tribe has to answer a calling deep inside. Do you feel it?"

Nodding with certainty, she smiled. "I know my answer."

"It's your destiny, Harmony."

She turned towards Bjorn and the Tribal Council and began to walk towards them. Raising her head confidently, she spoke with clarity and confidence. "I would be honored to accept your invitation to be a part of The Tribe of Light."

The room erupted in an explosive burst of claps and whistles, celebrating her decision. The crowd threw streamers and confetti, peppering the room in a snowstorm of paper and colors.

Bjorn smiled at her response. "We are delighted to have you join The Tribe of Light, Harmony Mendelson. Welcome to the family!"

She was surrounded by the Tribal Council, who began to introduce themselves individually. She could feel herself relaxing, her vibrations rising with each contact. The Tribal leaders gazed into her eyes and connected forehead to forehead with each welcoming hug. By the time she had finished hugging the Council, she felt lightheaded, her third eye expanded with energy and awareness.

She turned to the rest of the party and received welcoming hugs from everyone from Karl to Mr. Makai, who ended up being a warm, receptive and open man – so different from the client she initially met. Feeling a tap on her shoulder, she turned to find Tristan facing her, his eyes light with pride and joy.

"Welcome home, baby," he whispered softly in her ear as he pulled her close for an embrace. "I'm so proud of you."

"Oh Tristan," she smiled. "I know this is right."

"We'll celebrate privately later." His words held promise as his eyes darkened with thoughts of their erotic adventure.

She blushed at his pointed gaze, feeling the connection between them growing stronger. "I can't wait."

They both turned towards the party which had engaged in full celebration mode. Champagne filled glasses began to circulate the room as people began to talk and gather in circles.

Bjorn stood up, clinking his glass, drawing everyone's attention to him. "Ladies and Gentlemen, I'd like to propose a toast. We've fought a hard battle this evening and I'd like to recognize our valuable team for their hard won efforts. Tristan Alexander, our finest and most talented tracker, has done an outstanding job in preparing Harmony for this evening."

A round of excited applause filled the air. "And I'd also like to recognize Emily Morgan, our past Tribal Leader and Oracle, for her vision and direction in leading this attack."

Harmony turned to face Emily, clapping her hands with surprise. *She was their Oracle?!* She inwardly wondered what other magic tricks Emily had up her sleeve.

"And I'd like to recognize our team for their support during this evening, especially Mr. Makai for successfully infiltrating The Corona's E-2K program and embedding the light virus that destroyed their program. Your work, along with Ms. Mendelson, allowed a great victory for The Tribe and for the collective conscious. Thank you!"

The crowd cheered wildly as Karl and Mr. Makai flushed with gratitude. The applause died down as Bjorn began to speak.

"Tonight, The Corona leaders and the NET Media owners were arrested by The Special Forces and sent to a maximum security prison for psychic criminals. They will be held there until they complete their sentence. While we don't know how long they will be in this facility, we recognize a great victory this evening."

A hush filled the room at the mention of The Corona. "In fighting for the collective spirit of men and women of this planet, we ensure that our future generations have a chance to fight for their freedom and their place in this world. We cannot let our guards down, for we represent the next leap in evolution. In contributing to our collective consciousness, we ensure the survival of The Tribe of Light."

The crowd erupted in applause. Bjorn nodded in confirmation and stepped down from the stage. The Tribal leaders were led in a straight line out of the room, following Bjorn.

"Where are they going?" Harmony whispered to Tristan.

"They're returning to Terra Quattro."

She nodded in understanding, knowing that their appearance publicly was rare. "And what about us? What happens now?"

Emily came to join them, hearing Harmony's question. "We leave first thing in the morning, dear. Your training begins immediately. The Tribal Council has already prepared everything for our arrival. They will be expecting us."

Her eyes widened with joy. "You're coming too?"

"But of course. I will always be your Guardian. It's my duty to make sure your initiation and training are in alignment with your path."

She turned and hugged Emily fiercely, tears glistening in her eyes. She was filled with gratitude. Knowing that Emily and Tristan would be there made her feel more at ease with leaving.

"I'm coming too!" Clara's voice piped up. Harmony separated from Emily and reached out for her best friend.

"I'm so happy! We're going to do this together!"

Clara smiled. "There's no way I'm going to let you do this on your own. You're my best friend. I go where you go. Besides...I don't think I have a job at NET Media anymore."

Harmony burst out laughing. "Well if it makes you feel better, I don't have one either!"

The two women giggled as the guests milled around them. "I'll see you tomorrow," Clara chimed in. "I think you're going to be busy the rest of the night."

Harmony turned to see Tristan standing apart from everyone, waiting for her. With a quick squeeze, she let go of Clara's hand and walked towards Tristan.

"Are you ready to go?" he asked suggestively, taking her hand in his.

Her green eyes met his, answering his question with a glowing "Yes."

They quickly made their rounds and bid farewell to everyone, hugging them before heading out the door. Harmony could feel herself growing warm in anticipation of spending time with Tristan.

Instead of heading out toward the valet to pick up their car, he led her towards the elevator. When the doors opened, Tristan pulled her in and into his arms, planting a searing kiss on her lips. Intense desire coursed through her as she responded to his touch. She was grateful no one else was sharing their cab.

"Where are we going?"

"We're staying here tonight," he smiled, looking down into her flashing green eyes. "Everything is prepared for you to leave tomorrow."

"What about my apartment?"

"Glenda took care of that. She packed your clothes and your personal belongings. The rest of your stuff went to Sacre Tellus. They will be waiting for you after you return from your initiations."

She nodded. It was all too much to process at once, and she didn't have it in her to care or argue. Her evening with The Corona and The Tribe of Light had filled her to the brim with stimulation and information.

The door dinged open at the top and Tristan led her towards a penthouse room. When he opened the door, her mouth dropped in awe. They had a luxurious suite that overlooked the other skyscrapers. Turning, she eyed the large king-sized bed strewn with rose petals and the tea-light candles flickering around the nightstands. She felt Tristan's ravenous gaze and turned slowly to face him.

"This is beautiful."

"Not as beautiful as you are. I love how you blush."

He trailed a finger from her face down to her neck to her low cut gown.

"You seem to have that kind of effect on me," she murmured, her eyes flashing with heat.

"We seem to do that to each other." He pulled her close, capturing her full lips in his.

He kissed her passionately, his tongue seeking entrance into her mouth. She sighed in delight as desire began to course through her body. His hands began to unzip the back of her gown, loosening the straps. With skillful fingers, he removed the straps and slowly brought the crystal laden gown down so she could carefully step out of it. When they were off, he stepped away and admired her beautiful body.

She was wearing only a black lace thong, garter belt and black silk stockings. Tristan's sharp intake of breath informed her that he wasn't immune to her beauty. Her eyes gazed at him as he assessed her from head to foot. Harmony tried to cover her full breasts, blushing at her semi-nudity.

"No," he gently responded, pulling her hands to her side. "You look radiant. Don't cover your beautiful body."

He stepped away to admire her figure. "Thank God I didn't know you were wearing this under your dress. I think I would have gone crazy at the party knowing you looked this hot."

"Crazier than you already are?" she teased him lightly.

"Crazy for you, baby." She shyly looked up to see his smiling face and darkened eyes. With a brave smile, she stepped towards him and began to slide his tuxedo jacket off. He helped her by shrugging out of the jacket, waiting patiently as she undid his cummerbund and his tie. She unbuttoned each one slowly, placing a kiss on his bare skin with each opening. He gasped in pleasure as her lips touched his chest.

When she arrived at his pants, he assisted her in undoing his belt and fly. With sure fingers, she pulled his pants off along with his shoes, until he stood before her in his boxer briefs. His firm erection bulged out.

Without a word, Tristan scooped Harmony up in his arms and brought her towards the large bed. He gently placed her atop the scattered rose petals, crushing her with his weight as he swooped down to claim her lips again. Gone was the restraint that he exhibited earlier.

His hands urgently caressed her, squeezing her breasts and nipples, eliciting fire bolts of electricity to run up and down her body. She sighed as she raked his back with her nails, causing him to groan in pleasurable agony. She caught his bottom lip, sucking slowly as her hands reached down to grasp his firm erection.

He moaned, trailing hot kisses down her throat as he continued towards her breasts, massaging the sensitive globes in his hands. She was on fire, wanting him to take her to higher levels of arousal. He took one stiff nipple in his mouth, sucking voraciously as her back arched towards him. His touched opened the door for her wanton desire to unfold. He teased and sucked on her nipple while his other hand massaged the other breast.

A sigh of pleasure escaped her lips as she clutched his hair, holding him feverishly close. "Oh Tristan, I want you so much."

"Soon, baby. I want you as crazy as I feel about you."

She gasped as his fingers pulled the black string thong aside, exposing her full, wet lips to his seeking fingers. He plunged through her warm wetness, into her waiting pussy, which enveloped him tightly.

"You're always so ready for me," he said reverently.

Pulling his fingers out, he raised the wetness to his lips, licking them with hunger. "And you taste good."

"Oh you're so naughty!" she whispered.

"This is just the beginning," he answered. "Wait 'til your initiations. I will drive you over the edge with pleasure. Tonight is just a peek."

With a lascivious grin, he bent down and ran his tongue up and down her juicy opening. Her breath was sharply drawn as a burst of sensation spread through her loins at his onslaught. She brought her hands to his head, holding him closer as he licked and sucked her clitoris. A wave of pleasure grew in her.

"It's time to replenish your energy reserves. I believe you've used quite a great deal tonight."

"Ohhh."

She sighed as his tongue plunged deeply into her, moving in and out in a sensual rhythm. His fingers replaced his tongue as he continued to suck on her center of pleasure.

She felt a shocking bolt of electrical energy course through her as his fingers touched her deep inside. A blue light ran through her body as it activated each power center, causing them to turn in a clockwise direction and vibrate with activity. A torrent of sensations radiated through her, opening her mind and heart to his influx of life force energy. She felt her cellular matrix sizzling with vitality.

Her body began to constrict and tighten, getting closer to an orgasm. Wildly, she pulled his head, attempting to make him stop but he persisted.

"Tristan!" she gasped. His merciless onslaught triggered a wave of ecstasy to flood her body, a vivid blast of colors exploding in her mind. Her body was racked with pleasure as he pushed her over the edge into an orgasm. She cried out with desire as she felt her body turned into liquid fire, shaking her from the base of her spine to the top of her crown.

"I'm glad you're warmed up," he said in between licks of her creamy outpouring. "I've got so much more for you, baby."

Her eyes opened to gaze at him. He raised himself and pulled his boxer briefs off. His erection sprung freely, further fueling her fire. He reached down and slipped her black thong down her legs, pushing them apart as he came down to rest between her open thighs.

She could feel his hardness lubricating in her juices as he rubbed himself over her sex. She sighed in wonder, feeling her body ravenously responding to his touch. Tristan slipped himself inside of her, feeling her squeeze him as he entered.

He groaned with pleasure as he thrust himself deeper into her, filling her. She responded to his movement and ground her hips against his, a wave of sexual fever rising deep within her. She wanted him so bad, to feel his body respond to her touch. They continued to move in rhythm as he continued to drive her closer and closer to release.

"Look at me," he demanded. She moaned as he pushed himself deeper into her, awakening her nerve endings of pleasure.

"Oh baby, you're mine!" he whispered, thrusting into her with growing speed. She could feel her body rising with his growing momentum. Her fingernails clawed down his back, squeezing his buttocks and pushing him deeper into her.

"Yes, I'm yours," she replied breathlessly. She unraveled as he wantonly rubbed her clitoris. Her body was pulled tightly like a string about to snap. He was driving her senseless as he continued to ravage her.

"Harmony, come with me!" he urged. His hips moved more frantically in and out of her, and she thrashed beneath him. She could feel her body spring up like a coil, set to release.

"Tristan!" She called his name as waves of rapture engulfed her, inviting her to surrender. Tristan pushed her past the edges of control into an abyss of ecstatic bliss. He shook, releasing his seed into her. They bodies reverberated with orgasmic energy as they exploded into a sea of sensation and light.

Tristan gently fell on top of her, his breathing heavy and hard. She panted with exhaustion as her body began to relax. She relished the weight of him atop her and wound her arms around him, holding him close. They continued to lie in this position, allowing their breathing to regulate until a peaceful calm ran through their bodies.

Tristan hoisted himself off her and pulled her into his warm embrace. She snuggled closer to him, feeling radiant and well-loved. There was no place she would rather be than in his arms at that moment. As if reading her thoughts, Tristan pulled her face to look up at him.

"I love you."

She smiled, feeling a surge of love expanding around her. It was as sweet as the first time he'd said it. It filled her with joy and elation. "I love you too, Tristan."

He pulled her close, brushing the top of her head with his lips. As he sighed in contentment, he squeezed her reassuringly. "Tell me this is a dream come true, baby."

She pulled up to face him, her eyes smiling with tenderness. "It is. It's our dream."

"You know there's nothing we can't do together."

"I know. And...I believe you."

She smiled, feeling his love for her blanket her heart. Her root chakra was glowing with a rich maroon light, energized and catalyzed by their lovemaking. Her whole body felt infused with Divine Love.

Her hand found Tristan's, winding her fingers with his. She laid her head down on his chest, a small smile of contentment etched on her face.

What would tomorrow bring? She had no clue, but whatever the future held, her family - The Tribe of Light and Tristan - would be with her. For now, that was more than enough.

THE END

Stay tuned for the next novel in the Metaphysical Erotica series:
"Sacred Fire: Cultivating Power" due for release in March 2014

Made in the USA
Monee, IL
31 December 2023

50875933R00144